Shadow Doctor: The Past Awaits

Also by Adrian Plass from Hodder & Stoughton

The Shadow Doctor

The Sacred Diary of Adrian Plass:
Adrian Plass and the Church Weekend

ADRIAN PLASS

Shadow Doctor: The Past Awaits

Further Exploits
of the Shadow Doctor

HODDER

First published in Great Britain in 2019 by Hodder & Stoughton
An Hachette UK company

This paperback edition first published in 2021

1

A CIP catalogue record for this title is available from the British Library

Paperback ISBN 978 1 473 67526 1
eBook ISBN 978 1 473 67528 5

Typeset in Sabon MT by Hewer Text UK Ltd, Edinburgh
Printed and bound in Great Britain by Clays Ltd, Elcograf S.p.A.

Hodder & Stoughton policy is to use papers that are natural, renewable
and recyclable products and made from wood grown in sustainable
forests. The logging and manufacturing processes are expected to
conform to the environmental regulations of the country of origin.

Hodder & Stoughton Ltd
Carmelite House
50 Victoria Embankment
London EC4Y 0DZ

www.hodderfaith.com

This book is dedicated to all the Jacks and Jills
who have come tumbling down, and are looking
forward to getting back on their feet again.

Contents

1. Stalking the lion   1
2. The trouble with Sammy   11
3. In the lion's den   19
4. The small person inside   36
5. Laughing with Miriam   43
6. The myth of Sisyphus   51
7. Victor Morton   56
8. The list   66
9. Getting ready for Martha   71
10. Sign of the times   75
11. Meeting Martha   84
12. Martha's story   90
13. The road less travelled   106
14. The top of the mountain   112
15. A clue   123
16. Green Pastures   132
17. Elsie   146
18. Aelwen   159
19. Two questions   173
20. Conflict in the car park   180
21. An absence of colour   187
22. Flush it again, Sam   189
23. What happened to Alice?   201
24. A fondness for God   221
25. Understanding blue   236
26. Dying to live   249
27. The bottom line   259

Stalking the lion

'Today, Jack, I am planning to stalk a lion.'

Jack Merton stared. The bizarre announcement had come out of nowhere as the two men were enjoying their beloved morning coffee. After two months of close contact with the Shadow Doctor, he had become a little more comfortable with the older man's obstinate insistence on cloaking simple ideas in cryptic metaphor. Two problems remained. One was his experience of a few alarming occasions when it had transpired that typically bizarre statements were neither cryptic nor metaphorical. The other was a growing awareness that his very singular colleague was unwilling or unable to allow short cuts to the solid centre of his thinking, if and when it existed. Doc loved cryptic crosswords. Jack was hopeless at them.

'Stalking a lion? Are you serious?'

'Serious? Actually, I've been stalking this beast for some time. Today, my idea is to get right inside the creature's den.'

Jack sighed. It could mean anything. Doc seemed to believe (with Oscar Wilde, apparently) that a concept or a plan, or even a person, lost layers of essential quality and identity by being encased in something as banal as a name or a simple explanation. For Jack, it was a relief to have reassuringly clear labels stuck on almost anything.

Jack sipped his coffee; a moment in which to lean back before returning his mug with exaggerated care to the kitchen table. He looked up.

So, when you say you're planning to stalk a lion, are you talking about something that's – you know, flesh and blood? And hair?'

'Absolutely, Jack! Oh, yes. Breathing, walking, occasionally roaring, made of real flesh and real blood. Quite famous hair.'

'Dangerous?'

'Can be. Has been. Could be again.'

'With a mane?'

'With a mane? Of course, with a mane! A lion wouldn't be a lion without a mane, would it?'

'Actually, it would if it was a female. Only males have manes, don't they?'

'Correct. Thank you, Mister Attenborough. Well, the one that I am going to stalk is quite definitely male, and I know for a fact that this individual, masculine lion has an impressive mane, and can be extremely fierce. However, I shall do my best to battle with the creature, and if I manage to overcome it . . .'

Doc paused. A note of gravity and reserve entered his deep, gentle voice as he continued.

'If I manage to overcome it, there is a slim chance that I may be able to discover some sweetness buzzing around in the remains.'

Jack floated, resisting a temptation to drop a nice safe anchor in the biblical connection that the other man seemed to be making. Experience suggested that observations of that kind would not be welcomed. Mentally, he set aside the question that he really wanted to ask, the one about why the Shadow Doctor appeared to be excluding him from this latest expedition, whatever it turned out to be. Apart from anything else, Doc had hitherto happily expressed a preference for being a passenger in his big silver X-Trail, and Jack loved to be behind the wheel.

'So, excuse my ignorance, but do you have to go to Africa or India or somewhere in the Orient to sort this animal out?'

'No, none of those, unfortunately. I have to go to Eastbourne.'

'Eastbourne?'

'Yes, Eastbourne.'

'Eastbourne!'

Doc placed his elbows on the kitchen table and rested his chin on interlinked fingers.

'Jack, although it would make life much simpler, if marginally less interesting, we really can't sit in the middle of a forest in Sussex saying "Eastbourne" to each other for the rest of our lives.' He raised his hands in parallel, ready to chop down and package his plans to make them comprehensible. 'The lion that I intend to hunt is in Eastbourne. That is where I am going. It's about thirty miles from Wadhurst to Eastbourne.' He glanced at his wrist. 'I shall leave straight after lunch.'

Eastbourne. As far as Jack was concerned, Eastbourne groaned and glittered with memories. Recent ones abounded suddenly now. It was the place where Jack's gran, Alice Merton, had spent the last years of her life in a small flat near the seafront after the death of her beloved husband, William. Jack and Alice had adored each other, and loved spending time together, but the same persistent elephant had been stubbornly present in any and every room in which they met. The pachyderm was easily identified. It was Jack's Christianity.

Once, Jack had plucked up courage to ask his gran why she never showed any positive response to the things he said about his faith. Her devastating reply had been that, however hard she listened, she couldn't really hear him saying anything. In a letter written to Jack shortly before she died, Alice had apologised humbly for her lack of courage in avoiding every opportunity to tackle the issue after that. Ironically, it was shortly after his gran's death that Jack had finally begun to face the hollowness within himself that she had seen so clearly.

In that same letter, Alice had talked about an extraordinary meeting with a man who described himself as 'The Shadow Doctor'. The encounter had rescued her from an abyss of hopelessness, and, she added, something else had happened that she would tell him about when they met. Alice was gone by the time Jack got to read her long, final letter to him, but she had included the phone number of a person who would be able to connect him with Doc, the Shadow Doctor. If by any chance we don't get to meet again, she had said in a postscript, ask Doc, and he will tell you what happened to me.

With great fear and apprehension, and following a long, emotional splurge of a telephone call, Jack finally arranged to meet the Shadow Doctor at his cottage in a remote part of the Sussex countryside near Wadhurst. His experience on that wild and stormy night was surprising, to say the least. He seemed to have found a safe place to say dangerous things. The freedom was intoxicating, but he was shocked to find himself eventually agreeing, a few weeks later, to enter a living, working partnership with a man who conducted his faith, if faith it was, in a way that was almost unrecognisable. Jack had spent his Christian life in settings where, for the most part, nothing shocked, and spontaneity was carefully controlled.

The two men were very different, and there had already been battles, but Jack was hanging on to a belief that both of them had taken decisive steps into the no-man's-land between each other's heavily defended lines. Hopefully, the future lay somewhere out there where the mud was thick, and the bullets flew, and a good friend was what you needed most. That was the plan, but every panel within the mosaic of that plan seemed to be completely different, except to the extent that most of them were unpredictable, and, on almost every occasion, Jack had been allowed little or no involvement in their genesis or development.

Today was a good example. What was the plan? Where were the lions in Eastbourne? Why was his so-called colleague intending to travel alone? He thought of a question.

'What kind of weapon will you be using against this fierce creature?'

Swinging an arm, Doc pointed lazily to a rectangular object standing against the wall beneath the bow window. It was neatly wrapped in brown paper and tied with string.

'Over there – that's my weapon, Jack.'

Jack stared.

'Is it – it looks as if it might be a picture.'

'Good guess, that's exactly what it is. A painting. A copy of a painting.'

'You're going after a lion, armed with a picture.'

'Correct.'

'Is the picture – loaded?'

The Shadow Doctor smiled grimly. 'Oh yes! Fully loaded and ready to fire. I just have to make sure that my aim is dead straight.'

'Why can't I come with you?'

Doc appeared to be studying a small remnant of the biscuit he had been enjoying with his coffee. Jack raised his voice slightly.

'Do you mean that you're planning to do this stalking thing on your own?'

'Tell me, Jack, is this a genuine Choco Leibniz biscuit, or is it another miracle replica from the place in Tunbridge Wells that does a palatable single malt for a few quid?'

'Miracle replica. Why am I not coming with you? Why have you not mentioned this before?'

The Shadow Doctor popped the fragment into his mouth and dusted his hands together industriously before replying.

'Actually – I have mentioned it before, but not quite in the same terms.'

'What do you mean?'

'You recall that icy night on your first visit when you followed me into the forest? When we were back in the cottage later, I went right over the top with promises about things I'd tell you if and when you agreed to come and work with me. Remember?'

'Do I remember? I think about it all the time. I'll never forget it.'

He instructed himself silently. *Tell him. Tell him the thing that made all the difference.*

'I remember you telling me your wife's name.'

It had been an unforgettable moment. The two men were sitting before the open door of an oven on that freezing cold night in the early hours of the morning. The Shadow Doctor had spoken reluctantly but openly for the first time about his wife, telling Jack that she had died of a brain tumour fifteen years earlier. This unaccustomed openness seemed to be presented as a sort of hostage, perhaps a deposit of good faith in return for a decision about joining Doc in his attempts to help people struggling with a bewildering variety of problems. Although Jack had not realised it until much later, the question he asked in response to this act of vulnerability was probably a sign of his need to be sure that the man he was facing would not always be in charge of selecting the stretching points in their relationship.

'What was your wife's name?'

That had been his question, or words to that effect, and, to Jack's alarm, the Shadow Doctor had reacted physically and abruptly, almost as though someone had leaned forward and slapped his face. But he did answer the question.

'Her name was Miriam. My wife's name was Miriam.'

A strange moment. Electric. Significant. Unsettling and reassuring. That particular tension seemed to be an ongoing feature of their relationship. Had getting closer to this strange man become easier as the weeks went by? Ironically and illogically, he felt that he would eventually have to ask Doc to answer that question. Not now, though.

'I remember it all. I don't remember anything about lions, though.'

The older man hardly missed a beat, but he did miss one nonetheless, without any doubt. Jack smiled to himself. If they had been playing *Just a Minute*, it would be his turn now.

'That's because I didn't. I never mentioned lions. I said that I was planning to visit a famous Christian leader, and I think I made the point that—'

'That's right – you said you had something to tell him that might ruin his life.'

'Well, spoil his day, I think I said, but – who knows?'

'So, let's get this straight. The lion you're talking about is actually a Christian elder or minister or something.'

This time the ensuing pause was controlled and deliberate.

'His name is Trevor Langston.'

It was like being hit in the gut by a medicine ball. An unidentifiable threat of potential catastrophe rendered Jack speechless. For nearly half a minute he found it difficult to breathe and impossible to move. It was as though his present and his past were being fused together by a dangerous accident. He collected himself at last.

'Trevor Langston. *The* Trevor Langston? Are you serious? Trevor Langston who's moved his big shepherding headquarters thing down to the Old Town in Eastbourne? Up the hill from Meads Village? I've been there. Speaks and prophesies all over the world. Loads of books. Doc, you can't go chasing after him. He's an amazing man of God. Everyone says so.'

'Mm. Famous for his hair, is he not. A bit like a lion's mane.'

'No, you don't understand. He was very important to me when I was a young Christian. The things he said and

8

wrote. He was for real. I – I sort of leaned on him and his ideas.'

Jack was conscious that a note of pleading had entered his voice.

'I don't doubt it,' replied the Shadow Doctor quietly, a kind but quizzical smile illuminating his face. 'Don't worry. You don't have to come.'

Rising to his feet, Jack gathered up coffee mugs and plates and the empty miracle biscuit packet. Without speaking, he carried them over to the sink, dumped the empty packet in the bin next to the end of the work surface, and washed the mugs and plates thoroughly under the hot tap. Reaching up for a tea towel from the shelf next to the oven, he dried everything carefully before hanging the mugs back on their correct hooks on the dresser and returning the small blue plates to the top shelf of the middle cupboard immediately underneath. Only when these small tasks were completed did he turn and face the other man once more.

'Do you want me to come with you?'

Planting his elbows on the table, the Shadow Doctor pushed his hair back with both hands before lifting his head and looking rather helplessly at Jack.

'Oh, Jack, telling the truth is so not the simple matter that people say it ought to be. I want you to come with me because I'm a little bit nervous about doing this thing on my own. That's true. I don't want you to come because I am more than a little worried that if you do, you will almost certainly learn things about me that you won't like, and you'll have a pretty massive close-up view of me at my weakest. Less than attractive I can assure you. Look, I suppose I do, and I don't want you to come because – well, perhaps this is the most challenging thing of all, and it won't surprise you. You will end up further inside who I am and what I do than you have been before. Tough for you as well as me. Fear and trust and all sorts up in the air.' He stroked the surface of the table in rhythmic arcs with the palm of one hand. 'It's a big step for me, Jack. I need to want that. The child in me, the kid who would always rather run away, definitely doesn't want that.' He tilted his head to one side. 'So, it's up to you. Come if you want.'

'Trevor Langston?'

'Up to you.'

'If I do come, will you tell me what's happening before we get there?'

'No. No, you'd only decide to have a view. Don't even try to say you wouldn't. Everyone has a view. I'm not quite used to dealing with views yet. Are you coming?'

'I'll tell you after lunch.'

2

The trouble with Sammy

'Feeling nervous, Jack?'

'Yes. You?'

'Let's change the subject.'

Jack steered the X-Trail carefully towards the main Wadhurst road.

During a light lunch of ginger beer and ham sandwiches, one of the rounds with English mustard and one without, nothing had been mentioned about the forthcoming trip. It was a slight sulk on the younger man's part. In his mind he had been replaying as much as he could remember of Doc's complicated speech about whether or not he wanted company for his hunting expedition. Not at all easy to work out what that had all meant, but he had finally and determinedly whispered to himself, 'Jack Merton, you are going to be at this meeting with Trevor Langston whether Doc wants you there or not.'

At exactly two o'clock, without discussion or announcement, Jack had used one finger to ostentatiously pluck the ring with the car key on it from the hook beside the front door before heading across the yard to the X-Trail. Minutes later the Shadow Doctor had arrived beside the car, and after stowing his wrapped painting carefully on the floor at the back, had settled himself into the passenger seat ready for the journey.

There was a quick call to Trevor Langston's secretary to let her know that there would be an extra visitor, but Doc's question about Jack's nerves began the first conversation between the two men since leaving. Jack decided to abandon his sulk and be kind.

'Change the subject? Okay. Let's think. I know – what makes you laugh, Doc?'

'Hmm, interesting question. I have to admit I'm not very spiritually PC about the things that make me laugh. Maybe I just lack taste. Tell you what, I'll give you an example. There's this fellow called Sammy. I've known him for years.'

'What's he like?'

'Sammy? He's one of those wheeler-dealer types. They pop up all over the place, including in the church world from time to time. A sort of utilitarian charm. Adjustable morals. I quite like these characters usually. They sometimes morph into benevolent fixers. Very useful people. In fact, thinking about it, most people I've known who were wise enough to hand over their negative side to a wiser judge for recycling have turned out to be really good value. It's a lot better than stuffing faults away and pretending they don't exist.'

'Any faults?'

'Probably. Bad temper's a good one. I'd say we're seriously short of direct, assertive people who've given up things like selection and control but are still happy to speak out when the right time comes. It works brilliantly as long as they're equally willing to keep quiet when they feel like shooting their mouths off and know perfectly well that's exactly what's not needed.'

'Lust?'

'Lust is another one. Not something you or I have experienced, of course, Jack, but another good example. Give it away. Maybe it'll be transformed, or transfigured even, into a hunger, a muscular appetite for things that are worth doing or having.'

'I remember you saying on our way to meet the exploding lady that you thought appetite is one of the worst things to waste.'

'That's quite right. Thank you for remembering. All kinds of appetites. Just imagine, Jack, all the useful, juicy sins that are doomed to be buried or shelved. Must drive God mad. I once knew a man who gave away a bitter, horribly sarcastic sense of humour. He could be seriously nasty. Still makes people laugh nowadays, but no one gets hurt – most of the time. Old habits die hard, even if you've been transfigured. One day you might meet up with someone in heaven who thought he was transfigured but ended up terrified that he was being told to eat snakes and lizards and frogs and birds. A very swift and hugely positive move away from that negative appetite after that, I can tell you.'

'So, carry on about this wheeler-dealer of yours.'

The Shadow Doctor chuckled.

'Yes, Sammy was his name. He spent quite a lot of his time looking for ways to make a buck, especially in church circles. You know, Jack, it's frighteningly easy to learn the language and patterns of a tight little evangelical culture, and Sammy became a bit of an expert. Nothing illegal exactly, but a bit iffy.'

'Was he a Christian?'

'Who knows? If he was, he didn't allow his faith to impact too much on his life, as far as I could see.' Doc hesitated. 'I wouldn't usually tell anyone this, Jack, but I did ask if it was possible – for Sammy's sake, I mean – for him to learn a lesson.'

'Asked God, you mean?'

'God? No, of course not. I filled a form in and sent it up to Church House.'

'You mean that Anglican place in London?'

'And the people up there came good. One day, not so long ago, Sammy thought he was on to a winner. Sammy had a lot of contacts in the Holy Land tour industry. Big business, although security's more of a problem nowadays. Have you ever been to the Holy Land, Jack?'

'Never, I'd love to go. At least, I think I would.'

'Nor me. Ah, well, perhaps we'll go together one day.'

Jack was taken aback by the immediacy with which his heart leapt at the prospect, but he could think of nothing to say in response. *Concentrate.*

'So, what was Sammy's business plan?'

'He knew that one of the most popular items on your average Holy Land itinerary was a boat trip on the Sea of Galilee. Being where Jesus and his disciples had been. A contemplative feast. Surely, people would love to have a souvenir of that memorable, deeply moving experience. He contacted someone he knew who was able to produce printed tee-shirts for a ridiculous unit price. The start of the season was imminent, so he ordered and paid for a very large consignment of suitably printed tee-shirts, and shipped them off to hotels, tour operators and anyone else who was interested, then sat back and waited happily for payment and profit.'

'Something went wrong?'

'Oh, yes. Sammy's first mistake was trusting his supplier. He had been sent a sample of the product. The general quality was poor, but that was predictable. Not a problem. The brightly coloured scene of Galilee was exactly what he'd asked for. The supplier's mistake was in failing to ensure that the correct slogan was passed on to whoever was responsible for having the words embroidered on top. Presumably the job had to be finished by pathetically paid factory workers in some distant land.'

'The wrong words on the tee-shirt?'

'You could say that. Only one mistake, mind you. One tiny but crucially important mistake. Each tee-shirt made exactly the same announcement, in very, very large capital letters.'

'Tell me.'

Doc boomed the message.

'I SOILED THE SEA OF GALILEE.'

Jack threw his head back and laughed. There was something deliciously satisfying about the idea of huge consequences springing from very small mistakes.

'Wow! Not an achievement many of us would be keen to boast about.'

'Not really. Church House did well, didn't they?'

'God, you mean?'

'Well, I'm sure they're very estimable people, but I don't think I'd go that far myself.'

'So, Sammy lost all his outgoings.'

'He did, yes.'

'Happy ending? Did he then become a Christian and write a book about how wrong it is to cheat people, and afterwards find he was getting invitations to conferences and things?'

'No, Jack, he didn't. Despite Church House doing exactly what they were asked to do, the scheme Sammy came up with to repair his finances was illegal, and, I'm sorry to say, really quite despicable. He was caught and sent to prison. I visited him there a while ago.'

Jack spoke without thinking.

'Why?'

'A couple of reasons. First, he's my friend. He's never cheated me. It wouldn't really matter much if he had. He thinks I'm seriously odd, but we get on very well. Second, I'm grateful to him for giving me something that makes me laugh every time I think of it. Hundreds – maybe thousands – of tee-shirts sitting in great piles somewhere in the world, each one carrying the same message. I SOILED THE SEA OF GALILEE. Wonderful!'

'Will he become a Christian one day?'

'I think I've got his back, but it's not my decision.'

'Did you mean it about us going together to the Holy Land?'

'Jack, I think I've always known I would make that trip one day. I know a man who went every year for the last two decades of his life.'

'Gosh. Must have been keen on Jesus.'

'Worshipped the ground he walked on – not Jesus, you understand, just the ground he walked on. Myself – I have to confess that the prospect makes me feel a little scared.'

'Of terrorists, you mean?'

'No, not at all. Scared of myself. Miriam and I were going to do it together one day. We talked about it quite a lot. In a way we were saving it up as a treat for when the right time came – and we had a bit more money. I've got the money now, but I don't know if I can handle being in the Garden Tomb with God, but without Miriam.' He paused. 'I tell you what, Jack. You and I going to Israel might be a very good experience for both of us. I'll ask George what he thinks of the idea. He spends a lot of time out there. Yes, I'll see what he says.'

'That's another of the things you promised you'd tell me. George. George this, George that, you're always going on about him. So, is George a real—?'

The Shadow Doctor lowered his head and raised a hand.

'Not now, Jack, please. A bit too heavy. Not now. Speaking of heavy, we're going to be meeting Trevor soon, and there are a couple of things you need to know. First, I've known Trevor Langston for years. In fact, I used to know him very well – very well indeed. He'll probably use my real name. I doubt if he knows anything about the shadow doctor stuff.'

Jack felt cold and frightened and alone.

'I don't understand. Why on earth didn't you tell me—?'

'I'm telling you now, and you'll hear a lot more about him and me before the end of the day.' A brief silence. 'You might wish you hadn't.'

Jack balled his hands into fists and struck the top of the steering wheel in his frustration.

'But I still don't understand! Why would you think—?'

'The other thing you need to know is that I – sorry, we – have only been granted twenty minutes of Trevor's time. It's taken me weeks just to arrange that. I know you're angry, but please, please, just be with me in this. I'm so glad you decided to come. If it helps . . .'

Jack became aware that the Shadow Doctor had leaned forward and was hunting through the glove compartment in front of him.

'I know I had an old forgiveness voucher in here somewhere. I'm pretty sure it's still valid, but . . .' He stopped hunting and turned accusingly towards Jack. 'You haven't used it, have you?'

Jack's smile was slightly teary, but it was genuine.

'Probably, Doc, yes. Almost certainly.'

'You can get a whole book of them, apparently.'

'I know, I've seen it.'

3

In the lion's den

Trevor Langston glanced at the watch on his left wrist.

'I'm sorry, I can only give you fifteen minutes, then I have an important leadership discussion followed by our monthly Vision and Strategy session all the way through until six.'

Using the sat-nav for the last part of their journey, Jack had driven through Meads Village before turning right and heading uphill towards open country on the edge of the Downs. Batley House, described on a large roadside sign as the headquarters of Sustain Ministries, was a substantial Edwardian building at the end of a half-mile drive that turned right from Dean Lane just after it intersected with a road that Jack recalled would eventually take you all the way up to Beachy Head and back down to Birling Gap on the other side.

A number of more modern buildings had been erected on both sides of the original dwelling. One of these, a long, low church-like structure with a large wooden cross affixed to a gable at one end, was the place where Jack had once heard Trevor Langston speak at a bi-monthly open event entitled Growing Together. A turmoil of excitement and fear almost overwhelmed him as he braked to a halt outside the front doors of the main building and sat for a moment, abruptly ambushed by arrival.

Minutes later a professionally pleasant and efficient receptionist ushered the two men down a central corridor and through the open doors of a large office at the back of the building, gracefully decorated and furnished, and equipped with huge modern windows looking out towards green-carpeted hills rising against today's blue sky in the distance. Trevor Langston, moving out from behind his highly polished wooden desk, greeted the Shadow Doctor with a shake of the hand, but hardly seemed to register Jack's existence. Tall, elegant and supremely confident in movement and manner, the silver-haired leader of Sustain Ministries waved at two neatly positioned chairs and returned to his place behind the desk.

Despite having unexpectedly lost a few of his promised twenty minutes, Doc nodded co-operatively in response to Trevor Langston's firm establishment of time restraints. Reaching down beside his chair, he carefully lifted the package, unwrapped the heavy, framed print, and leaned it against a substantial table-lamp at the end of the desk so that it was visible to the other two men.

'Right. If you don't mind, Trevor, I'd like you to take a look at this print for a moment.' He looked across the table. 'Have you ever come across an artist called Gustave Doré?'

The silvery locks moved with silken elegance as Langston indicated an uninvolved negative.

'Quite an interesting character actually.' The Shadow Doctor chattered happily as the other two took in details of the painting, Jack with fearful curiosity, Langston with little visible interest.

'French, of course. Died when he was just over fifty years old. Never married. I think he lived with his mother for most of his life, apart from a short and startlingly lucrative time in London. Doré was paid an amazing amount of money for a professional artist in that age. Very talented. He did all sorts of things. Printmaker, lots of illustration. Intriguingly, he virtually imprinted the popular image of Don Quixote in our minds. Now, that's interesting, isn't it, Trevor? Comics, caricature, sculpture. Died in the early 1880s, I think. And this—'

Raising a hand, he signalled an end to the biographical detail with a jab of his finger.

'This is one of many Bible illustrations painted by Doré. They were very popular during his lifetime. Specifically, it's a print from a painting of Jesus delivering the Sermon on the Mount. He painted a few versions of the same scene. When I saw this one recently, Trevor, I immediately connected it with something else I'd seen, and then, for reasons that you'll understand in a moment, I thought of you. So, I brought it along.' He gestured cheerfully. 'Here it is.'

Doc leaned back in his chair, rather, thought Jack, with the air of one who has made his point and needs to say no more. Perhaps, he conjectured with scant confidence, no more needed to be said. In any case, the church leader must surely find the comparison flattering.

'May I ask why it made you think of me?'

It was the grudging tone of one who is unaccustomed to requiring clarification. In response, Doc continued in the same chatty voice that he had used before.

'Ah, well, what happened was, I was re-watching an episode of *Frasier*, my favourite American sitcom – Jack enjoys it as well, don't you, Jack?'

Jack nodded and murmured agreement. He had no script. He had less than no script. Doc's statement happened to be true, but he would have nodded and murmured if it had not been. He made a mental note to mention this to the Shadow Doctor later.

'There was this scene, you see, where Frasier Crane's boss, a very fierce lady, is in hospital after an accident, and Frasier is visiting. As well as the serious injuries that are keeping her in hospital, she's got this lesser damage to her finger. So, she holds up her hand with this injured finger on it and complains to Frasier that she won't be able to use her car properly for a while because that's the finger she needs for driving – meaning that she uses it for gesturing aggressively to other drivers when they annoy her. Big laugh from the audience.' Doc turned his head to glance at the man behind the desk for a moment. 'Are you with me, Trevor?'

Presumably Trevor Langston understood the words that had been said, but a slight tilting back of his head and a hardening of the expression on his hawk-like face suggested to Jack that, after that unsavoury little anecdote, he might consider himself to be with Doc purely in a geographical sense.

'And a couple of days later, I happened to see this picture, and that is when I thought of you, Trevor.'

Not for the first time, Jack aborted his feeble attempt to understand or guess what on earth his new friend could possibly be talking or thinking about. Since moving into the cottage in the forest he had certainly become less agnostic about the possibility of rigid parallel lines meeting at some unexpected point in the cosmos, or even in the world, and there was a sort of excited liberation about knowing that phenomenon to be possible. Nevertheless, the process remained as bewildering as ever. At times it was hair-raising. This threatened to be one of those times.

Doc, continuing as though Langston had responded with fascinated enthusiasm, leaned forward and pointed to the figure in the centre of the painting.

'Look, you see! Here's Jesus sitting at the top of the slope, light shining from behind him, as it often does in this more classical style of biblical art, and here at the sides and up at the back are all the disciples and a few others I expect, scribes and Pharisees, odds and sods, you know, standing or sitting around listening to that famous, amazing list of the types of folk who've won the spiritual lottery, and simply won't be able to believe their luck when they get the news. Quite a nice piece of work, don't you think?'

Jack raised a defensive hand to his face, aware that tears were misting his eyes. For once, here in this office of all places, the Shadow Doctor was actually talking about Jesus in a straightforward way, using words that were easy to understand, and with a passion that made his soul want to sing. Stupid, but true. *So, don't spoil it, Doc. Just mean it. Please don't spoil it.*

'But now, look at this.' He beckoned with a crooked finger. 'Hold on – Trevor, come on, get a bit closer, I really want you to see this.'

Moving forward with a barely stifled sigh, Langston slapped his hands resignedly on the wooden surface in front of him, extended his body across the desk so that he could see clearly. Jack, not wanting to miss anything, twisted to his right and pivoted on an elbow so that he could still view the picture between the heads of the other two men.

'Now, look at Jesus.' There was something new in Doc's voice, an intensity and, to Jack's ears, a note of authority. 'See how he's raising his right hand high and sticking his finger straight up as he looks in our direction. Remember what I said about the woman in that *Frasier* episode, Trevor? OK. Here's what I reckon. I reckon Jesus is doing what she does. I reckon he's using his upraised finger to tell you, at this precise moment, exactly what he thinks of your ministry.' The atmosphere changed. 'Any idea why he would want to do that?'

The three bodies in that room might as well have been frozen solid. Jack, motionless with shock, raged inwardly. Learning to trust the Shadow Doctor had been a gradual process from the very beginning, but it was certainly a process in progress, as it were. It had been happening. Now an abyss had opened.

After a miniature eternity, Trevor Langston cleared his throat and very slowly levered himself back into his swivel-chair. Regarding the Shadow Doctor with a steady, wide-eyed expression of something close to pity and scorn, he now appeared totally at ease. Jack lowered his gaze as he hunched miserably back into his own seat. No wonder his partner in foolishness hadn't wanted him along for this particular ride. The whole thing was ill-judged, badly conceived and pointless. It almost took his breath away. If Jack had felt able to drag any words from inside himself, he would have begged Doc to grab the stupid picture and its stupid wrapping, and let the two of them get their stupid, stupid selves out of there.

But the Shadow Doctor was clearly not finished yet. He spoke very quietly.

'I did ask you a question, Trevor. Why do you think Jesus might feel like that about your ministry?' He raised his eyes to check the clock on the wall behind Langston's head. 'We do have a few minutes left out of our fifteen. Plenty of time to answer my question.'

It was strange. Jack suddenly recalled a phrase that his father had mentioned to him, something that he had heard in the course of a trip to South Africa in apartheid days. The 'blue wall of silence' was an expression used by those who had learned not to put their trust in the police during those dreadful times. An unspoken policy of concealment by the ones who held the power. Why would those words come into his mind now?

Hardly daring to move, Jack watched as Trevor Langston vibrated his head in tiny, rapid movements from side to side. Perhaps Doc's words and general behaviour had been so shockingly outrageous that it was difficult to select just one of the huge number of appropriately crushing and eminently reasonable responses available to him. He succeeded in selecting one. His voice was perfectly assured.

'I am taken aback. I have no idea if this is intended to be a joke of some kind, but I hardly know what to say. To be honest, I find your veiled accusation towards me, and your vulgar, trivial misrepresentation of an image of the Lord Jesus, flippant, foolish and seriously offensive I'm afraid.'

The Shadow Doctor nodded slowly and allowed a humourless smile to stretch his lips.

'Mm! Two and a half out of three for alliteration, Trevor, but would you say, and would you imagine that the god you claim to serve would say that this little joke of mine, as you call it, is more or less foolish and offensive than an innocent person being deliberately and cynically used and manipulated by the very man who was supposedly committed to protecting and caring for her? A little bit more, would you say? Or a little bit less?'

Trevor Langston leaned back in his chair, a smidgeon of a gleam appearing in his eye.

'Am I to understand that you are actually accusing me of a specific sin, Michael? Because if that is the case, I would ask you to give careful attention to three verses in the seventh chapter of the Gospel of Matthew.'

The Shadow Doctor replied without a moment's hesitation.

'Oh, the ones about judging others, you mean? Motes and beams and all that stuff.'

Langston's face changed. Jack judged the new expression to be intended to convey duty and sorrow. His tone closely matched that of the Shadow Doctor.

'I am truly, sincerely sorry that the words I am going to say now need to be spoken, but I have little choice. The Spirit is upon and within me.'

He paused, his blue eyes, more piercing than any the young man had ever seen, fixed immovably on the Shadow Doctor's face. Jack remembered those eyes from a couple of large meetings he had attended in his very early twenties. Trevor Langston, a big name in the evangelical world, had been the main speaker. During one of those evenings, at the end of the talk, and immediately before a call to the front, Langston had announced with calm assurance, 'The Lord has just called six people to minister in the Sudan.' He then panned across the assembly, those brilliant, corkscrewing eyes missing not a single soul. Jack recalled the next period of his life as a tortuous time, in which any and all references of any kind to the Sudan, whatever its needs, and wherever it might be, filled him with a choking sense of guilt and confusion. Even now, those feelings slumbered quietly somewhere inside him. At no point had it occurred to him that the great man of God might have been mistaken.

At this moment all that filled him was an anguished, passionate desire to run like mad from a situation that seemed to be threatening his new-found, and still very slim hope of finding some kind of peace with himself and God. The Shadow Doctor appeared unmoved by the situation, and, as far as Jack could tell, by the amazing eyes.

'As you know,' continued Trevor Langston, 'and please believe me when I say that it gives me no satisfaction whatever to remind you of this, I have personally witnessed you on a number of occasions in the streets of the town where we once both lived, drunk and incapable, swearing and shouting to the entire world, regardless of whether they wanted to hear you or not, about the God who had failed you, and, as I believe you expressed it, had heartlessly condemned you to a life of misery.'

Jack felt himself entering a state of shock that was almost physical, but the Shadow Doctor's complete failure to respond seemed to goad Langston into new and rarefied heights of accusation.

'You may or may not recall, and I quite understand you having no wish to bring such things to mind, a Sunday evening during which I was obliged to accompany two or three of the brothers when we were urgently summoned by a panic-stricken young curate, and asked to remove you from the High Street Anglican church where you had ended up prostrated in a pool of your own vomit after staggering up the centre-aisle and collapsing across the altar rail.'

A pause.

'There is a great deal more. You know that. Much, much more. I have no intention of mentioning any of those other occurrences here. I think I have said enough. You speak to me about ill-using those who depend on my leadership and care. God alone knows how many believers came close to losing their faith because a man they had trusted and admired fell apart so comprehensively when faced with a challenge that, let us be brutally and I hope constructively honest, was far from unique. People lose their loved ones. You lost your wife. I personally know and have ministered to many who have suffered in that way.'

He lifted a pen from the pot on his desk, clicking the point into view as though signalling that the time had come to move on to the important work of the day. His blue-ray glance seemed to acknowledge Jack's presence at last.

'Forgive my frankness in speaking of matters that are normally best left unsaid, but perhaps it helps you to see more clearly why it is not easy or helpful for me to receive sermons or lectures from your friend on the subject of sin.'

Jack discovered that his jaw had actually dropped. An excess of unexpected and staggering information had temporarily robbed him of control over mind and body. He knew next to nothing about his new friend's past life. How was he to absorb Langston's brutally vivid accusations? Were they even true? Recovering the use of his faculties at last, he turned troubled eyes in Doc's direction. Still no change there. He appeared as serene as ever.

There was a sudden, hesitant knock on the door, a knock that would perhaps have preferred to remain unacknowledged. Paradoxically, it intruded like a thunderclap. Trevor Langston half rose in his chair, clearly resolved to dispense with his two unwanted visitors and proceed speedily to the impending and important meeting.

'Jack,' said the Shadow Doctor quietly, 'would you be kind enough to just answer the door, and politely tell whoever it is that Trevor will be held up for some time.'

Langston towered instantly and aggressively, but Doc continued in a relaxed, almost conversational manner.

'Trevor, we do need to have a chat about Julia Thomas. We can do that accompanied or unaccompanied by whoever is standing on the other side of that door. Your choice.'

It was extraordinary. After a moment of paralysis, the church leader's body seemed to deflate like a punctured dummy. Sinking into his chair, he remained motionless, apart from a rapid, rhythmic movement at the centre of his chest, perhaps betraying panic or shock, or both.

'Jack?'

Hypnotised by the magical transformation, Jack almost jumped when Doc repeated his name. After a formal handshake and a whispered conversation at the door with a quiet man who introduced himself as Ralph, he regained his seat and waited with bated breath to see what would happen next.

The pause before the Shadow Doctor spoke again seemed so long that Jack began to feel like screaming. When he did say something at last, his tone was almost conversational. At least it broke the interminable silence.

'Trevor, when I think about it, I do actually agree with you about the inappropriateness of having a discussion about sin. I don't really want to talk about that either. Let's not use that word. I know what it means, and I think I know what you mean by it, but a word like "sin" can so easily become like something printed neatly on a laminated list. Just another pulpy word to add to a very long and tedious list. No, let's not talk about sin. Let's talk about wrong-doing. Doing wrong. Wrongness. Let's talk about something that is hugely, vastly wrong, but is also, in the act itself, grimly trivial and personally indulgent. Let's talk about the infliction on a vulnerable person of something that is utterly inexcusable, in exchange for – what? Five minutes or so of physical satisfaction?'

Trevor Langston's tongue passed briefly across his lips.

'I have not the slightest idea what you are talking about.'

'Interesting. I've often wondered why people feel the need to abandon the use of verbal contractions when they feel threatened. I suppose a wall looks more impressive when the stones are substantial. Still a wall, though. Come on now, Trevor, you know exactly the sort of thing I'm talking about. You must have preached and written about stuff like this so often.'

Langston smoothed the palm of his hand with exaggerated care across the polished surface of the desk as though checking for dust. He took a breath like an inward sigh, as if he were about to say something. The Shadow Doctor continued before he could speak.

'Let me think. What about that famous king in the Old Testament, the one who also deliberately did something catastrophically wrong? And then, instead of owning up and trying to make things right, did something even worse and equally mean-spirited to cover up his first crime. My goodness, it must have become a daily nightmare for him, mustn't it, Trevor? Can you imagine having to grit your teeth and hope that your massive power and reputation will protect you from having to face up to your own selfishness? Can you even begin to guess how that feels? In the end, the choice was taken away from that man. A prophet arrived one day at the palace to tell him a story. Stories are power-ful, beguiling weapons, aren't they? They can trap and distract at the same time. And this guilty, self-deluding man, he plummeted, threw himself, into the prophet's trap – well, God's trap, I suppose. Everything changed after that. Any idea who I'm talking about, Trevor?'

Trevor swallowed, and as he did so, the words learned by rote long, long ago passed with a mildly hysterical random-ness through Jack's mind.

The Adam's apple is the lump or protrusion that is formed by the angle of the thyroid cartilage surrounding the larynx.

Langston took a deep, steadying breath before speaking. Perhaps, thought Jack, a last-ditch attempt to take the high ground. His voice was thin.

'I think you had better leave.'

The Shadow Doctor's voice was unemotional, and steady as a rock.

'No. I disagree. I think, for your sake, Trevor, and for the sake of those who look to you for leadership, and perhaps most of all for Julia's sake, that I had better not leave.'

The Shadow Doctor's words seemed to hang in the air, a heavy, invisible sword suspended by a thread.

Julia? Julia Thomas was the name Doc had used earlier. Jack was barely able to breathe. His could feel his own lips moving and twitching very slightly, as though something urgently needed to be said, but would never allow itself to be encased in puny words. Something to do with the fact that one of the giants in his life was shrinking visibly before his eyes, while the other was growing in stature and authority with every second that passed.

'If it helps, Trevor,' continued Doc, his voice resonant with certainty, 'I know exactly what's happening in your mind at this moment. You feel as if you're crouching in front of a very large, high-definition screen, watching with sick terror as scenes from your recent past and potentially horrendous future are played out before your eyes, and the eyes of many, many others. These scenes include a brief adulterous affair with a very young married woman who would have trusted you with her life because, in her eyes, you were and are an amazing prophet of God. After confusing and entrapping her into doing something that she will be ashamed of for the rest of her life, you managed to persuade her that she was responsible for what had happened because of what you described as her provocative behaviour. Later, she and her husband Peter were removed from your organisation because, according to you, and I am able to quote . . .' He reached into his jacket pocket and withdrew a small slip of paper. 'Here is your divine revelation to those two young people. "The Lord would have you seek important work for him in other parts of the nation." That absurdly spiritualised use of innocent words constitutes an extraordinarily cold and cruel wrapping for such a nasty little lie. Did a lot of earnest prayer go into that decision, Trevor?'

Langston said nothing.

'Finally, you warned Julia that if she told her husband or anyone else what had happened, she would be placing her salvation in jeopardy. She believed you. As far as I know, I am the only person she has ever told about this. It was over a cup of tea after a chance meeting in a charity shop, as it happens. Thank God, those are the kinds of places where Jesus still hangs around wasting his time nowadays. The best things never change, do they?

'That young woman was and remains filled with a shame and a bewilderment that threatens not just her marriage, and not just her desire to be alive, but also, now that she has spoken to me, a profound terror of death because you threatened her with eternal damnation if she spoke to anyone about what had happened. She is, to use a very apt modern phrase, in pieces. I should add that I believe every single word she said to me.'

Doc's voice as he continued was steady and gentle. 'Trevor, your reply to the question I'm going to ask you now will affect the whole of the rest of your life. Tell me I was wrong to believe the woes poured out to me by that heart-broken girl, and I promise Jack and I will leave you to whatever variety of peace you can cobble together for yourself.' He dropped his gaze. 'I know you too well to bother reminding you who is in the room with us.'

In the ensuing silence Jack grew aware of something that he could only describe to himself as an invisible energy in the air. He had felt it twice before in the company of the Shadow Doctor and had found the experience puzzling and vaguely exciting. It was akin to the buzzing sensation he had known in live theatre when a very dramatic or moving scene was in progress. Something else? Difficult to judge. The jury, if there was one, was out.

'Here is my question. Only two possible answers. Was Julia lying to me?'

33

By now, Trevor Langston's original relaxed, dominant posture was nothing but a hollow pose. The colour had drained from his distinguished features. He looked older, less dignified, perhaps even on the verge of tears, his eyes fixed wide with fear and defeat. Even the famous mane of silver-blond hair seemed to Jack to have lost some of its lustre in the short time since they had arrived.

The slow-motion shake of his head in response to Doc's question was almost imperceptible.

'Very well. We have to come up with a plan, Trevor. I think I can persuade Julia that she needs to hear the truth directly from you, and I must be there when that happens. In addition, you need to tell at least one person at the highest level of your organisation exactly how you mistreated her.' The Shadow Doctor waited for a second. 'I insist on being there for that encounter as well. You will absolutely not want that, but there is no alternative. If those two things happen I think I can help you to work through to the least disastrous outcome. No guarantees. I have no idea how Julia will react, and I have no control over her husband's response if she has the courage to tell him. Understand, Trevor, this is not a plan designed to save your neck. It's for Julia. You could at least end up feeling as clean as it's possible for any of us to feel after facing the worst of ourselves.'

He leaned back in his chair.

'If you are not willing to go along with those suggestions, I shall offer Julia quite different advice. The nature of that advice and its possible consequences will be none of your business. So, will you do as I ask?'

Jack estimated that the nod of Trevor's head was, if anything, even less perceptible than the shake, but it was definitely a nod. Doc turned towards Jack.

'Trevor and I need to have a chat about one or two things, Jack, so I'll see you back at the car. Is that OK?'

Jack nodded vigorously as he rose to his feet. Uninterrupted time with the contents of his mind was exactly what he needed. Doc lifted a hand.

'Sorry – if you don't mind, could you take the picture and the wrapping with you. Thanks very much. We might need an hour or more. I seem to remember there's a dreadful café down at the bottom of the hill. Why don't you get yourself a coffee?'

Turning to leave the room with a statutory whisper of farewell, Jack's last sight of Trevor Langston was the great Christian leader sitting motionless behind his desk like a poorly wrought statue of himself. He breathed a sigh of relief as the door of the office closed with a soft, expensive clunk behind him.

4

The small person inside

'What will happen?'

'With Julia and Peter, you mean?'

'Of course. Do you think Peter will go and punch him on the nose?'

'I have no idea. Julia may decide not to tell him. I think she will in the end, though. I'll help as much as she wants me to.'

'Will he forgive her?'

'I hope so. They were both so young – children really. Starry-eyed and vulnerable.'

'I really hope their marriage lasts.'

'So do I.'

'Do you think what's happened could cause more problems than it solves?'

'I'm trusting that it won't.'

'And what about Trevor Langston?' Jack was faintly embarrassed to discover that the residual awe and respect of his attitude to the great man still prevented him from using the Christian name alone. 'You know, Doc, we used to read his books all the time. Our Bible-study group in Bromley went through one of them from September right up to Christmas once. I liked them because he sounded so clear, and sure about things. I'd never heard anyone sound as sure as that. I certainly didn't, because I wasn't. I'm still not.' Jack blinked hard, as though clearing his sight. 'I can't believe what just happened. I mean – all of it. He was – he is so respected. How could he be so – so not what everyone thinks?'

Doc had emerged from the building after just over an hour. Jack had spent the whole of that time sitting in the parked X-Trail, attempting to make his way through a maze of unthinkable pathways. Neither had spoken as Jack steered out of the Christian centre and drove slowly down towards the Eastbourne seafront. Only as they passed the Victorian bandstand on their right had he spoken his first question aloud.

Glancing to one side now, Jack saw that Doc was leaning back in his seat, his face almost haggard with something that seemed akin to exhaustion. He raised a limp arm in response to what had been said and replied without opening his eyes. His voice, no longer authoritative, sounded weak but uncompromising.

'Easy there, Jack. It's not as simple as that, is it? Nobody is one thing. He's not. You're not. I'm not, thank God. You heard what he said about me. And to answer the question you're too polite to ask, it was all true. I was that person. I'm also, through an act of overwhelming and undeserved friendship, what I am now. I really, truly am.'

Risking another sideways look, Jack saw that Doc had opened his eyes. A solitary tear was trickling down the cheek that was visible to him in that glance. Driving on along Royal Parade past the Sovereign Centre and left off the roundabout in the direction of the north, he did his best to store the words that had just been said. Above and beyond them, the sky was an unsullied white, shining as though it was enjoying a secret. It was some time before the Shadow Doctor spoke again.

'I remember when Trevor's first book came out. I enjoyed it. It was a great read. He'd been working in this high street church in the Midlands, and things had suddenly taken off.' He waved his hands around in illustration. 'Everything became shapeless and exciting and glowing and full of possibilities. People got the feeling that God really did exist after all, and was right there in the middle of them, changing lives and situations and all sorts of things. Trevor was leading them through that and loving every minute of it. I knew him well, and I knew the church, and I knew the story was true. And that's who Trevor was then. He didn't quite know what had hit him, and he was all the better for that not knowing. And then, of course, the book flew off the shelves like parrots in a pet shop and changed everything. He became a bit of a star.'

Jack nodded. 'I read that book as well, quite a bit later than you I suppose it must have been. He became even more of a star after that, didn't he? Lots of books. Lots of speaking. Didn't he open that big ministry place in the north before he moved down to Eastbourne? I heard him speak a few times. Knocked me out. Festivals and what not – including up at the place where we've just been. Always packed out. Very powerful speaker. Fireworks of some sort guaranteed. It was – well, it was wonderful.'

Jack was about to describe the dismal way in which he had been affected by Trevor Langston's message from God about the Sudan but changed his mind. Too indulgent. 'In any case,' whispered the ghost of an evangelical imp who occupied his shoulder at the worst and most challenging

moments, 'perhaps you should be in Sudan right now.'
Unthinkingly, he gave his left shoulder a light smack. *Ask a question.*

'What went wrong?'

'Trouble with your shoulder?'

'Bit of an ache.'

'A bit of an ache? You should have that seen to.'

'What went wrong for Trevor?'

'Ah, Jack, it's not about one thing going wrong, is it? It never is. The problem is that we're all faulty mechanisms. Someone I know happily and hopefully described his own relationship with the creator as "God driving a battered old jalopy with a smile on his face". I'm sure Trevor did a lot of good for a lot of people, but something did change. He wrote one more book that I quite enjoyed, but after that – who knows? Maybe he wanted to be a cool religious roadster and choose the direction for himself. It happens to the worst and the best of us. He seemed to suddenly discover capital letters and exclamation marks, and began to express things in short, pithy, rather boring paragraphs that were never quite open to discussion or debate.

'I remember one book that was about the messages God had communicated to Trevor every day over a period of three months or so. In the introduction he said that, of course, he couldn't be 100 per cent sure that it was word-for-word correct and directly from the heart of the Almighty, but having read it myself, I did get the distinct impression that God agreed in just about every detail with Trevor over absolutely everything connected with faith and Christian living.'

'And this thing that's happened?'

'The business with poor Julia and her husband is probably, in one grossly distorted sense, a dismally small but heavily bracketed indulgence. Maybe Trevor was able to convince himself that his crucial big-picture mission to the world had to be protected from its consequences. Perhaps he confessed it to God and decided that the divine vibe was lining up with him yet again. People convince themselves of the most extraordinary things sometimes. I've known at least two women who were excluded from the place where they worshipped after their husbands had affairs with other members of the church. The husbands were too useful to lose apparently. Handy to have around. It beggars belief, but it happens. I tell you, Jack, when individual Christians vote out of their humanity there's always going to be trouble. Julia and her husband Peter might have been victims of that kind of nonsense thinking.'

'Then you came along.'

'Yes, then I came along – or rather, Julia came along and spilled the whole story out to me for some reason. I knew something had to happen after that, so I started working on setting up the meeting with Trevor.'

Ask the question you want to ask.

'Doc, can I ask you – did you enjoy getting to the bit about Julia after all the horrible things he said about you?'

Doc let out a little laugh, apparently welcoming the notion with equanimity.

'Sour grapes, you mean? Very good question. No, once upon a time I'd have loved every minute, every second of it. Not any more. As you know, I was pretty sure he would talk about those things. If I'd been looking forward to hitting back I don't think I would have been allowed to see him at all.'

Almost everything in Jack wanted to make sure that he understood exactly who was doing the allowing or not allowing in the Shadow Doctor's life. Later perhaps. Doc looked so defeated.

'There was a moment, earlier on when we were with Trevor, that made me realise something.'

Shifting uneasily, Doc used the knuckles of his left hand to limply knock a gentle rhythm on the window beside him.

'I do hope it's the realisation of something positive, Jack. Tell me it was, even if it wasn't. A friendly little lie.'

'No, it was a positive thing. A good thing – I think. You told Trevor that we both enjoy watching *Frasier*, and actually it's true. But I suddenly realised that even if it hadn't been true, I would have nodded and agreed. That's quite new for me. I just wanted to support you.'

'Thanks, Jack. That is positive, and I'm sorry I sounded so pathetic. I wanted to tell you all that about Trevor, but I'm afraid there's not a great deal of me left just at the moment. I am – what am I? I'm filleted. It's kind of OK when you're in the act of throwing out thunder and lightning and whatever on behalf of somebody else, but there's not a lot to hang on to afterwards. I don't see things like my jalopy friend does. I'm sharing some kind of horse-drawn vehicle with God. He does the steering when necessary, but after that the reins get put back in my sad little hands, and whatever you may think, I'm rubbish at steering for myself.' The hand on the window was stilled as he turned to look at Jack. 'Understand that I wouldn't take back a single word that I said to Trevor, but I do feel for him in a way. Being forced to take a good look at the small person inside you is never much fun. I know how true that is. And I'm hating it right now. If you must know, seeing as I've collapsed into a self-revelatory mode, this sort of thing can strip you of courage and confidence. That can go on right up to the point when the next job fills the horizon and you become a passenger again.'

5

Laughing with Miriam

Doc suddenly emitted a tired, mirthless chuckle.

'By the way, Trevor's wife is called Marigold. In our wicked moments, my wife and I—'

Miriam?

'Miriam, you mean?' Jack pretended to study something far ahead in the distance.

The Shadow Doctor flicked his young friend's shoulder gently with the tips of his fingers, a small, generous token of acknowledgement.

'I can tell you, Jack, that if my wife – Miriam – was here now, we'd be discussing how long it's likely to take for Marigold to get on my case after what's just happened. Miriam once said that, given half a chance, that lady could and probably would talk God into redefining the fall, and persuade him to invite Adam and Eve back into Eden. Save Jesus all the hassle later. I rebuked her, of course.'

'What would – might Marigold say to you about what's just happened with Trevor?'

Doc considered.

'I guess she would probably point out that those who do most for God are always targeted by the devil, and that it's very naïve of me to believe the things said by that young woman when it's almost certain that she wickedly lured Trevor into sin. And, she would definitely add, what business is it of mine anyway? She'd give me hell. And then she'd go home and, if she hadn't already done it, she'd give Trevor hell to the power of goodness knows how much.

'In our sillier moments Miriam and I would refer to that lady as Jezebel. "What time are Ahab and Jezebel due for dinner?" we would say with childish glee. Dangerous, Jack. A dangerous game. Miriam very nearly called her by that name out loud once. Terrifyingly, she was in the process of warmly sympathising with her over something fairly trivial to do with Trevor, I seem to recall. By some miracle I just about managed to grasp what was happening and inter-rupted. I prevented a potentially surreal outcome in the nick of time, a split second before she completed the first syllable of the wrong name. We both fell about. Had to pretend we were laughing at a hilarious salt cellar or some-thing, and then, the trickiest trick of all, double declutching back into the sympathy again. Ah, the skills you need for normal social interaction. Somebody once said, Jack, that when you scratch a Christian you find a human being. I tell you what, if you scratch a married couple you find a married couple, whether they're Christians or not.'

If Miriam was here now.

'Going back to Miriam – what else would she say to you if she was here?'

Yawning, Doc leaned his head back and stared at the roof of the car.

'I'm not exactly sure, but I can tell you that if my darling wife was sitting in this car now, and I really cannot begin to tell you how much I wish she was, she would know exactly what is happening in me. Let me think what that means. First, she would know I am feeling reduced and close to powerless. She would know I'm feeling that, just for the moment, I've had enough. And, just as importantly, much, much more importantly, she would know that my feeling is wrong. But she definitely wouldn't say anything so pointlessly positive until quite a bit later. She'd probably suggest that we go and have a drink and something nice to eat, and – actually, how about we pull in somewhere now and I'll grab us some tea and a large piece of very indulgent cake to have in the car. I know she would approve of that. Let's find somewhere where we can still see the sea in the distance.'

Doc was gone for longer than expected, and when he returned there was a thoughtfulness about his manner that disturbed Jack a little. He wondered if it would be best to get the subject off Miriam and the past. Talk about something a bit more positive.

The Shadow Doctor stared out towards the faraway sea as the two men drank weak tea from cardboard cups and ate disappointing slices of some indeterminate variety of cake. They were parked in a diagonal space overlooking a particularly dismal view of Eastbourne's eastern fringe. Jack was about to make a joke about the sad nature of their refreshment break, when Doc continued to speak about his wife as though he had never paused.

'I can tell you what Miriam would say if she was here. I reckon she'd do her very best to find something for us to laugh about. Lots of difficult moments ended up with us laughing.'

'Such as?'

Doc's brows were knitted as he stared into the distance, then he unexpectedly released a guffaw of laughter as a memory surfaced.

'Someone like you, with a soul more tender and highly principled than mine, might find this story a little shocking, Jack, but I'll tell you anyway. Miriam and I worked together for most of our married life. No children.' He waved a hand in dismissal. 'Please don't ask me to talk about that.'

I'm not asking you to talk about anything, thought Jack, *but you are, and I'm glad – I think.*

'What sort of work did you do together?'

The Shadow Doctor smiled.

'Privately, we called it blethering on to people. We led all sorts of things – all kinds of groups in every kind of setting you can think of. Mostly very informal. I suppose we had only one aim really. We set out to help people relax and accept themselves, to see that it was OK to fail and pick yourself up and start again. I expect we made all kinds of mistakes. Actually, I know for sure that we did.'

Doc's face clenched like a fist. He uttered a loud tutting noise.

'Good Lord, Jack, I curl up like a frightened armadillo when I think back to some of the things I said so pompously from the front, things that went way beyond what I was and what I was sure of. In a way, the worst thing was that, although my heart was sometimes pumped up with nonsense, my manner was not pompous at all. I was good at that. I think I said my piece with warmth and a sort of generous confidence. Very impressive, I was. You know a bit about that, I think, don't you, Jack?'

Jack tapped the steering wheel with one finger and nodded frowning agreement.

'Yes,' he replied, 'I suppose I do in a way. I haven't done all that stuff that you and Miriam did, but, as I've already told you, I know exactly how it feels to offer people things that I haven't got. It was really bad for me in the end. You and your wife don't sound like me, though. I'm sure a lot of the work you and Miriam did was helpful to people. Must have been, surely?'

'Well, we did all right, I suppose. As far as it went. Lots of laughter, a few tears. We were good at making friends with people – Miriam especially. No, both of us. I don't know . . .'

He seemed to fade, inwardly and outwardly.

'The story?'

Doc pulled himself together and smiled.

'Oh yes, the shocking story I wanted to tell you. We were spending a week at one of those Christian conference centres where people come for all sorts of different events. This one was a five-day thing, I think. Just us speaking in the mornings and joining in with some of the other stuff that the centre organised during the rest of the days. About seventy or eighty people putting up with us for a week in return for us putting up with them. Nice, friendly group, but as usually happens when people relax and discover that it's OK to tell the truth, there were lots of problems aired, endless chats, loads of people wanting to be prayed with. All that was part of what we did in those days – we accepted that – but by the end of this week I'm talking about we were worn out, finished, sick of the sound of our own bleating voices. At lunchtime on the final full day we devised a cunning plan.'

'More cunning than dear old Baldrick's cunning plans?'

'Less colourful, and not at all funny, but yes, much more cunning. We decided to escape as quickly and quietly as we could after the meal to our wonderful room at the top of the back stairs, complete with bathroom and toilet. En suite was a rare luxury in those days, I can tell you. Up there, we reckoned we could hide for a couple of hours from the world in general, and our little fiery furnace of a Christian world in particular. So off we went, and you need to move fast in these situations, Jack. You're lost if you don't. It's essential to look as if you're on your way to do something important, useful and preferably godly.

'And that is what we did. It worked, right up to the point when we reached the peak – the summit of the stairs – and were about to step into the en suite Shangri-La that this conference centre had so kindly provided. Only one, solitary step needed to achieve our aim, when suddenly, as if by magic, a lovely, fluffy, elderly lady called Brenda, who was a member of our group, appeared to the right of us and began to talk about her life just as seamlessly as though we'd arranged to meet her there, just outside our room.

'Miriam really was the kindest person in the world, and we both worked hard at giving full attention to this dear lady, but I knew my wife was having as much trouble concentrating as me. The problem when you make all that extra effort to keep your eyes open and sympathy radiating is that you can end up looking slightly mad and weirdly rigid. We got by, though, until Brenda, in mid-flow, began a sentence with, "As I said to my husband just before he hung himself . . ."

'Oh, it was terrible, Jack. Truly awful. At the precise moment when I needed to appear deeply shocked and profoundly sympathetic . . .' He clutched his stomach. 'This maverick laugh started to rise from somewhere down here inside me, and it gained such momentum that I really thought I would not be able to control myself.' Doc wagged a finger triumphantly. 'But I did. I did it, Jack. It was hard, but I'm proud to say that I did it.'

'So, all was well.'

A wry smile appeared on Doc's face.

'Actually, no. All was not well. It might have been but for the fact that Brenda, probably noting the expression of horror on Miriam's face, volunteered an extra piece of information. "I have to tell you, Miriam my dear, that Kenneth hanging himself was the best thing that ever happened to me." I developed a coughing fit and had to disappear into the bedroom. Miriam managed to join me shortly afterwards, claiming concern for my physical well-being. We collapsed back on to our comfortable king-sized bed and lined up a couple of pillows in case we needed something soft to make noises into.'

Jack managed to produce a sound in the back of his throat that might have been laughter, but his heart was not in it. In his mind he rehearsed a lightness of tone, rubbing his left earlobe before he spoke. He had been trying to eradicate the habit for some time.

'Anyway, let's make a move. This really is the armpit of Eastbourne. I've got a bag here for the rubbish. We'll dump it when we get home.'

Jack reversed carefully onto the coast road. Traffic could be disturbingly fast moving just outside the town. He formulated a sentence in his mind as he pulled across the road and headed east.

'So, you and – your wife, did you beat yourselves up about the business with Brenda afterwards?'

He sensed rather than saw a glance of total comprehension from the Shadow Doctor. Damn the man! He always knew. Even sideways he knew.

'Not really, no. I seem to remember we had a chat with Brenda later on that evening. She was fine.' He paused. 'Sends shivers down your spine, doesn't it, Jack?'

Jack shrugged and shook his head. 'I just – I just hate the idea of someone saying something so . . .' He shivered. 'Something so dreadful, and me reacting like that. I think I'd have – well, I think I'd have wanted to die. I get guilty as hell about next to nothing, as it is. I mean – I mean, if it's not a silly question, what do you think God would have thought about that?'

6

The myth of Sisyphus

Doc sighed and shook his head slowly. 'Not a silly question at all. And you're right to put guilt and hell in the same bracket, Jack. Guilt belongs in hell because that's where it comes from. Difficult to say what God would have thought, though. He doesn't communicate with me in triplicate as he seems to with some folk I've met. I suppose, looking back from my advanced years, clinging to a new temporary ledge, and with a completely fresh lack of understanding, I guess he might have said to any gawping angels hanging around at the time, "Look at my two nice, silly children laughing their heads off on that bed. No problem, they'll get their act back together in a bit."

'Of course, that's only my idea. I don't really know what God would have said. Something like that, perhaps. Actually, I think, even back then, a long time before – before the darkness came, Miriam and I had begun to get our heads round something important. It's to do with one of a list of tyrannies that seem to have screwed Christians up from about three o'clock on the afternoon of the day after the resurrection.'

'That early?'

'Well, possibly a little after three, perhaps.'

'A long list?'

'A list containing any one of those nasties would be far too long, Jack. I can think of a few off the top of my head.

51

I'll tell you about the others some time, but the one that my wife – and me as well, coming up in her slipstream as usual – were just beginning to escape from was to do with the tyranny of spiritual success. More accurately, it's the tyranny of a belief that if you work hard, or pray constantly, or learn the Bible backwards by heart, or whip yourself three times a day, you'll be able to match your message. Then, when God does something amazing, well, you can feel good about yourself as well. Ironically, its foundation is more often vanity than humility. In fact, it tends to be one of the last vanities to go. But when it's gone – then, like poor old Sisyphus—'

'Is that the mythological bloke who was doomed to go on pushing a boulder up to the top of a mountain for ever? Mrs Williams told us about him when we were in year six. He was a king, wasn't he?'

'Yes, full marks to Mrs Williams for teaching it and you for remembering. He was the king of Ephyra – Corinth, it became in the end. He was so big-headed and crafty and deceitful that the gods condemned him to roll this massive boulder up a hill again and again, without ever managing to get it over the top. In fact, I think he lost control and it rolled back and hit him every single time. So, when we say a job is Sisyphean—'

'Not very many of us do.'

'No. True. Can be useful in a crossword, though, Jack. All right, if a pretentious person such as myself were to say that a task was Sisyphean, what would we mean?'

Jack rocked forward over the wheel, and as far back in the seat as he could go, struggling to stretch his back and his arms and his brain.

'We – or rather you, you being the pretentious one: no offence.'

Doc expelled air through his lips and gestured that none was taken with two outspread hands.

'You would mean that the job, whatever it might be, was very hard work.'

'Precisely.'

'And a complete waste of time.'

'Yes, that's it. The task would be laborious and futile.'

'You'll be eaten alive by a wild thesaurus one of these days.'

Doc's eyes brightened.

'Think so? I would love that. Swallowed alive and intact with a bit of luck. What interesting innards a creature like that must have. Fascinating. Intriguing. Captivating. Enthralling. Don't you agree?'

'Doc, I think I've lost the thread as usual. Maybe I didn't have much of a grip on it in the first place. Now it's gone altogether. Something about tyrannies. How did that link up with Sisyphus?'

'Ah, yes, the tyranny of spiritual success. Having to match your own message. That was it. Miriam and I spent a few years labouring under the weight of feeling too grubby and unholy to represent God. We were, of course. How could we not be? As I've said to you before, God is so annoyingly, unremittingly perfect. But we probably spent as much time moaning and groaning about our unworthiness as we spent getting on with the job. Like old Sisyphus, we dismally rolled what we had been taught to regard as the weight of our personal inadequacy to the top of every success that we saw in the work we did, then gave up and let it roll back over us, crushing a lot of the satisfaction we might have enjoyed and appreciated in the good things that happened. And that went on for quite a long time, until I read something by Albert Camus.'

'Never heard of him.'

'Philosopher, journalist, enemy of nihilism, all sorts of things. Died in his mid-forties. And he actually wrote a book called *The Myth of Sisyphus*.'

'Ah!'

'It's a long time since I read the book, but as far as I can remember Camus reckoned that there was a moment in the eternal repetition of rolling that tiresome rock up towards the summit of the mountain and seeing it come tumbling down again, when Sisyphus was actually in control of his own destiny. Think about it. As he yet again watched his massive boulder plummeting to the bottom of the slope, he knew exactly what would happen next. He would trudge to the foot of the mountain, put his wearied shoulder against that solid weight, and begin the process all over again. The gods had ordained this grim pattern of existence, but, even though he was trapped in an inescapable routine, there was, for Sisyphus, an obscure satisfaction to be gained by surveying and comprehending the inevitability of his own fate.'

Jack nodded sagely.

'R-i-i-i-ght. Got it!'

'Have you?'

'Not in the slightest. Not even a little tiny bit.'

'Oh. OK. Well, Miriam and I worked out that we were well ahead of old Sisyphus. The God we believed in, the only God around as far as we knew, had never asked us to do anything as useless as carting a boulder up a hill and failing to get it over the top for ever and ever. We were the ones who were putting ourselves through the misery of believing that we had to create a burden that was never supposed to be there. We must have been mad. All that hard work and angst for no reason at all.'

He leaned back and closed his eyes once more.

'No more about Miriam for now, if you don't mind, Jack. She's coming back to life. I can't handle it at the moment.'

Jack replied quietly, 'No problem. We'll get home.'

'OK, but I just had a thought. We'll make a little detour on the way. Look out for somewhere where we can get a couple of bottles of half-decent red wine. I think we ought to drop in on Victor.'

7

Victor Morton

Jack decided that he would probably not argue with Doc, but he was surprised and concerned. Victor Morton was a retired clergyman in his seventies who had got in touch with the Shadow Doctor some weeks before. In his letter, relished by Doc as a real-life handwritten one in an envelope with a stamp on it, he had talked about his recent discovery that terminal illness was eating him away from inside with ominous rapidity. Now, after more than forty years of ministering to others with what anyone else would have regarded as great success, he was experiencing panic and confusion as he faced the fact that, as far as he, Victor Morton, was concerned, only one person had consistently failed to turn up. That person was God.

Jack had been deeply moved to hear that, in a recent attempt to speak to the creator who had never put in an appearance, Victor had told God that he would address him as Father, because that was what he most wanted him to be. It had been a sad letter to read, and it asked for little more in return than to be heard, and perhaps to receive a quick visit if the Shadow Doctor was ever passing on his way to somewhere else.

Jack tried conscientiously to identify the real reasons for his concern as he drove onto the A47 and headed in the direction of Lewes. The man sitting next to him was clearly feeling weary and diminished after his encounter with Trevor Langston. It was the first time Jack had seen him in this state. Yet now, Doc was suggesting that they visit an extremely needy, elderly man who would undoubtedly use up whatever energy remained in him. It made no sense. Why did it need to happen today? Should he say something?

Glancing to his left he saw that the Shadow Doctor had found a pen and was writing something in large block capitals on a sheet of A4 paper taken from Jack's mileage notebook that lived in the side-pocket.

'What are you doing?'

Doc looked up and for a moment seemed to be asking himself the same question.

'Oh, it's just something we might need if we get to see Victor. Show you later.'

Jack grunted to himself. Making sense never seemed to be a high priority in the Shadow Doctor's world. *Keep your mouth shut, Jack. Just drive.*

Thirty minutes later Jack found himself and Doc sitting in Victor Morton's dining-room, a space largely occupied by a hospital bed and a selection of medical paraphernalia, presumably connected with the elderly man's illness. Victor's second team of carers for the day had just left, leaving their patient clean, tidy and settled in a room that smelled of fresh flowers and disinfectant. Victor was a shrunken presence in the big bed, his slight form raised mechanically at the touch of an electric button by the carers before they gathered their equipment and left. Through the glass panel in a door that led to a little kitchen, and through the large window at the far side of the kitchen itself, it was possible to just see the imposing bulk of Fennerley Beacon rising towards huge puffy, cumulous clouds in a sky as blue as a hedge sparrow's egg.

'Still got a little bit of my view,' announced Victor proudly, raising one trembling hand an inch or so above his coverlet. The voice lacked strength and resonance, but the sick man's eyes were bright beads in the mottled grey skin of a fleshless face. 'I told you in my letter that I would be able to show you my view. Now I have. What do you think?'

'Beautiful,' said Doc. 'I used to walk around here a lot with my wife. We loved it all, Victor. The valleys breed humility. Hilltops adjust the balance. I think someone famous wrote something about those things.'

'Chesterton, but he said it a lot better than that.'

Doc laughed appreciatively. The creaky voice joined in.

'I shan't be able to enjoy my view for much longer, though,' continued Victor. 'I believe that my removal is imminent, either to the grave or to the hospital. I'm not sure which I would prefer. Lacking this view of mine, the grave seems a cosier option. What do you think?'

'Almost anywhere where I don't have to be washed by somebody else,' replied Doc seriously.

The creaky laugh again.

'What should I call you, Mister Shadow Doctor?'

'Well, most people call me Doc, but I was thinking, that's probably what you have to call most of the people you meet nowadays. So, just call me Michael.'

'Thank you, Michael. And who is your good-looking assistant?'

Doc gestured towards Jack.

'He's not my assistant. This is my very good friend, Jack. We work together most of the time.'

'Hello, Jack.'

Jack, warmed immeasurably by Doc's words, lifted a hand as if to wave, then felt silly and put it down again.

'Hello, Victor. It's very nice to meet you.'

A silence fell. Victor slowly revolved his head to gaze once more at his precious view, then turned back to Doc, and after a short coughing spell, asked a question.

'Have you come to do good to me?'

Rising to his feet, the Shadow Doctor lifted his chair and set it down in a place where he could sit very close to the plump pillows that supported Victor's head and shoulders. Reaching across the cover, he took both of the withered hands in his.

'I have come to ask you to pray for me. Today I had to do something simply because I was told that it had to be done. It has nearly broken me into pieces. I need a gift of peace or strength or both to protect me. Jezebel is on my heels, Victor. Be an angel, will you?'

It seemed to Jack that an expression of something close to alarm or fear or even panic was misting the bright eyes of the sick man.

'You read my letter.'

'I did.'

'Then you know that I – I'm nothing. I can't do anything for you.'

'Thank goodness for that. I don't want you to do anything for me, Victor. I want God to send me peace, but someone has to deliver it. Whatever you think about yourself, on this occasion, you're the chosen one. Please stop arguing and pray for me.'

Doc lowered his head onto the bed, its covers obscuring his face. Jack watched, motionless, as Victor slowly detached one of his hands and let it hover for a few seconds. Finally, he allowed it to descend very slowly and carefully until it was touching the Shadow Doctor's shoulders. He closed his eyes and spoke.

'God, if you are here – or there, or anywhere where you can hear me, I have a friend of yours underneath this hand of mine. He's been obedient, but for some reason it has hurt him right deep down in the middle of who he is.'

For one confused moment, Jack thought that the heaving of Doc's upper body was caused by a fit of laughter. But the muffled sounds were all wrong for that. He wasn't laughing. He was crying. In fact, he was sobbing his heart out. And it was indeed happening somewhere deep down in the middle of who he was. As Victor continued to pray, the air in the room seemed to vibrate with an energy that promised the possibility of anything and everything.

'He has asked for a gift of peace from you. I can't give that to him. He believes that you can, and that it will come through me. I have not the faintest idea if that is true, but my hand is touching him, and I want it for him as well. Press the button, God. You told someone once that there's no trouble your end when it comes to healing. Help us with our end. Please give this man enough peace to make sure he has the confidence to be obedient again next time. That's all I can say. In the name of Jesus, I suppose. And if you have done what I ask – thank you.'

'I shall be too tired to do anything at all very soon. Is it possible for you to say a prayer for me before you go?'

It was a few minutes later. Doc had dried his eyes and used the washbasin in the hall toilet to splash some water on his face. Whatever the cause, Jack judged that he did seem to have found a measure of peace.

'Of course I will, Victor. Just at the moment, I think I'd do almost anything for you. Before I start, I want to ask you something. Is that OK?'

Victor nodded, his brows contracting with curiosity. 'Ask away.'

Doc's short pause amplified the gravity of his next two words.

'What happened?'

After passing his pink tongue over thin, dry lips, the old man shrank a little more, and replied so quietly that Jack had to lean close to hear what was being said.

'He never came. That's what happened. He never ever came.' Black pinpoints darkened the very centre of Victor's bright eyes. 'The man who called himself my father did things to me when I was very small. I asked God again and again and again to come and rescue me – to make it stop. He never came. That's what happened. There's nothing else I can think of to say about that.'

'It's enough, Victor. Thank you. Now I will say a prayer for you. We could start by reading the words of a song a friend of mine wrote. I love it very much.'

Doc passed Jack the square of paper he had been writing on in the car.

'Jack, are you happy to sit by Victor and hold this so that you can both read the words? This is the chorus. We can all say it together. Some of these will be familiar words for you, Victor – just joggled around a little. Have a look before we start. Get the hang of it. It comes before the verse and then again after it. We'll all say the choruses together. I'll say the verse. Don't worry about me. I know the whole thing by heart. OK, Jack?'

Victor was already reaching a shaky hand out towards a pair of glasses in a dish on his bedside table. Helping the sick man to safely retrieve his spectacles, and making sure that they were gently but firmly settled on his nose, felt to Jack like a tiny capsule of intense and unaccustomed privilege. Holding the sheet of paper carefully in a position where both of them could view the carefully written capital letters, he watched Victor's lips twitch and move as he scanned the lines, his eyes wide and unblinking with the effort of absorption. This, he thought, is a man who, certainly for this moment, is determined to remain in the land of the living.

'Ready?'

The reply came in a voice that sounded to Jack's ears just a little less faded.

'Ready.'

All three of the men began to read, the pace steady, the concentration on each word absolute.

Lighten our darkness, we beseech thee, oh Lord,
In the name of your son, Jesus Christ.
For we know there will be troubles before we see the
    morning light,
So, defend us,
Please defend us,
Lord, defend us,
From the dangers of the night.

As long as we can stand,
Like children hand in hand,
Together,
We'll see the tale unfold,
And love will make us bold,
Together.
Together we stand today,
Tomorrow is far away,
But sometimes we long to know,
The end of the story.

So, lighten our darkness,
We beseech thee, oh Lord,
In the name of your son, Jesus Christ.
For we know there will be troubles before we see the
    morning light,
So, defend us,
Please defend us,
Lord, defend us,
From the dangers of the night.

Doc sat on the side of the bed to take Victor's hand as he
continued to pray.

'Thank you for helping Victor to use his quartermaster
skills so well for me. He delivered a package of peace from
you. An efficient courier. Thank you for that, but what will
happen to him now? That's what we want to know. What's
waiting for our friend at the end of his story? Will he
disappear into nothingness, just as he has always feared
and suspected? Will it be the grinning imps and the tridents
and the lake of fire for eternity? Or will he be recycled and

taken apart so that bits of him can be used to repair other broken-down Anglican priests?'

It was a joy for Jack to hear the scratchy laugh squeezing itself from Victor's lungs once more, presumably as he pictured his depressingly functional end.

'As far as we know, you didn't turn up even once when little Victor cried out to you. You offered him nothing as he lay awake night after night, asking you to tell him why he was not important enough to be rescued. Strange, that after such a wretchedly disappointing beginning he spent more than half of his life speaking about you, doing his very best to comfort and encourage hundreds of people on your behalf, and hoping against hope that the day would come when you would be as real to him as you were to so many of those people he helped. And he did love you in his own way. He did, you know. It was a love born of hope and fear. I remember the words he spoke to you when he became so ill, and despair was closing in.

' "I have always loved the you that is either there or not there."

'His great desire was that you would let Jesus be born again in the scruffy stable of his soul. And now we three are hoping that it might be possible for you to answer that prayer. In his last letter to me, Victor was kind enough to say that he felt confident I would never offer him anything that has not been given to me. Please may I have a gift for my friend that has a chance of matching his gift to me?'

In the silent minutes that passed, Jack checked any outward display of emotion, but inwardly he wept a word-less yearning into the cosmos. When the Shadow Doctor spoke at last, his voice was filled with quiet confidence.

'Victor, you are going to die. When that happens you will find yourself at a destination you could never have imagined. This time, he will come. He will turn up, he will thank you for all you have done, and if you wish you will be able to have answers to the questions you have been waiting all your life to ask. I am reliably informed, though, that as he takes your hand and walks you into your new home, you will probably not want to bother.

'Thank you. Amen. And two–thirds of God's people said—'

'No, all three of them.' Victor visibly summoned all the breath left in his lungs to send one word singing into heaven. 'Amen!'

'Amen,' echoed Jack. It was little more than a breath. 'Amen.'

8

The list

'What are you up to, Jack?'

'Me? I'm making a list.'

The sun had finally descended behind the trees to the west, leaving a pink wash above the encroaching darkness of the forest. The evening continued warm. The air buzzed quietly with life. Sitting at the circular garden table on the stone flags outside Marlpit Cottage, the two men drank contentedly from large glasses of a particularly smooth Merlot. The Shadow Doctor was frowning over his cross-word. Jack was busy with a pen and a sheet of paper.

It was a peaceful moment at the end of an extraordinary, emotionally turbulent day. Those contrasting encounters with Trevor Langston and Victor Morton had taken Jack on a breakneck journey from extremes of fear and shock in the expensive and impressive office of the religious leader, to tearful compassion in the adapted dining-room of a man who had spent his life battling to distribute gifts from a benefactor who gave little evidence of actually existing.

Most confusing, deeply warming and, Jack decided, ultimately reassuring, was his memory of Doc allowing his own, life-giving vulnerability to puzzle Victor into the possibility of asking himself new questions about an invisible God who, it appeared, might have more than one way of turning up.

Stored in his heart, strictly inaccessible to anyone else, including his friend and colleague, was also something approaching love for the Shadow Doctor. It had filled Jack's heart when Doc took Victor's hand and spoke to him as a loving parent might speak to a hurting child. That moment of love and admiration was accompanied by a feeling that even Jack himself, heavyweight champion in guilt as he was, could not be harsh enough to describe as envy. It was a wish. A need.

Doc didn't look up from his paper. 'I'm glad you're only making a list. You were working so intently, I thought for a moment that you might be doing something.'

'What do you mean? I am doing something. I'm making a list.'

'Jack, I have nothing against lists, but those of us who are sane know perfectly well that when we make a list, we are simply collecting together all the things that we wish to postpone. I make lists myself sometimes. It saves a lot of work. Very important not to leave anything out. Otherwise I might end up having to do it.'

'That doesn't make sense. What do you do with all the useless lists you've made?'

'Ah, this is where I score. I make them into paper aeroplanes – I'm good at that – and I fly them off into the woods.'

'That's litter. You need to clear them all up.'

Doc nodded solemnly. 'I never thought of that. You are so right. I shall make a note on the bottom of my newspaper to add it to my list.'

Jack laid his pen and paper down.

'More wine?' He poured the fragrant liquid with reverent care. 'I know for a fact that you often make lists and then go and do the things you've written down. And you never make paper darts – well, you do, but you certainly don't throw them into the woods. You do strange things, but I know you wouldn't do that. Why don't you tell the truth?'

'I suppose I'm just trying to be more like Jesus,' said Doc piously.

Jack stared.

'What does that mean, assuming it means anything?'

'It may interest you to know, Jack, that there are two occasions recorded in the Gospels where the Son of God says things that are definitely not true.'

'Where?'

'I think I'll leave you to find that out for yourself.'

Jack picked up his pen.

'I see. Well, in that case I'll add it to my list of questions that still haven't been answered. There, it's on the list.' He twizzled the pen with his fingers for a second. 'Doc, I just wanted to say that I thought today was amazing. I still have a problem with the Sermon on the Mount picture. I don't like the image that's been left in my mind. Maybe I shouldn't feel like that, but I do. Apart from that, though, I thought – I thought you were so brave. You were so very brave to take Trevor Langston on, knowing there was a fair chance that he would chuck all that stuff back at you. In front of me too. I thought I was going to fall off my chair.'

'To be honest, I was not feeling any too stable myself, Jack.'

'And taking the time to be with Victor.' Tears filmed the young man's eyes as he remembered. 'To tell you the truth, I thought you were mad. I couldn't think how it could be a good plan to go and see someone so needy when you were – how did you describe it?'

'Filleted.'

'Yes, filleted. Crushed. And it was so – so sweet. You really, really needed him, and he really, really needed you. Did you know that it would end up like that?'

'Not really. What I am very slowly learning, Jack, is that doing the thing that works is sometimes a bit like riding those trick bikes that go left when you steer right, and vice versa. Have you ever seen one? They used to have them at the school fetes when I was a kid. Five pounds to anyone who could go fifty yards without touching the ground with their feet. That was a lot of money then, but it didn't matter. No one ever won – except the bloke who owned the bike, of course. He must have made a fortune. I practise a bit. Fall off sometimes.'

'You really do care about the little people, don't you?'

Doc laughed immoderately. 'You make me sound like an over-imaginative Irishman. But, yes, I do. Someone certainly does.' He rubbed his hands briskly together. 'Anyway, this terrible list of yours. What's still on it?'

Jack suddenly felt a little embarrassed. *Never mind.*

'Well, actually, it's just the rest of the things you promised to explain to me if I came and worked with you.' He fluttered his hands at the sides of his head like birds flying away. 'It doesn't matter just now – but, you know, when there's a moment . . .'

The Shadow Doctor rubbed his face with both hands and groaned loudly.

'O-o-oh no, come on, Jack. Pick one out and hit me with it. Not the one you've just added about Jesus not telling the truth. That's cheating. One of the others.'

'Are you sure?'

'No. Yes. Go on.'

'OK. The lady who answered the phone when I first got in touch—'

'Martha.'

'Yes, Martha. Who is she, and how does she fit into everything?'

Doc sat up straight, his face alight with relief.

'Jack, this is almost certainly nothing but a bog-standard coincidence, only she texted just after we got back. She's coming round next Tuesday morning for coffee and a strawberry tart. She'll be here about eleven. She says she has a favour to ask, but she could have done that over the phone. It's the strawberry tarts from our wonderful bakery in the village that she's really after. You can put all your questions to her then.'

'Will she mind?'

'Mind? She's been longing to meet you. And it's very important that you do know how she connects with everything else, so I'm glad she's coming. I have to warn you about something, though, Jack.'

'What?'

'You'll fall in love with her.'

Jack started to laugh, then stopped nervously on noticing that the Shadow Doctor wasn't even smiling. He could feel worry lines gathering on his own face.

'Not really?'

A slow, serious nod.

'Oh yes. You will.' More, quite vigorous nodding. 'Really. You really, really will.'

9

Getting ready for Martha

Jack slept fitfully on the night before Martha's visit. Events of the previous week had excavated the centre of him like a mechanical shovel. In particular, something about the collision of icons he had endured in Trevor Langston's office was still haunting him.

One dream persisted throughout that Monday night, not precisely a nightmare, but an experience of grindingly repetitive, shadow-laden frustration. It featured the two pictures that hung on the walls of his bedroom. One was the small painting entitled *Pals*, inherited from his gran. It showed two male friends sitting side by side, appearing awkward and nervous as they posed for the artist. The other was a very large and intensely vivid black-and-white photograph of a young, supremely confident Vanessa Redgrave, an overwhelmingly evocative gift to Doc from his wife. It had been consigned by him to the spare bedroom of his cottage shortly after her death.

In the mysteriously authentic world of his continually repeated dream, Jack was presented with the urgent task of fitting the huge Redgrave print into the relatively tiny frame of the painting that had once belonged to Alice's beloved husband William. The job needed to be done, and some slightly scary person in authority had selected Jack to do it.

There was no question of avoiding responsibility, and mere logical impossibility was no excuse.

Again and again Jack awoke to a breathless, panic-stricken awareness of failure. However hard he tried, however feverishly he struggled, he knew in his heart that he was certain to disappoint the nameless luminary who had foolishly placed trust in him.

He returned to full consciousness only when his phone alarm sang to him at seven in the morning. For at least two blurry-eyed minutes after that, the shadow of failure darkened and threatened his real world. It was as though the heart and fundamental life of the dream had been roused by the same alarm. In the end it was the familiar sight of Vanessa's sardonically lifted eyebrow in the blessedly real picture that brought a flood of relief.

It had been a dream. Certainly, in some way it was inside him. It was a part of him. But it had definitely been a dream. So good to be awake. But why had he set the alarm for seven o'clock, an hour before there was any real need to leave his bed and get on with the day?

Vanessa's cocked eyebrow and knowing smile invited an honest answer to that question. He knew why.

Since moving in with the Shadow Doctor, Jack had begun to see and reluctantly acknowledge an almost automatic editing process that rummaged through his thoughts and feelings and reactions. This process deftly removed anything that seriously disturbed his image of himself as a Christian or challenged the hard-won, fragile self-respect that had allowed him to survive as a human being and as a man. It was a strange business. A shock, but a positive one. He thought it might be a little like finding the courage to finally confront a bully who had threatened him for years, only to discover that the threats were mostly bluster. He could learn to disregard bluster. He had definitely made a start.

Jack knew that he was getting up early in order to feel ready to meet someone he might fall in love with. Sacking his internal editor had not necessarily removed embarrassment. He coloured a little as he owned his motivation by slowing his thinking down and employing a deliberate effort of the will. However silly it might seem, even to himself, Doc's solemn prediction a few days ago had, as it were, put him on his mettle.

'So,' he said quietly to himself as he swung his legs over the side of the bed, 'better not waste your extra hour.'

After a careful shower and shave, Jack chose the clothes he would wear. The short-sleeved shirt with faint grey lines on a white background was one that he had bought for ten pounds in a supermarket. Casual but considered. The price had turned out to be a bonus. It was a perfect fit. The rather limited male consensus was that it looked good on him. Trousers? No contest. Dark blue in a thickish material with buttoned pockets just above the knees, pockets that he was unlikely to ever unbutton or use. Comfortable and substantial. Exactly the right length. Socks? Only got black. No problem. Shoes. Nearly new Merrells. Expensive, but so much more than a trainer.

On his way to the stairs, Jack smiled at himself in the mirror on the landing.

'Idiot.'

Still, he looked OK. Perfectly dressed for falling in love. Mind you don't drop any marmalade down yourself, and don't forget to clean your teeth after breakfast. Hearing the door opposite his own begin to open, Jack turned quickly away from the mirror and clattered down the narrow cottage stairway to lay up for breakfast.

10

Sign of the times

Breakfast and teeth-cleaning were completed by nine o'clock. The kitchen was cleared, and coffee beans were ground in anticipation of Martha's visit with the assistance of a new coffee-bean grinder, shipped, according to Doc, who had received the package at the door on the previous day, directly from the Amazon. All that remained was for Jack to drive to the village to pick up fresh strawberry tarts to go with the coffee. At the last moment, Doc climbed into the car and said that he might as well come along.

As they set off along the track towards the lane, Jack could sense his companion thinking. He had discovered that this could happen quite often when you travelled with the same person in the same car all the time. Something about the power of sideways communication? Perhaps you learned to recognise and interpret differences in breathing or body movements. Easy to get it wrong, of course.

'What are you thinking about?'

The Shadow Doctor shifted slightly uneasily in his seat.

'I was thinking about a question you asked me the other day.'

'Oh, good, was it the one about who George is? I've been looking forward to finally knowing what that's all about.'

'Do you want to hear what I've got to say or not?'

'Go on.'

'You asked me if I thought you'd changed for the better in any way since we've been together?'

'That's right. And I told you I'm not fishing for rubbish compliments. Not that you'd be any good at those. I really want to know what you think. I know it seems a bit childish, but even a little thing would do. Something encouraging. Just to keep me going. But it has to be true.'

'Well, first, I ought to ask you the same question. I guess we're supposed to be adapting to each other. So, have I changed for the better? There's a question. You have a good think about that and let me have it later with both barrels if the answer's messy.

'Right now, though, it occurred to me, as we were enjoying our breakfast earlier, that as we have to go up to the village for a spot of tart-hunting anyway, there's an ideal opportunity to point out something that suggests to me you've changed quite significantly.'

'To do with my driving, you mean?'

'No, that still has a bit too much Champion the Wonder Horse about it for my liking, but—'

'Champion the what?'

'It was a programme in the sixties about – oh, never mind. No, it's nothing to do with driving. Look, let's pick up a paper at the garage on the way.'

Jack smiled. 'You'll be saying next that my significant improvement is something to do with buying newspapers.'

'It is. That's exactly right. It's all to do with how you actually buy a newspaper.'

Here we go again, thought Jack. *It's like being taken on a trip without any warning of how the weather's going to be or what sort of terrain you might have to face or who you're going to meet. You just have to go as you are and hope for the best. Ah, well, maybe I can solve the clues for once.*

'OK, let me get this straight. You're going to tell me a way I've improved, and it's to do with how I buy a newspaper. Have I understood that much?'

'You have. I mean – a bit of it depends on me not being up the creek with one or two guesses based on observation, but yes, it's basically about how you buy a newspaper.'

Jack leaned an elbow on the ledge beneath the side window and rubbed his chin. How could that possibly make sense?

'It's not about which paper I buy, because we nearly always get *The Times*.'

'Correct.'

'And it's not just about me being nicer to the person who sells it to me or engaging with them more than I have done in the past – your sort of constructive time-wasting style?'

'Both of those things may well be true, Jack, but they have nothing at all to do with the improvement I've noticed.'

'So, you're saying it happens before I pay for the newspaper. In the queue, do you mean?'

'Not at all. Never in the queue. Before that. Always before the queue.'

Jack resettled himself in his seat, both hands on the wheel, leaning forward and peering hard at the road ahead, as though it might be possible with intense concentration to drive himself into the heart of a solution to Doc's puzzle.

'But, Doc, nothing happens before I join the queue. I just pick up a paper and troddle off to pay for it. Is it something to do with when I pick the newspaper up off a pile? No, it can't be. How could the way I take a paper in my hand tell you anything at all about me?'

'Let's wait until we get to the garage, Jack. Easier to explain on the spot.'

Five minutes later, parked in a space at the side of the garage forecourt, Jack presented Doc with a newly purchased copy of *The Times*, sat back in his seat and folded his arms.

'Right. Here we are. Explain.'

The Shadow Doctor placed his newspaper on his lap and nodded solemnly.

'Very well.' A pause. 'Jack, ask yourself this. Why do we buy *The Times*?'

Jack drew in a breath and shook his head.

'Same as anyone else, I suppose. News, of course. *The Times* has turned into a bit of a tabloid, but still not bad. Sport. We both read quite a lot of it, and you enjoy doing the crossword. Is that what you mean?'

'That is exactly right, and because the last thing you said is true, the way that you pick up the paper has changed — for the better. And that's what I've noticed.'

'Am I more careful how I handle it?'

'In a way, but that's not really the point.'

Jack raised a hand to slap something, but ended up touching the dashboard lightly with the flat of his hand.

'All right. OK. I'm baffled. I have no idea what you're talking about. I give up. Come on then, tell me. And it had better make sense.'

'OK. It's to do with something I've been thinking recently, Jack. How can I put it? I've been amazed by the way human beings like us seem to be blindfolded when it comes to patterns of behaviour that have somehow got installed in our lives, I don't mean through planning or anything like that, but because what we might call a habit of attitude is bound to have an automatic effect on the way we make decisions. Are you following me?'

'No, I'm not following you. Actually, I don't want to follow you any more. I've gone off down a nice, flowery little side-road to find a place under a tree where I can lie down and have a nap after wasting all this time trying to understand what you're talking about.'

The Shadow Doctor smiled patiently.

'Fair enough. Let's take you as an example, Jack. Both of us have these patterns of attitude, as I call them, but here's one of yours that's been a part of your life for quite a long time. Over the years you learned to police yourself, and others at times, quite sternly over matters of morality and general Christian outlook. Correct?'

Jack sighed. 'Correct.'

'And the problem with that perspective, if it gets out of hand in the lives of people who call themselves Christians, is that the rules and regs can end up being applied at the expense of care, love, flexibility – all those things. And when you think about it, trying to stay safe through an obsessional adherence to not getting things wrong is never going to work properly. Agreed?'

'Agreed.'

'You run out of steam in the end. That's what happened to me once, and I know it's happened to you because you've told me. Are you following me now?'

Jack signified reluctant assent. 'Yes, well done. You've managed to drag me back from my flowery little whatnot. I know that way of looking at things has been part of me. Still is quite often, and I know I don't want it to be. Do you remember that time when we met the posh lady in the car park near Battle?'

'She'd just been to the doctor's surgery.'

'That's right. She offered us her parking ticket because there was quite a lot of time left on it. I don't know if I ever told you this, but my first response to her offering us that ticket was to refuse it because we would be cheating if we took it. Stealing money from – I don't know – Battle council, or whoever owns the car park. Stay true to your faith in the small things, we were taught, and you won't go wrong when it comes to really big challenges. For most of my Christian life I would have said it was the Holy Spirit who told me what to do when I had to make those kinds of decisions.'

'Oh dear, I messed that one up for you and the Holy Spirit and the wise person who told you that, didn't I?'

'Yes, you did, particularly because the words she said when she passed over the ticket across the bonnet of her posh car told you something important about her state of mind that I didn't even notice. You smiled and took the ticket and asked her a question. Then you and she had a little private talk and she ended up laughing and giving you a hug. That annoyed me. I remember that. I was confused, and grumpy about being held up when we were supposed to be meeting the exploding lady. And how come you got hugs from posh ladies you'd never met before and I didn't? Everything about you confused me in those early days. Quite a bit still does. Come on then, tell me about the newspapers.'

'OK, well, this is where, if my original conclusions were mistaken, the whole thing falls apart, and you haven't improved at all, not in this way anyway.'

Jack laughed out loud.

'Oh, this is just great! A massive build-up, all for nothing. I should have stayed among the flowers.'

'We'll see. I could be wrong. You must be honest.'

'Do get on.'

Jack consoled himself yet again with the reflection that it was good to at least role-play being the person who did the driving.

'It began the first time I saw you collect a newspaper. It was from one of those plastic-covered bins like the ones over there where you just got this paper. I was standing right behind you that first time, and I noticed something a little odd. Try to picture this. You picked up the paper from the top of the pile, glanced at it for a moment, then picked up the next paper in the pile and put the first one back in the bin. Then, curiouser and curiouser, you pondered for a moment, picked up the one you'd just put down, and put the second paper from the pile back on top.

'After that, I watched with interest each time to see if you would do it again. You did, but there were three variations. Occasionally you went through the whole palaver I've just described, but every now and then you simply took the top copy of *The Times* straightaway. At other times you slid out the second paper in the pile and left the first one on top. I have to say, it baffled me for a while. I got it in the end, though – I think. Can you remember why you went through all those variations, Jack?'

Jack shook his head in wonderment.

'This is all so strange. No, in one way I don't remember. At the time I never really focused on what was going on.' He smiled ruefully. 'Now that you've been good enough to describe every fascinating little detail of my strange behaviour, I'm pretty sure I know exactly what I did, and why I did it.'

'Thank goodness for that – if I'm right. It all made sense when I remembered one thing. Pay close attention, Jack. I wouldn't want you getting bored. The top paper in those piles has often got quite scruffy because of people picking it up to glance at the headlines, and then putting it back and getting a nice clean, smooth one from underneath. Then, along comes Police Constable Merton – that's you – to buy a copy of *The Times*. He detects himself rejecting a messed-up copy that may become the one remaining option for some poor soul at the end of the day, so he makes the personal sacrifice accordingly. Thereafter, on other occasions, he takes the paper straight from the top of the pile when it's clearly not scruffy at all, and the second one down when the temptation is just too great to resist. Am I close?'

Jack threw an arm up in mock despair.

'Do you know, I'm not sure I come out of this with a great deal of dignity, Doc. My only consolation is that you've obviously taken as much time obsessing over the way I choose newspapers as I have in choosing them. Perhaps we could share a room with nice soft walls to bang our heads against when we get older. We could count coloured objects together.'

'Did you want to hear about the improvement?'

'I need to.'

'For quite a long time now, as far as I can tell, you've chosen a pristine copy of *The Times* on every single occasion without hesitation. Now, why would that be? I think it's because you noticed that the scruffiest bit of the paper on top of the pile is usually the back page. It's the way people pick it up. They look at the headlines, then quite a lot of them turn it over to glance at the sport. What else is there on the back page of *The Times*?'

'The crossword.'

Doc spread his hands in congratulation.

'Grace has once again galloped up on the rails and won by a short head from Law. Thank you for your kindness to me, Jack.'

Jack was suddenly embarrassed.

'Ah, well, I do know you love your crossword, Doc. Can't be easy filling it in when it's all scrunched up.'

'Right, let's go and do our shopping. Martha deprived of her strawberry tart is not a pretty sight. Well, that's not strictly true. Martha is always a pretty sight, but the metaphor is—'

'Don't worry. I understand. Let's get the tarts.'

Meeting Martha

Martha was late. She arrived at twenty past eleven, just after Jack had nervously put the kettle on for the third time. He was sitting awkwardly at the kitchen table with Doc, twisting his hands together and wondering if the strawberry tarts needed to go in the fridge to avoid them going mushy, when a crunching of tyres on the gravel outside, followed seconds later by the slam of a car door, signalled her arrival. As Doc disappeared outside to do the initial greeting, Jack rose slowly to his feet and glanced at the kettle. *Now, perhaps? No, just wait.*

Martha entered the cottage with the happily relieved sigh of someone who has finally arrived at the place in the world where they most want to be. Tall, fair, slim but strong, dressed with casually stylish confidence in blue jeans, a soft grey pullover and a delicately flowered grey silk scarf, she stopped just inside the door, beautiful and at a reassuringly comfortable distance, with her arms outspread and her head tilted to one side. Gazing at Jack through the kindest, most absorbent and grown-up eyes he could remember seeing, she said just three quietly impassioned words.

'Jack! At last.'

The Shadow Doctor's prediction was accurate. As the morning wore on, Jack did fall in love with their morning visitor, but it was the type of instant attraction that rather surprisingly swept him straight back to memories of Miss Watson, his very first infant school teacher. At the age of five he had given this dark-haired lady his heart, more profoundly and completely, he reflected later, than to anyone since, certainly in any kind of romantic sense. Martha must have been a good twenty-five years older than him, but she projected an ageless radiance that left Jack captivated and, for the early part of her stay, virtually tongue-tied. He felt like a young fan suddenly discovering that his favourite film star had dropped in for morning coffee.

'Jack was hoping to ask you some questions, if you have time, Martha.'

'Oh, I would love that! I'm really hopeless at thinking of things to ask, but I can bore anyone to death with answers. Are they very clever questions, Jack? I hope not.'

The strawberry tarts had been admired and consumed. Martha and the Shadow Doctor were still sitting at the table drinking coffee. Jack, relieved to have a practical task, had removed plates and cutlery, and was busy washing up. He turned from the sink, his own coffee mug dangling from a finger of one hand, and a wet cloth in the other. Martha had swung round in her chair and was gazing at him with bright expectancy. He gave an embarrassed little laugh.

'Oh, no – honestly, not clever at all. I just wondered if—'

Without changing her expression at all, Martha had transferred her gaze to the cloth and the mug, both of which were dripping water onto the kitchen floor. *For heaven's sake!*

'Sorry, just put these back in – you know.' He cleared his throat. 'No, it's just that I wondered – I'm not sure how to put this. I wondered how you fit in to all this. The stuff Doc does. You were the first person I spoke to on the phone, and you were so friendly that I thought perhaps—'

Martha clasped her hands together as she interrupted.

'Jack, that's kind of you. It was easy to be friendly, though. Doc had spoken so warmly about your gran, who he became very friendly with, of course. And I knew he was really hoping you might get in touch, so when you phoned I thought, *Wow! Yes! It's Jack! Things are happening.* And they were. And they have, haven't they?'

'Well yes, but no thanks to me, I'm afraid. I've got a lot of catching up to do. I'm still not sure where I am in all this. So I thought I might at least find out something about you – if you don't mind, that is.'

Martha turned and addressed the Shadow Doctor as though he was a naughty five-year-old. The ghost of Miss Watson made a fleeting visit to the kitchen of Marlpit Cottage.

'Michael, you are useless. What are you?'

'I am useless.'

'What should you have done?'

Doc looked very abashed.

'I should have explained more to Jack. Filled him in on more things.'

'Exactly! Right. You never do learn, do you? We're all going to go into the sitting-room now and Jack can ask me whatever he likes.'

'Right.'

Finishing at the sink, Jack shot a glance at the other two as they rose to their feet and turned towards the sitting-room. Doc's arm slid comfortably around Martha's waist. He could see her smiling before she allowed her head to rest for a moment on his shoulder. He felt a stab of jealousy. Who or what was he jealous of? A friendship like that, he supposed. How do you become part of something as downright lovely as that?

'OK, here we all are. We've been catching up a bit, Jack. I've just been asking Doc for a favour.'

Washing-up completed, Jack had hesitated to join Doc and Martha in the sitting-room. He felt nervous and awkwardly intrusive. He told himself that it was more to do with him than them, and hoped he was right.

Martha laid a hand on the younger man's arm. 'The thing is, Jack, my lovely gran, Elsie, who's in her nineties, lives in a really excellent nursing home over in Kent, in the Pembury area. Doc's visited with me a couple of times, so he's met her and knows the place.'

She turned back to the Shadow Doctor.

'I had a call from Aelwen, Doc – you remember, the lovely Welsh girl who has a lot to do with looking after Gran?'

'Of course. Brilliant girl.'

'Well, apparently Gran's suddenly gone all silent and worried. You know what she was like the times when we visited. A little bit confused, but marbles intact and very smart and fit for her age. Loves to talk usually. Aelwen says it's as if there's something very heavy bothering her, but she just can't get it out.' She choked on an emotion and swallowed hard. 'I'm worried, Doc. I'm sorry to bother you, but I wondered how you might feel about paying her a visit.'

87

'You don't think it should be you? She adores you.'

'You know I'd go like a shot if I thought it would help, but I know it won't. I'd cry and have to go out of the room, and then I'd come back and suggest something stupid like a cruise or a trip to the hairdressers, and then cry again when she doesn't know what I'm talking about and have to go out again, and—'

Doc raised both hands in surrender.

'Yes, yes! I get the picture. You're right. I will go. I'll go. How about next week? Wednesday OK?'

'Oh, Michael! Really? That would be wonderful. The doctor comes on Wednesdays, and he'll want to see her, but that won't be for very long. Any time after that. Mid-morning probably.'

'Fine. You set it up and give me a call. Fancy coming along, Jack?'

'Of course. I don't know that I'll be much use, but I'm happy to come.'

Martha turned her radiance onto Jack.

'I would be so happy to think that you were going as well. Thank you!'

Doc clapped his hands loudly once, perhaps signalling a change of direction.

'That's settled then. Now, Jack. Where do you want to start?'

Jack patted the arms of his chair briskly.

'I'm really not sure. I'd just like to know where Martha belongs in the story. I mean, was she a big part of what happened?'

'She was a huge part of it, Jack. In fact, without her, it might never have happened at all.' He stared into the distance for a little while. I tell you what – I think we could start with that trip I made to Ripon. What do you think, Martha?'

Martha folded her long legs comfortably into the armchair beneath her and smiled reassuringly.

'Perfect place to start. Couldn't be better.'

Martha's story

'OK, so one day, some while after my wife died, I drove up to Ripon Cathedral in Yorkshire. Ever been to Ripon, Jack?'

Jack controlled a startled response. Ripon Cathedral. That was the place where the first hint of a possible change in his life had come to him. For some reason he had never told Doc about the experience, probably, he realised with a little shock of awareness, because he had not entirely made that connection for himself.

One rainy day, after a long drive to the north and a failed appointment in connection with the Bromley Church Centre where he worked, Jack had sought refuge in the cathedral on Minster Road. Jack's father had taught his son to love cathedrals. After a dreamy circuit of the building he had succumbed to a temptation. In the church circles Jack had known, the lighting of candles in such a setting tended to be regarded as an unwise and inappropriate surrender to crudely visible worship or prayer aids. Nevertheless, a wordless prayer had sobbed its way out of the centre of him as he daringly lit a small candle and placed it in a holder next to others on the rack. Something unexpected happened as he studied the little flame. It was especially his. It danced and flickered and changed without reference to anything or anyone else. Uniqueness. For a few moments the promise of liberation had filled his heart. At that point in his life he had understood neither the nature of the promise, nor the need for freedom.

He found himself silently asking a question now. If he had known what the future might hold, would he have extinguished the flicker before it had a chance to become a flame? Whatever the answer to that question might be, now was not the time for sharing his memory with the Shadow Doctor.

'I've been to Ripon, yes, just the once when I was supposed to be buying stuff for the church. They cancelled the appointment. All that way north for nothing.'

'For nothing?'

Well done, Jack. Idiot. He cleared his throat.

'So, why did you want to go to Ripon Cathedral in particular?'

The Shadow Doctor raised his eyebrows but obviously decided that Jack's uncommunicated truth could wait.

'Miriam and I loved it. It wasn't just the cathedral itself, although it is a magical space to spend time in. It's very good at being majestic and cosy at the same time. Not bad for a place that goes back to the seventh century. We were able to relax in that building. We got into the habit of going there when we were up in the north to sit and talk through stuff that was going on, say some prayers if we weren't sure about something that was happening in our lives – that sort of thing.

'This was the first time I'd found the courage to visit Ripon without my wife, and as I drove, I repeated the same words over and over again. *This will be the last time. This will be the very last time.* Last time for what? Well, I suppose for what I vaguely hoped – feared – thought – might be my final angry confrontation with Jesus. I'm not sure what I imagined was going to happen after that. I have to say the one or two options that were staring me in the face looked pretty dismal.

'When I stepped inside the building I wanted to walk straight out again. I didn't. I walked slowly up the centre-aisle and stood staring at the altar for a while. Then the difficult bit. I moved over and sat where my wife and I always used to sit, and I did a bit of hurting. After that I said – well, I hissed – my piece. It didn't make much sense, but that didn't matter. "My wife and I came here to sort things out. Why isn't Miriam sitting here beside me to sort out the problem of her not being alive any more? You took her away, you heartless bastard. You just took her!"'

Jack seemed to hear and feel the continuous murmuring echo of the cathedral inside his mind and body.

'What did you do then?'

'Cried. I cried and cried and cried.'

'But you don't cry.'

'As you saw very recently, Jack, I lie about things like that.'

What did Jesus do?

'What did Jesus do, Doc?'

'What did Jesus do? That is a good question. That is a very important question. What did Jesus do? I can only tell you rather tentatively what I think he did while I was slumped miserably on that familiar old seat beside the pillar in Ripon Cathedral on a cold autumn afternoon. I think he wept as well. Yes, he wept. Jesus wept. He wept just like he did 2,000 years ago when two of the people he loved most in the world stopped him on the road one after the other to tell him he'd let them down. And as I thought about that, I knew in my heart that on that long-ago day, if there'd been anyone around who could have held him and genuinely done their best to find out what was wrong, he would have said, through his tears, "They're so angry with me. Those two. They're disappointed in their friend. They want to know why I didn't love them enough to turn up in time to heal their brother. I don't know if I can do this. I'm not sure I can handle being torn apart over and over again. But I have to. I was given a choice. It was a real choice. I made it. It stands."

'And I realised then, in the cathedral, a place that had never failed to be an island of peace for my best friend and me for so many years – well, I was doing exactly the same thing to him, because he'd done more or less the same thing to me. I was beaten up and bruised by shock and loss and disappointment, and he was wrenched in half yet again by what was always theoretically possible on one side, and what could not be allowed on the bloody, inscrutable, impenetrable other. So there it was. That couldn't be changed. It couldn't be different. And then, everything went kind of still. At the time it seemed as if – as if we might have been weeping quietly together. And, Jack – for the first time, probably in my life, if I'm honest, I genuinely felt for him. I felt so sorry for him. I really did.'

Complete stillness for several seconds.

'And then,' said Martha softly, 'I turned up. I was a bit late. That was a good thing in a way, wasn't it, Michael?'

'Perfect timing.' The Shadow Doctor smiled. 'You padded in and sat on the row behind me, and I didn't even know you were there.' He looked at her for a moment. 'You brought me a gift.'

'I did. It was an odd sort of thing though, wasn't it? I was quite nervous about giving it to you at first.'

'I've still got it. Do you want to have a look, Jack? It's upstairs.'

Jack looked a question at Martha.

'Go on – go ahead, Michael. I think it's a good idea. I don't think I've seen it more than a couple of times since that day.'

As Doc rose to his feet, Jack asked, 'Did you like the gift?'

He appeared to give the question serious thought.

'Did I like it? I don't know if I'd use that word, but it turned out to be probably the second-best present I've ever been given. Maybe the third. Definitely in the top three, anyway. Back in a jiffy.'

Two minutes later he reappeared in the sitting-room holding a small soft leather bag fastened with a drawstring. Placing it on the table, he regained his seat and turned to Martha.

'I'll let Jack see what's in the bag in a minute. Why don't you tell him all the stuff that happened to you first? Is that OK?'

Martha nodded and leaned forward to place a hand on Jack's arm for a second, focusing all her attention on him as she spoke. Obscurely enabled and overwhelmed at the same time by the extraordinary rush of her personality, he listened like a hypnotised child for a few seconds before starting to relax.

'I was a shadow doctor myself at the time, Jack.'

She smiled at the expression on his face.

'Sorry, I think I've shocked you a little bit, haven't I? I enjoyed saying that, Jack. You probably think I'm about to announce that Michael and I belong to a race of aliens who are visiting earth so that we can use our super-powers to help people in trouble. No, nothing so interesting, I'm afraid. I was a completely different kind of doctor. You probably know what a radiologist is?'

Jack nodded. 'Sort of. I think a friend of mine called Andrea – from school – went on to do that. Took her years to qualify. It's a specialist doctor of some kind, isn't it? Looking at X-rays and that sort of thing.'

'That's absolutely right. I've been out of it for quite a while, but that was my job. I used to be part of a team who spent most of their working days in darkened rooms, literally in the shadows, looking at people's images and X-rays and coming up with advice for the medics who were treating them. That's the simple version. And we did sometimes call ourselves shadow doctors. It was rather an affectionate term among us team members – not so much when one or two of our clinical colleagues used it as a bit of an insult. I think there might still be a tendency to see radiologists as shadows instead of real doctors, people who are just names on a report or voices on the end of the phone. A bit irksome at times.

'Having said that, I'm told times are changing in the shadow doctor world, Jack.' She counted a list out on her fingers. 'Ultrasound, CT, MRI, lots of different stuff. It's all about shades of grey apparently – to use an unfortunate phrase. In fact, you may be interested to hear that the whole thing involves the interpretation of shadows. And I think the clever old radiologists do get to see actual patients much more nowadays.'

She paused and smiled at Jack as though she was taking a moment to drink in the wonder of his presence. It took his breath away.

'Anyway, that was me. That's what I was. Spent quite a bit of time working in the dark, but I did have a lot of fun. And I think we were useful from time to time. Did our best.' She leaned back in her chair. 'So, speaking of interpreting shadows . . .'

Martha turned her head to glance at Doc before continuing. He was listening intently, sitting with one leg crossed over the other, arms folded across his chest. He said nothing but shrugged and made a very slight movement of encouragement with one lifted hand.

'Speaking of shadows and interpretation and all that, I'll try to tell you what happened with Michael – sorry, Jack, I know he's Doc to you, but I'll have to call him Michael if I'm going to get through this.

'Where shall I start?' She smiled ruefully at her own hesitation. 'Sorry, I know where to start really. Miriam and Michael were my great buddies. I met them at a point in my life when I was crawling through a crappy, stressy pit of a time that ended up taking all my job and most of my confidence away from me. Bad days.

'In the middle of my crawl I was on a private retreat in a conference centre somewhere down in the West Country, wishing that I hadn't come. Nothing against the place. Nice people. Well organised. It was one of those spiritual joints that make a lot of noise about being ecumenical but turn out to be more—'

'Ecumanglican?' suggested the Shadow Doctor smilingly.

'Something like that, yes. To be honest, that's irrelevant. Nothing would have been right for me around then. And I couldn't think why on earth I'd gone. Anyway, Michael and

Miriam were there for the same week, but with a group of people who seemed, from my wrecked perspective, to worship the two of them as much or more than they did God. I wanted nothing to do with them, especially as I couldn't help noticing them glancing at me occasionally at meals and in the chatty-chatty times between sessions. I was horrified. To slightly sanitise the inelegant thoughts in my head at the time, I was buggered if I was going to become prayer fodder for those two ego-stuffed holy creeps. And then—'

With startling emotional and physical abruptness, Martha placed one hand across her mouth and thrust the other one towards Doc, who took it and held on mechanically for a moment or two – rather, Jack found himself thinking, as though his hand was some kind of regular refuelling source. She took a deep breath and steadied herself. Her face opened like a recovering sunflower once more.

'Sorry, Jack. I'm OK now. I really, actually am. Just – the memory of the next bit punched me in the face when I wasn't expecting it.' She gave herself a little shake. 'Right. Got it! And then . . . where was I?' She shook a decisive finger. 'Holy creeps, that's right. I was sitting on a bench several yards away from the front of the house – the conference centre – looking out over a beautiful, peaceful valley towards the sea and idly wondering whether to do it by drowning or with pills or a noose, when Miriam and Michael appeared and sat down on either side of me. No invitation. And – look – I'm talking close, Jack. Squashed up. Right in my sodding, hurting space! I was furious, and I was about to express – in Russian as it happens, because I can – an offer to show them where the crayfish spend the winter. But then they began this weirdly intensive, unsmiling double-act. As far as I can remember, this is roughly how it went:

Michael: Excuse us, we've seen you around the place over the last couple of days –
Miriam: And we think you look sane.
Michael: So we wondered –
Miriam: As we're slowly going mad ourselves –
Michael: Could we walk down to the pub with you this evening?
Miriam: And drink a little more than is sensible?
Michael: And give everyone back here the impression –
Miriam: Without actually lying, of course –
Michael: That it was ministry you needed, not alcohol?'

She looked across at Doc for a few seconds before turning back.

'You know what they did? They saved my life, Jack. Not right then, and certainly not that night. The three of us were laughing too much in the pub to bother with anything so trivial and irrelevant as saving lives. But over the next few months that's what they did. From that day, they loved me. And I loved them. I love him now. And I love her so much now, even though I can't see her. Those two travelled stubbornly with me from pit to post-pit and far into the wild country beyond. Fair old journey it was.'

'Never hard work,' murmured Doc; 'we loved that journey.'

'After Miriam died and Michael . . .' She pushed the hair from her face as though she was repelling an attacker. 'When Michael dropped into his own horrible swamp of a pit, there wasn't a day when I didn't feel like vomiting with grief and fear and worry. I'd lost one of them. What was going to happen to the other? I reached a point one Monday morning when I just dropped to my knees on the kitchen floor to pray, the sort of naff Christian cliché I'd sworn to avoid. Why is it always kitchen floors? What's wrong with sitting-rooms? Or conservatories? Anyway, first of all I graciously forgave God for ignoring my frantic pleadings for Miriam to be healed, and then I got all weepy and disgustingly snotty and asked him if he would be so kind as to let me be a part of this person I loved, not just going through hell but coming out the other side as well.'

'And then?'

'I waited.'

That invisible energy once more. A childhood recollection of being frightened at the seaside entered Jack's thoughts. He had been stranded on an old, slippery plank of wood among the rock pools on the beach, terrified that if he took a step forward he would fall and crash against a rock or drown in one of those salty pools that might be bottomless for all his little heart knew. The fear might have lasted no more than two seconds, but the memory was a vivid, technicolour image in his mind. Every colour, every texture, every sound as clear now as it had been in Eastbourne all those years ago. And that was how it was at this instant, here in the sitting-room. Fizzing reality. Every visible object meaning more than it did – or as much as it was supposed to, perhaps? Not because of fear this time. Something else.

'Did God answer your prayer?'

Martha broke the spell by throwing back her head and laughing aloud.

'Shame on you, Jack! How could you even think of using such language in front of the Shadow Doctor?'

For Jack, it was an encouraging mark of the way things had changed that he and Doc were able to smile at each other with relative comfort on hearing this.

'Forgive me, Martha. What I meant to ask was – what happened next?'

'OK. Better. I said this prayer in the kitchen. And I waited. Those two things definitely happened. Two weeks later I had a dream. That definitely happened as well. There's a bit in the Bible where some sexist old prophet says that a day will come when old men will dream dreams. I'm not a man, but I don't think that matters, and I was kind of creeping up to the point where it could be said that I was on the edge of getting on a bit. Do you want to hear about my dream, Jack?'

'Please. I really do.'

Martha lifted both hands and placed her palms against the sides of her face, almost, thought Jack, as though she was steadying the picture in her mind.

'I don't want to add anything, and I certainly don't want to take a single thing away. I'll do my best. In my dream it was dusk-ish, and I was sitting in my own house, in the conservatory actually, which is where I sit a lot, and there was a man standing beside me in the same room. He was just – there. I didn't recognise him at all, but I wasn't frightened – more interested than frightened. He seemed nice.

Said he had something to give me, and in my dream I knew for sure he wanted me to pass this something on to Michael. He never said any of that. I just knew it, like you do when you dream. Then he held his closed fist out towards me. I opened my eyes really wide and stared at it, and as his fingers slowly opened I saw a flat white stone resting in the palm of his hand. When I bent my head and peered more closely, I could see words written in black on the stone, but frustratingly I couldn't read them at first because – this is going to sound idiotic – I hadn't got my glasses on. I don't wear glasses, Jack. I don't need them. But in my dream I did. *I was frantic. I must, must, must, must work out what those words are.* And it was getting darker. Then, suddenly, magically, my non-existent glasses were on! I don't know how – they just were. And I could see properly. Everything bright and clear. At last I was able to read those two words on the white stone. They simply said *Shadow Doctor*. Then I woke up.' Pause. 'It's all right to breathe now, Jack.'

Jack took the advice. It helped.

'That's extraordinary. Did you have any idea what the dream meant?'

Martha leaned back and flapped a hand in the air. 'Not a clue. Not a wisp of a germ of a wild guess. Obviously I knew I'd sometimes called myself a shadow doctor once upon a distant time, but that had nothing to do with anything as far as I could fathom. I did remember my kitchen-floor prayer, though, and Michael's name had been in the dream a bit, so I decided to do some obvious things and just see what happened.'

'Did you think God was guiding you?'

A don't-bother-saying-it glance at Doc.

'He didn't let on if he was.'

'What were the obvious things?'

'Well – I went to a couple of garden centres and in the second one I was able to buy three little flat white stones. Two to mess up, one to get right. Then I went back into town to get a tube of that silver nitrate, indelible ink stuff, drove back home, spread a sheet of newspaper out on the kitchen table, and tried to write *Shadow Doctor* on two of the stones. On the first one I only got as far as *Shadow Do* because I didn't leave enough space. The second one was simply a disgrace. It lacked dignity. Deeply embarrassing. Despite the fact that I now knew there definitely was no God, I had another go. The third one was not bad. It was about as close to how it had looked in the dream as I could get it. So I put that one on the side to dry and hunkered down into my very aptly named basket chair for a while, wondering if I had gone bonkers. Then I thought of one more thing to do. I often need a thing to do, Jack. I texted my friend Stuart, who knows everything – except what he's worth. Described my dream, did a long row of question marks, and waited for him to get back.'

'Did he?'

'A lot more quickly than God, I can tell you. Very briefly, though. Typical of the man. No curiosity. Just a Bible verse. Revelation 2:17. That was it.'

The Shadow Doctor leaned forward in his chair and quoted softly, '"Whoever has ears to hear, let them hear what the Spirit says to the churches. To the one who is victorious I will give some of the hidden manna. I will also give that person a white stone with a new name written on it, known only to the one who receives it."'

'I looked it up,' continued Martha. 'No one seems to be sure what the white stone thing is all about, but there was one theory I really liked. Apparently the Romans used to give these things to men who came first in athletic competitions – races and things. Their names were written on the white stones, and they were allowed to use them as a sort of ticket to get into the victory banquet.'

'And you decided then to give your stone to Doc – Michael.'

'Not straightaway. You understand, there was nothing very victorious about Michael around that time. On the contrary.' She continued quietly. 'He wasn't victorious. He was defeated. And I was still hung up over the Shadow Doctor thing. I mean – I knew he was a bright fellow, but he wasn't suddenly going to become a radiologist, was he? I know that might sound extraordinarily thick of me now, but how was I to know how it would turn out? I did give it to him in the end, though. I read something else in what straightforward people like you and I call the Bible, and Mystery-man in that chair over there might nowadays call a collection of old books. It was something about putting on a new self. And I thought, – yes! Just what my dear friend – one of the two people who loved me and helped to rescue me – just what he needs. A brand-new self. A new name. And, I said to myself, *if this isn't just rubbish, and God's got a plan for him to win some species of race or competition, and then to collect a ticket for the boozy old heavenly knees-up afterwards, that's more than all right with me.* As for the name itself, I still didn't know what it meant, but suddenly I didn't need to.' She shook her head. 'Odd or what? In the end I rang him – got him on his mobile, and found he'd gone all the way up to Ripon. I think I swore. I like things to happen straightaway. Then I said, *Martha, pull yourself together. Get your arse up to Ripon.* I said I'd meet him there the next day.'

Doc picked up the story.

'I told her not to bother, but she got as awkward and contrary as only she can, thank God, and said she had something to give me and was coming anyway. We made an arrangement. If she insisted on doing that long journey, I'd be in the cathedral at four o'clock the next day. That's all I knew for sure. She got there at four-thirty. People talk coyly about God having perfect timing, but he seems happy to adjust it when he has to.' He pointed. 'Martha gave me that. Take a look, Jack.'

Easing the strings of the little leather container, Jack pulled out a small oval stone. He studied the inscription, vivid against its white background. Strange to hold it in his own hand. The beginning of it all. In Ripon Cathedral. He glanced up at Doc.

'How did you feel when you saw it?'

Leaning across, the Shadow Doctor picked up the stone. Studying it on the palm of his own hand, he shook his head and released a sigh of uncertainty.

'How did I feel? Hard to pin down. I suppose I felt as though – as though I'd very quietly been given a message. Someone like old Elijah might have understood. A tiny, huge thing. It looked as though I might have been given or at least offered a new something. A new name? Maybe a new job. A new chance to be – all right. I had no more idea than Martha what it might mean, but that didn't seem terribly important right then. I really wanted it to mean something, but I hadn't a clue. No, that's wrong. There was one clue. One clue. One thought. In the middle of that night I lay awake in my Premier Inn hotel bed trying to bring to mind all the bits and pieces that Martha had told Miriam and I over the years about the work she used to do. With only partial success. So, in the morning at breakfast—'

Martha interrupted with passion and a dramatic waving of arms.

'Oh, it was cruel, Jack. When we met for breakfast, he made it impossible for me to attack my scrambled eggs and drink my coffee. And he knows how much I love those things first thing in the morning. I suppose that made me realise it must be important. I had to go through all the stuff I told you just now about being a radiologist, and a lot more besides. I didn't really mind. I mean, after everything that had happened I was quite excited. When I ran out of things to say and he ran out of questions, he just sat staring into the distance for ever – well, long enough for me to eat my depressingly tepid eggs.

'We didn't say anything else about what had happened the day before, which was a bit frustrating for me. I was like a child, Jack. I just wanted to know for sure that my kitchen-floor prayer had been answered. But that wasn't going to happen, not then anyway. I think I knew that really. After breakfast we gave each other a big hug, and pushed off in our separate waggons. I don't think I drove very well that day. I know I didn't.'

13

The road less travelled

The Shadow Doctor swayed gently in his chair.

'Of course, I knew Martha desperately wanted me to say everything was going to be fine from that day on, and I didn't blame her. But I couldn't. I didn't know what was going to happen, and there was so much anger and grief still washing around in me. Things could still have gone badly wrong.'

Fleeting memories of Christian testimony books he had consumed in the past appeared and faded in Jack's mind. The feeling inside him was not so much nostalgia as a yearning for clear pathways. Why could Doc's story not be a little more thrillingly consequential and less ragged at the edges? A dream. A new name. It wouldn't need much pumping up to become more like one of those great Christian sagas. How to transform this unworthy thought into a reasonable question?

'But that day in the cathedral, the dream and the stone and everything – that was important, surely.'

The quizzical expression on Doc's face was annoyingly familiar. Jack knew he was cogitating on whether to answer the spoken or the unspoken question. He must have decided to be kind.

'It was crucial, Jack. But, as I've already said, I didn't know what it meant. I can tell you this, though. Looking back I can see that when I took that stone in my hand, something new was conceived in my mind. Not exactly born, you understand, just conceived. Birth was a possibility.'

Martha giggled quietly.

'Michael, I do think Jack might have managed to grasp the significance of your vividly gynaecological metaphor.'

The Shadow Doctor raised an innocent eyebrow.

'Oh, OK. Well, my pre-embryonic decision came out of two things that happened on that day. One was the strange experience of sharing grief with the very person I wanted to shout and scream at. That turned me upside down and inside out. The other was dear Martha loving me enough to chase me all that way up to Ripon to bring me a gift that she hoped might change my life.'

Martha executed a formal bow of the head in acknowledgement, but when she looked up her eyes were shining.

She murmured, 'You still owe me for the petrol, Michael.'

'You've been paid in strawberry tarts over the years,' responded Doc solemnly. 'No, my reaction to those things was the faintest breath of a decision that if – and it was still very much an if – if I was ever going to have some kind of future as – how did I put it to myself at the time? – a person who did things for God, a line would need to be drawn under almost everything I kidded myself I had known or understood until then.

'And as the days and weeks passed, an awareness of the need to leave the past to look after itself grew stronger and stronger. That horse had bolted, Jack. It was gone. Long gone, that horse was. I had no excuse for organising a solitary pity party for myself, or for looking back and getting more obsessed about mourning the loss of what looked like lots of great big fat mistakes than pushing on along towards the place where I was supposed to be.

'You remember that famous poem by Robert Frost, the one about a man who's making his way through a wood and comes to a place where two roads go in different directions and he has to decide which one to take? In the end he takes the one that hasn't been travelled as much. It's a popular poem, and people get a bit sentimental about it. I can easily understand why. The whole thing sounds dramatic and romantic and meaningful.

'The hard truth wasn't like that at all. I couldn't tell you exactly what Frost himself was talking about, but I do know what it meant for me, and for Martha at the most difficult time in her life – although I didn't fully understand it at the time – and increasingly for you now, Jack, as well as lots and lots of others. The fact is, there's quite a lot of company down the path towards that fork in the road. Christians of every shade and shine walking side by side with each other – and atheists and agnostics, because their doubts and problems can be shockingly similar, sometimes precisely the same.

'Eventually, like me in the months after I first held this stone in my hand, you reach that fork. There's no avoiding it. No escape. One way or the other: a decision has to be made. If you've been wearing a label with "Christian" written on it, but can no longer stomach the fact that an omnipotent God allows appalling, heart-wrenching catastrophes to happen, or that coincidence has become more significant than experience, or that aspects of Christian behaviour and outlook are just plain flat-footed and silly, or that the gap between what happens and what is supposed to happen has become too wide to comprehend or tolerate, you might well opt for the path more travelled and get on with life, equipped with some kind of rationalised faith, or with no faith at all, as best you can. After that day in Ripon Cathedral that was one of the choices I could have made. I know that for sure.'

Tears had begun to shimmer in Martha's eyes as she listened to Doc. She dabbed them with a corner of her scarf and turned apologetically to Jack.

'Sorry, some of this I've never heard before.' She managed a smile. 'Perhaps it really did have to be the kitchen floor.'

Jack wanted the answer to his next question as much as he had wanted anything in his entire life.

'What's the other choice?'

'Jack, the fact is that there will always be people who, despite possibly having exactly the same reservations and frustrations – or different ones for that matter – are going to press on along that uninviting, less travelled road for one overwhelming reason. It's a simple, irreducible fact. They want God.'

An unaccustomed passion entered his voice.

'They want God whatever, Jack. They want God! They want Jesus. They want Christ, but they don't necessarily want Christianity. In the marrow of their bones they might not find words to make sense of the hunger they feel, because that's not where you find words, but they know for sure that the hunger is there. They want God. That is the fact. And that fact can be enough – in the end it was for me – to keep them going along a route that's characterised by a sad lack of signposts and contracts and guarantees and neat refreshment points at regular intervals. Not only that, but at some point along this path that people like me are mad enough to choose, we may well find ourselves shouting out like children lost in the desert, "My God, my God, why have you forsaken me?" And we might even believe that he really has. It does seem, though, that moments like that are a fairly common feature of the not-so-romantic but far more ultimately exciting and productive road less travelled. As Jesus himself had to discover – if you never leave, then sure as eggs, you're never going to arrive. An old story. No risk, no reward. No pain, no gain.'

He paused to draw breath.

'Obviously, those who are generally labelled unbelievers will make their own decisions, that's their business, but I'm fairly sure that one day we'll be amazed to discover how many men and women who would have called themselves non-believers have actually gone for the path promising nothing because, in the end, it has a ghost of a chance of offering everything. Is that gratuitous nonsense – meaningless metaphor? Or is it a mystery? If we think it might be a mystery, it's worth chewing on.'

'So in the end you made the decision you're talking about.'

'I did. Those fishermen took a similar step into the unknown 2,000 years ago. They got called. They went. Fishing for men, becoming a shadow doctor – we hear the words, or we read them like I did, but we're not usually allowed to have a significant grasp of what we're signing up for. We get called, and if that call comes from someone we want to be with – well, there's just one question. Will we be wise – or foolish – enough to go? It begins with relationship. Always did. Always will. Who can tell where it will end? The good news is the same as the bad news. Once you've said yes, that's no longer your business.'

14

The top of the mountain

'So what exactly happened after that day in the cathedral?'

'Nothing, for a long time. Martha told you how I asked her all those questions at breakfast the next day. I left all that to roll around in the back of my mind. After that I came home to Sussex and did exactly what she did after her kitchen prayer.'

'You waited.'

'I waited. Nothing happened. After a bit it occurred to me to wonder if the ball might actually be in my court, and a couple of months on I reckoned I might be on the edge of arriving at my final decision. Made my way down to the clearing where you found me that time soon after we first met and spoke to someone I called God. It was raining quite hard that day.'

'What did you say?'

'What did I say? Oh, lots of things. Can't live with you, can't live without you. What's a shadow doctor? Why couldn't Miriam have stayed and been one as well? Can I stay in my cottage? What will I live on? I'm getting very wet. Loads of things. Stopped talking after a while and just stood still in the middle of the clearing in the pouring rain, summoning up the courage to say the only words that would really mean anything.'

You had to give in.

'You had to give in.'

Doc nodded appreciatively. 'That's correct, Jack. That's what I said. I give in. No conditions. No more questions. No arguments. I said, "Okay, I'll do what you want. If you want me to be a shadow doctor, whatever that turns out to be, I'll be one. Blank canvas. First day at school. Forgive the mixed metaphors. Teach me."'

'Did the rain stop after that?'

'No, Jack, sorry to disappoint you. It was an encounter with God, not a bad American film, nor one of those old-fashioned testimony paperbacks. I went home, had a large whisky, then went to bed rather early. I think I was a little bit afraid that I might start scribbling on my own blank canvas if I stayed up any longer.'

'Did your life change after that?'

'No, not straightaway. Not for a while.'

Jack sighed inwardly. *Majoring on the gaps again. Why?*

Martha broke the silence.

'You took yourself off to Scotland a couple of weeks after that, didn't you, Michael? You said you wanted a chance to get away from people and concentrate on God.'

'Thank you for quoting me so exactly, Martha. I believe I did say something slightly strange and rather pompous like that, yes.'

'Did it happen?'

'Sort of, Jack – and no, and yes, depending on how you look at it. After a long morning of walking uphill on the second day I ran into somebody else at the top of my private devotional mountain. Apparently he'd more or less wound his way up the less steep path on the other side. Quiet sort of fellow. About the same age as me. Something a bit unusual about him. Hard to read. We got talking in the end. He was called Derek. Two things I learned quite quickly about Derek. First, he was a Christian. Nothing very remarkable about that. Christians seem to spend an awful lot of time roaming dismally through bleak country-side areas hunting for God under rocks, especially when they've got problems. And that was the second thing I learned. Derek was a man with a lot of problems. He told me about some of them while we ate our sandwiches and swapped fruit and shared Derek's flask of coffee and enjoyed the view. I listened. Still doing my best to stay in blank-canvas mode, you understand. It took an effort, because there were all sorts of things I could have said, stuff I would definitely have come out with in the past. Scripts of a kind. Useful stuff mind you. I'd use that stuff now. I do use it.'

'But—'

'But, by an act of will, I'd placed myself under orders, so I waited. And I'm glad I did, because, as so often happens, it turned out that none of those things he'd talked about were the important problem.'

'What happened?'

The Shadow Doctor tilted his head and seemed, for a moment or two, to be lost in the memory.

'It was quite odd. I noticed that, every now and then as he spoke, Derek touched the shirtsleeve on his right fore-arm with his left hand for – well, for barely a second. And certainly not more than three times in total while we were sitting there. It definitely wasn't done for my benefit, but it was so very deliberate. It stole most of my attention. After a bit, it was all I could think about. In fact . . .' He spread his hands and gazed at the ceiling. 'Ridiculously, I was trying to push it out of my mind in case I missed a message in the sky from God. And then, suddenly, it was hutzpah time, and all I can tell you is that the gall was not mine. I interrupted Derek in the middle of him saying something and asked why he kept touching his arm.'

Martha shook her head in wonder. 'I would have punched him. That's what I said when he phoned that night and told me what had happened. Cheek!'

'He didn't punch you?'

'He looked as if he might have considered it, Jack. He was one of those very serious, inwardly forceful men. Just stared grimly at me for a few seconds. Said nothing. Then very slowly and tidily he unbuttoned his cuff and rolled his sleeve up to the elbow. Still not a word. He just touched a mark on his arm with a finger. It was a tattoo. A very simple, fairly small one. It was a black circle with a capital "J" facing across his arm in the middle of it.'

'Did he tell you what it meant?'

Doc shook his head. 'Still didn't speak. Just looked me straight in the eyes. Strange atmosphere between us. The first time I'd known anything quite like that. Then this question . . . burrowed into my mind.'

Martha knitted her brows in puzzlement.

'I don't think you used that word at the time. Burrowed?'

'That's how it felt, yes.'

'Like a mole, you mean?'

'A mole? No, of course not. It was—'

'A question from God, you mean?'

'I had no idea, Martha. I did tell you at the time – it was just a question begging to be asked.'

Martha clicked her tongue. 'A begging mole! You do spoil your stories, Michael. I know how wonderful it is that the truth will set us free, but there are times when it doesn't exactly add to the entertainment. I mean, who precisely was begging you to ask this question?'

Doc just smiled. It was a fond smile. Jack was once again fascinated and slightly threatened by the easy relationship he was witnessing. These two old friends were very relaxed with each other. Was it possible, he found himself wondering once more, that he might enjoy a similarly comfortable rapport with the Shadow Doctor in the future? Perhaps, but not easy to imagine.

'Well, regardless of whether it was sent by God or by a mendicant mole,' continued Doc, 'it ultimately changed his life, and I suppose I have to say that in a very real sense it changed mine as well.'

'Michael, for goodness sake, just tell Jack the question you asked.'

'Okay. That is not a problem. I remember it word for word. I said, "Derek, what would happen if you had your tattoo removed?"'

'And he said—?'

Doc brought the heels of his hands together and clapped his fingers together gently.

'Can't tell you, Jack. Sorry. I made a promise. Tell you what, though, if we ever meet Derek when we're together, and we almost certainly will for reasons that I'll tell you about in a moment, I think he might tell you himself. I hope he does. I can tell you that, as far as I was concerned, two very important things happened as a result of that encounter.

116

'One was a sort of confirmation of that original blank-canvas instinct. If I really was going to be of any use to other people in the future, I would have to abandon any thought of being in charge of what was going on. My job would be to make sure I was in . . .'

He extended a hand to give Jack his cue.

'The flow?'

'Thank you. Exactly. The jolly old flow. Keep my ears and eyes and everything else open and ready to make the appropriate contribution, as opposed to my idea of what the right contribution might look like. Tricky. That was a work in progress for a long time – still is. Not made easier by the fact that common sense is needed just as often as stuff that's more bizarre and surprising. Hard to sort out sometimes. And the brazen truth is that it can be quite annoying and diminishing when someone else is usually calling the shots.'

'Someone else?'

'Someone else, yes.'

Jack nodded as though Doc had explained at length.

'You can't help people unless you know what's going on inside,' said Martha softly. 'Michael is the Shadow Doctor.' She reached across to touch his arm. 'I'm proud of him.'

'What was the other very important thing that happened?'

The last comment from his old friend seemed to have temporarily silenced Doc. Martha turned in her chair to answer Jack's question.

'It was to do with Derek. By the time he and Michael reached the bottom of the hill . . .' She flapped a hand in Doc's direction without looking at him. 'It wasn't a mountain, Michael, it was a large hill. I've been there. I know.

You really should learn to tell the truth. By the time they got back down, Derek had come to a decision that, I'm pleased to say, has seriously and dramatically affected his life for the better from that day to this. He took Michael's details before they parted and a few weeks later he wrote a letter that began with these words: "Dear Michael, you have passed the Nebuchadnezzar test . . ."

'If you don't know what that means, Jack, you'll just have to read the story of Daniel. That's what I had to do once I'd worked out where Nebuchadnezzar comes. In the letter, Derek said that he'd always wanted to be able to help with Christian projects that were genuinely effective, but most of the ones he'd looked at were not impressive. Good people, but not much practical experience or knowhow. More optimism than substance, was the way I think he put it.

'Anyway, on the way down the large hill or small mountain, Michael had told him all about my dream and the shadow doctor stuff and all the rest of it. He said he wanted to meet us both and find out if there was a way he might be able to help. We had no idea what that could possibly mean, but we said yes, let's do it. So, a while later, he drove all the way down from Bolton to Sussex, and we got together here, in this very room actually, and he had a piece of paper with a zillion questions written on it. When he'd run out of his questions, he sat quietly for a while and then – well, you tell him the next bit, Michael.'

'Okay, well our guest left the cottage saying that he'd love to be involved, and he'd have a think about how best to help. A week later he wrote me another letter. Turned out Derek was a very rich man, Jack, with vast business interests. I googled him. Couldn't believe it. He certainly hadn't looked or sounded anything like that, but it was true. That's what he was. He wasn't just a millionaire. He was a multi-millionaire. He was a multi-multi-millionaire. He asked very politely if I would allow him to be part of financing what he called the "Shadow Doctor Project", and, to cut a long and quite intensive and complex story short, that is exactly what he ended up doing.

'He looked at the whole business of setting up a charity or trust or something equally complicated, but after looking at all the options decided to simply put me on his payroll. He suggested a frighteningly high annual salary and promised that finance would be ready and available if another wage or salary needed to be paid. I argued a bit.'

'Why?'

'Temporary misplacement of bottle, Jack. I pointed out that, as far as I could see, the kind of solutions I was likely to offer people would never get through the committee stage in any sane organisation.

' "Like the things Jesus did, you mean?" he said.

' "Well, OK, but I could end up offending as many people as I help."

' "Like Jesus?"

'There were other excuses, but in the end I gave up. So there it is. I am now an officially registered, tax-paying employee of Reed Enterprises, in one of Derek's private business initiatives.'

'The other wage or salary turned out to be me,' smiled Martha delightedly. 'I can't imagine why you haven't heard all this before, Jack. I'm Michael's call filter, admin person, sounding board, general assistant, printer and laminator of contact cards and anything else he needs me to be. I've enjoyed every moment of it.'

'Derek knows about you. He'll pay your salary as well if that's what you choose,' added Doc, 'and he'll go on doing that for as long as we work together. So please don't worry about spending my money. It's not mine. It's his. Some of it will be yours. Martha and I meet Derek's terminally scary non-Christian accountant once a year, and Derek joins us for a meal way up in Alnwick every six months or so. We all love Alnwick. Any excuse to get to the best bookshop in the world. He loves to hear the stories – the ones we're free to tell.'

'And we really love to tell them, Jack. You'll be coming with us for the next one – if you stick around.' No one had ever looked at Jack with the expression of hope that he saw in Martha's eyes as she leaned imploringly towards him at that moment. 'Do please decide to stick around, Jack. Please.'

Later, just before leaving, Martha used a moment when Doc was upstairs to whisper a few more urgent words.

'Jack, very quickly – I can see that you still feel confused and inadequate, and heavens above, I know from my own experience that insecurity like that doesn't disappear like magic. But I so want you to hear this. Since the whole shadow doctor thing started, I have never heard Michael speaking so openly and so trustingly with anyone but me, especially about Miriam. You are definitely the reason for that. So please, somewhere in the back of your mind, however dark and difficult things seem to get, remember how important you are, not just to Michael, but to all the people you and he will be able to help. Sorry to go on. I've truly loved meeting you in person. Please give Elsie my love next week. Goodbye, Jack.'

Late that night, just before heading for bed, Doc and Jack exchanged questions. Doc's was predictable.

'So, was I right? Did you fall in love with Martha?'

Jack had rehearsed his answer, but it was an honest one.

'She's probably the most immediately attractive person, man or woman, that I've ever met. And, yes, in a way I did fall in love with her. But I'd describe it as more of an instant crush than anything else. I felt like a little kid in reception falling for a big girl in the top class. I'm looking forward to seeing her again. I might be a bit braver next time. I've got another question for you now.'

'Go ahead.'

Jack knew that he had less than half a second to conjure up a fake question before consigning the real one to the bin for ever. He failed.

'Have you ever been in love with her?'

The Shadow Doctor seemed unruffled by the question, but he finished the wine in his glass to the last drop before answering in musing tones.

'It looks very possible, doesn't it? Very tidy. While Miriam was alive the off-switch was firmly applied to emotional distractions. I wanted no one else, and then, quite abruptly, I didn't even have her. Martha was our friend. We loved her. Of course, she was and is a beautiful woman, but mostly she was – Martha. So, no, I don't think I would ever have been mentally able to push Miriam a body's width away so that Martha could slide into the gap. No, I value our friendship more than gold, but nothing else will ever happen.'

'I've got one more question before we go to bed.'

'Should I pour more wine, Jack?'

'Not for me, no. Thanks. I just wanted to ask you a question about Derek. You said he had a tattoo on his arm with the letter "J" in a black circle.'

'Correct.'

'I know you're not allowed to tell me what his problem was, but can I just ask you – if it had been you with the same problem as Derek, and you'd had a tattoo like his—'

'Yes?'

'Would the letter in the middle have been "M"?'

The Shadow Doctor swung his empty glass gently as he quoted, ' "This is the promise that I will make to them after those days, says the Lord, I will put my teachings in their hearts and write them in their minds." We need space in our hearts and minds, Jack. And you're right. In my case "M" would have been for Miriam. A heart-breaking task to do the clearing, especially after losing her, but nothing's possible if you don't.'

'Thank you, Doc.'

'Not a problem, Jack. Oh, by the way, I meant to tell you, I've been asked to preach at a church in Eastbourne in a few weeks, and I've said I'll do it. Fancy coming along?'

'You amaze me. I find it quite difficult to imagine you standing up at the front of a church. I wouldn't miss it for the world. We don't have to dress up, do we?'

'No, Jack, this place was messy long before they invented Messy Church. Goodnight. Sleep well.'

'Night, Doc. See you tomorrow.'

15

A clue

'We'd better swing round by Station Road and feed the creature. We can pick *The Times* up there as well.'

'As long as you aren't planning to make any more comments on my newspaper-buying habits.'

'I promise.' He raised one hand. 'Scout's honour.'

'That's the Cub Scout sign you're doing. Two fingers. They stand for Akela's ears. She's the leader of the pack – the wolf. Scouts use three fingers. And it's the right hand, not the left.'

'Thank you, Jack. I would not mistakenly offer you two fingers for the world.'

Minutes later the car was fuelled, and Jack was back in the driving seat, newspaper in hand. He passed it across to Doc and started the engine.

'OK, let's go.'

Doc reached a hand towards the glove compartment.

'Sat-nav?'

'No need. Elsie's nursing home is on Tonbridge Road, part of my old hunting grounds. I could do it with my eyes shut.'

'Please don't do that, Jack. I'm not sure anyone's ever come up with a sat-nav programmed for that sort of trip. I take your point, though.'

Doc folded the newspaper in half and hunted around in the glove compartment for something to write with. A biro emerged.

'OK, leaving all that other stuff aside, how about if I give you one of the clues from this pristine back page, and you see if you can work it out as we go along?'

Jack grunted hopelessly as he steered the X-Trail round behind the Shell garage towards the main road exit.

'Well, you can if you like, but if you're talking about the cryptic one, I think we both know the chances of me working it out are about as remote as the possibility of you providing a straight answer to a simple question, however pristine the back page is. Read it out. I'll have a go, seeing as you said something nice about me last week. Choose an easy one.'

Doc smiled to himself, tapping his teeth with his pen as he studied the crossword.

'OK, here we are. Eight down. "The Alpen wild creature". Eight letters. Do you want me to read it again?'

'Go on, then. I still won't get it, but you might as well.'

Doc repeated the clue, reading slowly and enunciating each word clearly. 'Right. The Alpen wild creature. Eight letters.'

'Is that Alpen as in mountain ranges and that sort of thing?'

'I would imagine so. Unlikely to be anything to do with Muesli. Capital A – l – p – e – n. Alpen.'

'Read it again.'

'The Alpen wild creature.'

'Right, I've got it.'

'You've got the answer?'

'No, of course not. Come on! I just mean that I've achieved the immense feat of memorising the clue. This is my brain we're talking about, remember, not yours. Anyway, you've got the paper in front of you. I have to drive.' He threw a quick glance to one side. 'Presumably you've already solved it, have you?'

'I think I might have got eleven across. And if I have that right, the sixth letter of the one we're trying to solve would be an "a". Does that help?'

'It might. Doc, don't patronise me. I know perfectly well you've worked it out already. You don't need to pretend. Just leave me to think about it for a moment.'

Silence reigned for a few miles. As the A21 unfurled before them, Jack silently repeated the four-word clue to himself. He wasn't even sure which questions to ask. What kind of wild creatures were you likely to find in mountains like the Alps? Would information like that be helpful?

'I'm trying very hard, but all I can really think about is goats,' he announced eventually.

'We can tackle your personal problems later,' replied Doc very seriously, 'I thought you were working on this clue.'

'You know exactly what I meant. The only Alpen creatures that come to mind are goats. Maybe different kinds of deer. I did think of roebuck and chamois, but neither of those has eight letters, so – probably not.'

Doc reached across to borrow Jack's mobile, and punched a question in.

'Mm! Interesting. According to this the French Alps are teeming with wild creatures. Listen to this. Brown bear, lynx, wild cat, wolf, red deer, fallow deer, roebuck, chamois – well done for remembering those two, Jack. Then there's ibex, bouquetin – not sure how you say it, but whatever that is – marmot, snow-vole and shrew. Amazing. Quite irrelevant, though, because you're—'

'What do you mean?'

'It's a cryptic clue, remember. You're being a bit too literal. The answer has got nothing at all to do with Alpen creatures.'

'How can it possibly have nothing to do with the very thing it talks about?'

'Do you remember me telling you once that this sort of crossword has its own set of unwritten rules?'

'I do. That was in connection with the chap we met who needed help because he was being blackmailed, wasn't it? I think I've forgotten the rules you told me, all but the one you used to work out that he'd given us a false name – the anagram thing.'

'Correct. Here's one I probably didn't mention at the time. Not always, but quite often, when you see the word "wild" in a crossword clue, it means that the word or words before or after it are likely to be an anagram of the answer.'

Jack considered this for a moment.

'Ah, so the answer to this clue must be an anagram of "creature", because that's the only word with eight letters. And it has to mean "Alpen". Am I nearly there?'

'No. Remember what I just said? It can be made up of letters from more than one word.'

Jack forced himself to concentrate.

'Right. So, in that case, it can only be an anagram of "The Alpen", and it must mean creature, or actually be an example of a creature.'

'Perfect reasoning, Jack.'

'So, are you going to tell me the answer?'

'No. let's leave it.'

Jack slapped the steering wheel with one hand. He was running out of ways to vent his frustration while driving. The Shadow Doctor seemed determined as ever to lead his new colleague along lengthy, twisting paths, before dumping him for reasons that were rarely divulged at the time.

'Would you like to explain to me why you thought it was a good idea to start this tortuous exercise with someone like me who's hopeless at it anyway, lead me along and then cut it off at the end as though it means nothing?'

The Shadow Doctor swayed with frustration as he wrestled with this request. Then he became still, gazing out of the side window as he spoke very quietly and calmly.

'I cut it off because I believe it may or may not mean something. I could be completely wrong about assigning it any significance at all. I suspect we shall find out later today.'

Inwardly, Jack cursed himself, Doc, and the entire population of Kent and Sussex, just to make sure that nobody got left out. This was always the problem about falling out with the man sitting next to him over issues like this. Soon after their first meeting, the Shadow Doctor had said that he was reluctant to offer anything to people unless he was quite sure that he was actually in possession of whatever he was offering. Help, answers, explanations, resolutions, insights, he simply refused to display or share any knots that he had not yet untied. On most occasions, the stubbornness was eclipsed by the result, as had happened with Victor two days earlier, but Jack wanted to be involved with the process as well as the outcome. It was beginning to annoy him. He decided to be mean. There was a speech he had often rehearsed but never delivered. He was very close to being word perfect.

'We're back to your bloody flow, are we? Flowing around all over the place and waiting to see whether you end up in a muddy puddle or a beautiful ocean or an interesting little tributary before you do your spiritual Sherlock Holmes act, and allow thickheads like me to be amazed by your special relationship with the cosmos. Well, flow away. Just let me know when we arrive somewhere. After all, what am I? Just the driver.'

It was a tribute to the developing relationship between the two men that, after two seconds of chilled silence, Jack began to laugh out loud at himself, and Doc, after batting the young man's chest with his folded newspaper, chuckled companionably in his turn. He sounded genuinely apologetic when he spoke.

'We've journeyed our pointless way around that circular route a few times, haven't we, Jack? Nothing's changed much. You've seen over the last couple of days how vulnerable I can be. The little person inside is still anxious about pulling apart something that might turn out not to exist after all, and you perfectly reasonably object to being made a victim of my anxiety, stranded in the dark until someone switches the light on. A problem for both of us is that we've spent quite a long time hunkered down in our own little worlds, coping and surviving by whatever means we've cobbled together. Someone, hopefully not someone like Donald Trump, who only thinks he created the universe, has decided that Martha is right. We need each other for our own good, and for the benefit of lots of folk we might be able to help if we get the right assistance. Your speech was brilliant, by the way.'

'I've said those stupid words in my head lots of times,' confessed Jack ruefully.

'Nevertheless, one thing is for sure. As I too often say without doing anything about it, our own pet expressions do come back to haunt us. The "bloody flow", as you so vividly and horrifically described it, has definitely passed its sell-by date. I shall put it out in the stale-metaphor bin. Which reminds me, I've got tons of hyperbole to dump as well. Been in the drawer by my bed literally for ever.'

Jack just smiled and nodded. Surely the Shadow Doctor would not be kind enough to explain what hyperbole was.

'I am sorry, Doc, I suppose I'm a bit impatient, and worried that all of this – being with you I mean – might come to nothing. It's strange. I get quite excited, but it's a lot harder than I thought it would be. Don't forget, I didn't have all the exciting dreams and white stones and stuff that you and Martha had. It's tough sometimes.'

'Real things usually are. When I was younger, we were often told that life would be straightforward because God has a plan for our lives.'

'Hasn't he, then? Say he has. I hope he has. I want him to have a plan for my life. Sorting it out on my own hasn't worked very well so far.'

'He might have a plan for your life, Jack, but that doesn't mean he's going to tell you what it is. He may be omniscient, but he's not silly, certainly not silly enough to spoil your sleep by going into detail.'

'What do you mean?'

'Have you ever heard of a man called Paul – chap who went around preaching to the Gentiles?'

After witnessing the banter between Doc and Martha, Jack felt more able to distinguish rudeness from deliberate provocation.

'Don't be silly, Doc.'

'All right, let's try to imagine how it might have been when Paul went to Philippi with his friend Silas. I suppose he might have said brightly to God, "Lord, could you just fill us in on your plan for the time we're spending in this place. Just the broad brushstrokes, if you know what I mean?"'

'And God might have replied, "Yes, if you insist. You are sure you want to know, are you?"'

' "Oh, yes," says Paul, "we can handle it. Can't we, Silas?"'

' "Err . . ."'

' "OK," says God, "well, let me see. You'll meet a woman called Lydia down by the river, and she'll be converted, and ask you to stay at her house and that will turn out to be really good and useful in the future." Pause. "You don't need to hear any more, do you?"'

' "Yes, I think we do! Don't we, Silas?"'

' "Err . . ."'

' "OK, this fortune teller woman will follow you in the street, and she'll keep shouting things about you, and you'll get really troubled and call a spirit out of her, so she won't be able to tell fortunes any more, and the people who've been making money out of the stuff she does will drag you to the magistrates and they'll order you to be stripped and flogged to within an inch of your lives, and then you'll be locked in the deepest, darkest dungeon they can find, with shackles on your ankles, and then there'll be an earthquake, and then – well, everything works out for the best after that – sort of."'

'So, what do you think, Jack? Do you want to know God's plan for your life?'

'Err . . .'

'I honestly don't think our visit to Elsie will involve any of those horrible things, but you never know. At least we feel fairly confident that helping Martha with her gran is the right thing to be doing for now.'

'You know I agree with that. Of course I do. But, on that same subject – and I know I'm going to wish I hadn't asked this – how exactly are we going to help Elsie? I mean, I know zilch about how you help elderly people to unlock themselves, or whatever the expression is. The only elderly person I've ever known well was my gran, and I'm sure she was sharper than me right up until the day she died. What about you? I don't suppose you're a qualified expert either, are you? What are we going to do?'

'I do have a bit of a plan, Jack, but I'd rather keep it to myself for now. I don't want to worry you. Getting to Green Pastures is our priority for now. Do the next thing. Not a bad motto, I think.'

No, thought Jack, *not if you're not sure what the next thing is. You* might *be, but I've got no idea. Mind you, if I had, it would worry me.* He settled down to drive, inwardly laying his head on the miniscule cushion of an awareness that he had taken a step forward in the context of buying newspapers, and the fact that he might have helped the Shadow Doctor to open up a little. Ah, well, those things must count for something. *What was that anagram again? 'The Alpen'. What species of little creature was skulking behind the undergrowth of those letters? Not a clue.*

16

Green Pastures

The last part of the journey took them off the A21 through Blackhurst Lane, and then left along Tonbridge Road, an area broadly familiar to Jack from his church-visiting days. An unexpected pang of nostalgia hit him somewhere in the pit of his stomach just as Doc raised a finger to indicate a sign on their left announcing that they had reached their destination. How odd, he thought, that such a dysfunctional and distressing time in his life should suddenly beckon like an old friend. As he steered the X-Trail carefully between ancient-looking stone gateposts and into a space in the Green Pastures car park, he found himself picturing the rough track up to Doc's cottage, and the forest that now seemed to cloak his life and possibly much of his future. Was that home? Did he want it to be home? Wasn't it a bit limited? More of a retreat than an advance? Perhaps. Maybe. Maybe not.

Green Pastures presented itself with confidence, a beauti-fully converted two-storey building. Pristine white walls and sky-blue window frames. Like a picture in a child's book. Jack peered up at the front of the nursing home as they waited outside two big frosted-glass doors for some-one to answer the bell.

'It's in good nick, isn't it?'

'No expense spared, Jack. You heard what Martha said. They really look after their ladies and gentlemen here. You'll see in a minute. It's just as smart inside.'

A ghostly figure looming from behind the frosted-glass doors turned out to be a very attractive young lady dressed in blue overalls. She ushered her guests into the reception area with a welcoming smile and spoke with a soft Welsh accent.

'Good morning. You're here to visit Elsie, aren't you?' She studied Doc's face for a moment. 'Yes, I thought so; I was here the last time you came with Martha. I'm Aelwen. It was me who gave Martha a ring. Miss Carlton, our manager, asked me to meet you and let you know that the doctor was late getting here to see Elsie, and she's only just gone up to her room. Would you be all right sitting here in reception until she's finished? She's got one or two others to see after that, so I don't think she'll want to be too long. And then someone will come and let you know as soon as Elsie's free. Can I get you some tea? We've got tea. Or coffee? I think we've got some instant.' She giggled. 'I'm afraid you won't like that if you're used to decent coffee. We ran out. And we never run out. I shouldn't say that really, should I? We are due more of the proper stuff later today. Soon as someone has a minute to pop down to the Co-op. Miss Carlton says she can't wait. She hates instant coffee.'

Smiling, Doc shook his head to interrupt the flow.

'That's very kind, Aelwen, and thanks for the warning. I think we probably take our coffee as seriously as Miss Carlton. Jack and I have actually crossed the line and started grinding our own beans.'

'Goodness me!'

Aelwen looked fascinated.

'In any case, if it's OK with you, we'll wait and have a cup of tea with Elsie when she's free. You all right with that, Jack?'

Jack wrestled his hypnotised attention from Aelwen's smiling face.

'Sorry? Oh, yes – yes, of course. Thank you.'

It seemed to Jack that the Welsh girl's eyes lingered on his face for an instant longer than necessary as she left. Probably just his imagination.

The reception lobby was indeed smart and well-appointed, but the table in the centre of the seating area was strewn with what Doc described as an embarrassed-looking, ill-fitting array of tatty magazines and half-completed word-search books. Jack checked the time on his phone and looked around for a few moments.

'I suppose there's nothing we can do until the doctor's finished her visit.' He cleared his throat. 'So, while we're waiting to see Elsie, would you mind if I asked you a couple of things quickly?'

The Shadow Doctor eyed Jack doubtfully.

'In my experience, Jack, when people say they want to ask something very quickly, they avoid finishing the sentence.'

'I didn't think I did. What is the end of the sentence?'

'Well, the whole sentence goes something like this. If I ask you a very quick question, will you take as long as it needs to answer it?'

Jack feigned hurt.

'I was just going to ask when the MOT's due.'

Silence.

'On the car, I mean.'

'O-o-oh, that MOT. The one on the car. Not the one on the lawnmower, then?' He smiled amiably. 'Jack Merton, you have just told a deliberate lie.'

Jack grimaced and scrubbed his face with one hand. 'Well, yes, that was a deliberate lie, designed of course to protect you from my annoying question, but—'

'Don't worry, Jack. Although you and I are both great champions of the truth in theory, it is also a gold-plated fact that no human being above the age of about three, including us, tells the truth all the time. Nobody.'

'Nobody?'

Doc shook his head decisively. 'Nobody.'

'Including Jesus, according to you.'

'I think I've already said as much about that as I intend to. I'll repeat it once more if you wish. Here it is. To my certain knowledge that particular gentleman makes at least two statements in the New Testament account of his life that are clearly not true.'

Jack mentally adjusted his inner police uniform and pursed his lips.

'I've been meaning to say to you that I just don't believe that.'

'You think I'm lying?'

'I didn't mean to – no, you're laughing at me. You know that's not what I meant. Come on, then. I give up. Where in the Bible are the two places where Jesus doesn't tell the truth? Which book? Which chapter? Which verse?'

The Shadow Doctor made a great play of looking at his watch.

'We might just have time for that question you wanted to ask, Jack. The other thing can wait, can't it?'

'I shan't forget.'

'Forget what?'

'The business about – oh, for goodness sake! OK, it was a serious question. When we were in the car after coming away from Trevor's place the other day, I asked you what you thought God would have said about you and Miriam laughing after hearing the elderly lady talking about her husband hanging himself. You said that God doesn't tell you things in triplicate, so you had to make a sort of guess about what his reaction might have been. Remember?'

'I do remember that, yes. What did you want to know?'

'Well, leaving aside all the stuff about hearing things three times over, I don't think it's true that God doesn't tell you anything. He does. I've been with you and seen what happens. Remember the first couple of weeks I stayed?'

'You were on approval,' said Doc tartly.

'So were you,' replied Jack spiritedly.

'Touché, Jack. And we both passed, me by the skin of my teeth.'

So far, thought Jack.

'During that time,' he persisted, 'there was a day when we set off to meet someone neither of us had met before, and you suddenly had to urgently – urgently, mind you – run back indoors to get a random piece of red silky stuff that you'd found in a charity shop the week before. Remember? In the middle of speaking to Sam in the café, you pulled it out of your pocket and used it to make her laugh when she got upset and started to cry. You told her it was your "joke handkerchief". In the car afterwards, I asked you why you brought it along in the first place, and you just said that it was part of your "flow". I still don't altogether understand what that's all about, but whatever it is and wherever it comes from I'm sure there are times when you know things. You know what to say. You know what to do. What about with Victor the other day when you asked him that question right out of the blue? Extraordinary. I know it doesn't happen all the time, but it's often enough to make me think that there's more to it than you thinking outside the box and turning ideas on their heads to shake everything up. You do that as well, like no one else I've ever known, but despite all the things you said yesterday, I still don't really get it. Where does the *you* part of it end, and – something – someone – else begin?'

The expression on the Shadow Doctor's face as he gave the impression of staring into himself in search of an answer to the question reminded Jack of something. Years ago, at university, on turning over an exam paper, he had discovered that, despite quite a profound knowledge of his subject, none of the set questions appeared to relate to any of the material he had studied. He had felt like the man in the ancient joke who asks a yokel for directions, and is told, 'I wouldn't start from 'ere, if I was you.'

In fact, the Shadow Doctor looked a little sorry for himself.

'I really do appreciate what you're asking, Jack, but it's such hard work explaining. I suppose the problem is that it – whatever it is – is something like learning to ride a bike or drive a car. When you're a novice you need to think about every single, blessed, component part of what you're doing. It's like a list in your mind. You tick the things off mentally in your head as you go. Seatbelt, mirrors, handbrake, all the rest of it, and that's before you even start moving – goodness me, I'd probably fail miserably if I had to take my test today, particularly as you so selfishly insist on keeping all the driving to yourself. Then, when you've been driving for a while, you don't have to think carefully through that list any more. It comes naturally. It's part of you, part of what you do.'

Jack sighed and waited. It appeared that nothing else would be forthcoming.

'OK, I think I see that, but there are two problems with your car metaphor.' He used a forefinger to count them out. 'One, it only explains why you find it difficult to explain. We have been through that before, haven't we? Two, whatever this thing is that you've learned to do automatically, it's not really like driving a car, is it, because it's never the same twice? Or very rarely.'

Doc crossed his arms and twisted his body from side to side like a child wrestling with an impossible maths question.

'So . . .' continued Jack, battling to retain a hold on his own logic, 'if the automatic bit isn't about what ends up happening, it must be about how you make the decision about what you're going to do.' He rapped a hand on the arm of his chair. 'Mustn't it? Doc, you're inclining your head very seriously, but you're not saying anything.'

Silence.

'OK, let's take another example. The picture you brought along when we went lion-stalking. You didn't have to take a picture at all, did you? You could have just gone in there and told Trevor you knew what he'd done, and that would have been that. Same result? Probably. Why was the picture of Jesus important? Have you used anything like that before?'

The Shadow Doctor came to life.

'Goodness, no. I find the idea of Jesus making a gesture like that with his finger quite abhorrent. Vulgar and disrespectful.'

Stopped in his tracks, Jack stared uncomprehendingly.

'But if you think that, why did you take it? What was the point?'

'Interesting, Jack,' he replied musingly. 'I have asked myself the same question.' He continued to think for a moment. 'You know, I suspect the picture was needed because we were dealing with a man of very great import-ance and reputation in his own well-appointed world. He'd done something that was mean and small-hearted and dismally unkind in the tiny universe of a vulnerable girl who, to quote our ruling premise, Jack, we must remember is no less valuable than any other person in the world. I would imagine that Trevor, who is no more or less import-ant than she is, might have forgotten that the little individ-ual living inside himself is no bigger or more important now than he was before he gained all that public stature. Put bluntly, he had started to think that he was in charge of what he did.

'Let's face it, Jack, postmen like us are not employed to write letters, nor to edit them. We just deliver them, whether they're bills or cheques. Maybe, in Trevor's case, the nature of the revelation had to match the crime. A shock and a rebuke. He'll never forget that painting. But no, in itself, the picture thing was all most unpleasant.'

Jack made the obvious point.

'Doc, you speak as though the picture was someone else's idea.'

'Do I?'

'Someone else's responsibility?'

Doc shook his head very definitely. 'Oh, no, absolutely not, Jack. Deciding to go ahead with the whole picture episode was entirely my responsibility. I've never been forced to do anything.'

'Your responsibility, then, but whose idea was it?'

The Shadow Doctor gazed with troubled eyes at Jack for what must have been half a minute.

'Jack, we'll probably have to go through soon, but I promise we'll talk more about this later on. In the meantime, I will tell you something that might begin to answer your original question.' He frowned thoughtfully. 'I'm just trying to think how to make it easy to grasp. OK, this might get close. My way of doing things has got quite a lot to do with not looking over my shoulder too much.'

Jack passed a hand across his forehead. 'Phew! What a relief. Thank goodness you made it so simple. I understand completely now. It's to do with not looking over your shoulder too much. I'll do the same from now on. I won't look over my shoulder too much, and everything will work out just fine.'

'Patience, Jack,' rebuked Doc mildly, 'I haven't finished yet. There is a man I respect greatly. No longer with us, which is a shame because he was wonderful, though actually I'm not sure he and I would have got on if we'd met in the flesh. Someone wrote to this chap, asking for advice on things like guidance and living the Christian life. One day I read the reply to this letter, and I have to say that the central argument of his reply helps to underpin my life, now that I've begun to get my head round it.

'What did he say?'

'He describes following Jesus as being something like rowing a boat. People like me, and you as well, perhaps, have only got to row. Someone else takes the tiller. I don't have to worry so much about that side of things. Just put the effort in. I'm not in charge of steering, I've only got to row well. So, and this is the important point, Jack, the future journey is behind my back. Mustn't look over my shoulder too often. No need. Keep my eye on the helmsman and become an expert with the oars. Make sure I don't mess things up by pulling too hard on one side or the other and end up going round in circles. Bright conscience and a clear brain. I'm in good hands. Do what I'm told and keep asking questions. That's about it. I know it doesn't cover everything, but it's not a bad start.'

'Yes, it is. In fact, it's rather fascinating in a way, but it still doesn't begin to explain—'

'Elsie's free now, gentlemen.'

The manager of Green Pastures, neat and bright-eyed, had appeared as if by magic through the internal security entrance and was holding the door to the corridor open as she spoke. A rectangular badge with the words MISS F CARLTON – MANAGER printed upon it was fastened to the lapel of her blue jacket.

'She'll be brought down to sit at the table by one of the windows in the little sitting-room. You can go and wait for her if you want. No one else will come in while you're there. I'm afraid, as you'll have heard, Elsie's not at all chatty at the moment, and hasn't been for a while. That's why we wanted the doctor to take a look at her this morning. He says she seems fine, but I think Aelwen, whom you met just now, might be right. Definitely something playing on her mind.' She pointed. 'So, straight down this corridor until you get to the far end, then through the swing doors on your left.'

A thought occurred to her.

'By the way, you'll almost certainly meet Doreen before you get there. A pretty little lady holding an old-fashioned dolly. If she asks you a question, you only have to answer truthfully.' She glanced at Doc as the two men rose to their feet. 'I spotted you from the window when you were coming in earlier. You've been before, haven't you? You came once or twice with Martha to visit Elsie. You probably met Doreen then.'

Noting delight on the Shadow Doctor's face, Jack smiled to himself. It was genuine. Never faked. He did at least know that now. The blessing and the burden of being a follower of Jesus, Doc had often declared, was the certain knowledge that there are no unimportant people in the world. No exceptions allowed. Not Trevor Langston, not anybody. Maybe, reflected Jack a little dispiritedly, that was part of being a dependable oarsman.

'That's absolutely right. Thank you so much for remembering. Yes, Martha's an old friend, and, as I think you know, she was keen for me to meet her beloved gran, so I've popped in with her on a couple of occasions. Doreen ambushed us both times. Martha loves the way you run this place, by the way. We were asking ourselves how on earth you do it.'

The faintest of flushes brought colour to the efficient set of Miss Carlton's features.

'It's very nice of her to say that. We do our best. I have a wonderful team.'

Jack smiled a neutral, parting smile in Miss Carlton's direction and almost took a step away, but it appeared that the Shadow Doctor had a thirst for further information. If Doc was right in his conviction that Jesus enjoyed and valued opportunities to waste time with people, he was a true disciple, at least in that respect.

'I'm fascinated to know how you train or persuade a staff group to be loving and caring towards elderly folk who come from all sorts of backgrounds and, with the best will in the world, can probably be very difficult at times. What's the most important thing about making that happen? Tell us your secret.'

Miss Carlton is about to enrol in Doc's virtual community, thought Jack, as he watched the manager's face. *How does he do that?* Certainly not, as far as he could tell, with something as crude and splashy as a pair of oars.

'Actually, I suppose I do have a sort of secret,' replied the manager, wrapping her arms around her chest and retreating a little from her tone of polite officialdom, 'but it's only a secret because nobody's ever asked me before.' She smiled and shrugged. 'It's not very exciting, I'm afraid. Rather obvious really.'

'Tell us.'

'After making too many mistakes in the past, I realised that I had to work very, very hard at making sure that I only employ nice people. People who enjoy being nice to others. Still one or two disasters here and there over the last five years, you won't be surprised to hear, but successful in the main. Thank you for asking.' She hesitated. 'You're the gentleman that Martha calls Doc. Am I right?'

'Yes, I'm Doc. And this is my friend and colleague, Jack. And you are?'

Jack sensed a small, private battle.

'Felicity. I don't put it on my name badge because – well, I don't know why I don't. Perhaps I should. Anyway – when Martha told me you were coming to see Elsie, she said, "If anyone can find a way into Gran's lost world, it's Doc." She thinks very highly of you.'

'Well, I'm flattered – and a little nervous. We'll do our best, Felicity.'

'Would you like me to ask someone to bring you both some tea? It's no trouble.'

'Tea would be lovely,' glancing at Jack. 'Yes, two teas, no sugar for either of us. Thank you.'

'It's a pleasure – Doc.'

The off-white painted corridor was divided along its length by a grey moulded strip that Jack vaguely recognised as something called a dado rail. Halfway down they were met by a small, rosy-cheeked lady with long grey hair caught back in an Alice band, wearing a dressing-gown and clutching a child's dolly to her chest. Emerging from a bedroom and hanging on to the doorframe with one blue-veined, transparent hand, she addressed the two men in urgent, childlike tones, her eyes wide with hope.

'Hello, my name is Doreen. What's your name?'

'Hello, Doreen. My name is Doc, and this is my friend, Jack.'

'Oh. My mummy's coming to see me this afternoon to take me home. Have you seen her?'

'I haven't seen her. Jack, have you seen Doreen's mummy?'

Jack shook his head, wishing with all his heart that he could give this little lost soul what she wanted.

'No Doreen, I've not seen your mummy either. I'm so sorry.'

'Oh. All right. I expect she's late. I'll go back and wait for her in my room, shall I?'

'I should, Doreen,' Doc said gently.

'It breaks my heart,' whispered Jack, as they continued down the corridor. 'Poor Doreen. I do wish she could find her mummy.'

'Me too, Jack.' Stopping for a moment, he turned his head to look back along the corridor. 'It's OK, I have a feeling she'll turn up before too long.'

17

Elsie

'Doc, Elsie will be here in a couple of minutes. You said you had a plan. What is it?'

The two men were sitting in their designated places at an oval, pedestal pine table beside a window in the small sitting-room. No one was occupying the chintzy three-piece suite that took up quite a lot of the rest of the room. On the longest wall, the one opposite the door, hung a large print of a picture known well to Jack. It had been a favourite of his grandad's. Susan Crawford's vividly engaging portrait showed Desert Orchid, Red Rum and Arkle, three of the most famous winners in the history of racing. Jack had always loved what he fancied he saw in the eyes of those three kings. Confidence. Specialness. Staggering beauty.

The window looked out onto a perfectly flat and immaculately tended lawn projecting from the west wall of Green Pastures. At the far side of the lawn sat a single figure looking like a character in a painting from the 1950s, her legs slanting from a knee-length skirt in a very straight line, and her head tilted in the opposite direction. As far as Jack could tell, she had not moved a muscle since their arrival.

The Shadow Doctor placed a hand flat on the table and gazed steadily at Jack.

'My plan is very simple, Jack. I think you should ask for a question that you can put to Elsie. Something that will jog her into a place where she wants to talk to us. That's my plan.'

Jack had rarely been so utterly suffused with horror.

'No, no, wait a minute, that's not a plan. That's the opposite of a plan. That's not anything. That's ridiculous. That's—'

'We may only have two minutes, Jack. Close your eyes and ask.'

'I've never—'

'Close your eyes,' repeated Doc soothingly. 'Just ask.'

Perhaps the whole thing would go away if he gave up fighting and did what he was told for a few seconds. Eyes closed. *God, I know I'm wasting your time as well as mine, but could you either tell me a question to ask Elsie or not tell me anything at all so that my nightmare can finish? Amen!*

He opened his eyes.

'Anything?'

Jack stared at the ceiling, his legs stretched out, arms hanging at the sides of the chair. If only someone would beam him up – to any place in the universe other than this room and this ludicrous situation. He rolled his head in anguish from side to side along the back of the armchair.

'Exactly what you'd expect. Nothing. Nothing sensible.' He heaved himself upright again. 'Doc, this is rubbish. I feel stupid. This is someone's life we're talking about. Martha's gran. You're the one that everyone's expecting to work the magic. Including Martha. Not me. I don't do that sort of stuff. She'll be here in a few seconds. Do something different. Have another plan. There's nothing in my head.'

'Nothing sensible, you said.'

'That's right. Just rubbish.'

'Interesting rubbish?'

Jack emitted a wild laugh.

'Right! Right! OK, if you insist. Here's a meaningless question that parachuted into my head straightaway and needs to . . . parachute right out again.'

'Parachutes can't parachute in and then out.'

'Do you want to hear this or not?'

'Tell me the question.'

'Have you ever ridden an elephant?' He waited for Doc to laugh. 'That should work well, shouldn't it? Ask a confused ninety-year-old lady if she's ever ridden an elephant. I don't think so.' He stared at the Shadow Doctor. 'Why aren't you laughing? You're not even smiling. Why is that not funny?'

Doc shrugged.

'Nothing to smile about. I'm fascinated. So should you be.'

Jack's panic propelled him to his feet.

'Look, this is insane!' He shot glances around the room, hunting for legitimate escape routes. None materialised. 'All right! Suppose I did go ahead with this, do you think I should tell her that God's given me a question to ask her?'

The Shadow Doctor replied with some passion.

'What? Of course not!'

'Why not?'

'Because you don't know whether he has or not.'

Jack clasped the top of his head in both hands.

'Doc! You drive me crazy. She'll think I'm completely bonkers.'

'Well, she'll know for sure you're completely bonkers if you tell her God wants you to ask if she's ever ridden an elephant and it turns out she hasn't.'

'It's not fair on her, and it's not fair on Martha, and most of all it's not—'

'I think I can hear them coming. Go and open the door.'

Jack stood, irresolute. He had only seconds.

'All right.'

The pleased smile that Aelwen threw Jack as he swung the door open almost deflected the nightmare. As Doc had predicted, he had fallen for Martha on the previous day in the same way that you might fall for an unattainable film star, or a beloved teacher. Aelwen was different. Even in this ludicrously short time, she had become something else. Not that he was in love with her. Come off it! Of course, he wasn't. How could he be? He just wanted to sit and look at her smiling face. He wanted to talk to her. He wanted to make her a really nice coffee. He wanted – something.

'Here's Elsie, everybody. Elsie love, this is Jack. Jack, this is Elsie. Shake hands, dear. And over at the table there, that's Doc. You've met him before, haven't you? Do you remember? He came to see you with your Martha, didn't he? We're all going to have a cup of tea together.' She looked across at Doc. 'Is that all right if I join you? I won't say much, but Elsie and me, we get on very well, don't we, my love? You know my face, and I know yours. Elsie's got her posh Liberty frock on just for her gentleman callers, haven't you, my sweet?'

Elsie was a tall, slim elegant lady, and, as Jack's gran would probably have put it, beautifully turned out, but her fine-boned, delicate features were constrained by tension and worry. It was, thought Jack, the expression of someone who has carelessly lost something so crucially important that there is little point in giving attention to anything else.

She did, however, take the Welsh girl's hand gratefully between both of hers for a moment, as if to acknowledge the bond.

Aelwen helped her nervous charge into the chair nearest to the window and was about to sit down herself when there was something between a knock and a kick at the door.

'That will be our tea and biscuits.' She chuckled. 'You'd have to be a rhinoceros or something to get through that big old door with a tray in your hands. As you were. Rhinos don't have hands, do they? Sorry. I'll go and help.'

At last they were all seated. Conversation was limited. Elsie uttered no actual words, but Jack found himself touched by the classy combination of a nod and polite smile with which she responded to all questions or observations. Perhaps, somewhere inside, the echo of a long-ago parental voice was gently reminding her that, however blank one's mind might become, the need for good manners is never less than paramount.

There was one moment when, as if abruptly reminded of something urgently important, the elderly lady swung her head and shoulders towards the window, an expression of surprise and alarm in the fearful shifting of her eyes when she turned back. Who was that sitting out there so still and all alone on that seat, and who on earth were these people drinking tea at her table?

The Shadow Doctor chatted warmly as he helped people to tea and biscuits. Aelwen smiled and said little, but Jack noticed that, after that sudden turn towards the window, she had taken Elsie's hand and was holding it gently on the table between their cups of tea.

It was only as he was about to bite into a custard cream that Jack found himself caught by the Shadow Doctor's quizzical eye and was hit by the full force of the situation facing him. For some reason, after it became clear that Aelwen was going to join them, he had assumed that the dreaded question would be shelved until the two of them could see Elsie on her own. Why had he believed that? He knew why. More than anything else in the world at this particular moment, he did not want to advertise his idiocy in front of the lovely girl sitting just over there. God could wait. Lovely Martha could wait. Even Elsie could wait.

That left the Shadow Doctor. In theory, Jack had lined himself up, or been lined up, by that man on the other side of the table, to say something utterly absurd to a lady who would do her polite little nodding and smiling thing and not have the foggiest idea what he was raving on about. Doc was looking at him now, his face completely devoid of expression. A meaningful and effective silent exchange was impossible. Retreat with honour was certainly not possible. Anti-climax without honour was absolutely on the cards. Could the Shadow Doctor wait? Jack glanced up for an instant at his grandad's equine heroes framed on the wall in front of him. He laid his biscuit down. *Right.*

'Elsie.'

He said it quite loudly. A courtesy acknowledgement lifted the elderly lady's chin for a moment.

'Elsie, I know this is a bit of a strange question, but – I just wondered – have you ever ridden an elephant?'

The smile, the nod, the retreat into troubled vacancy. The silence. Aelwen was frowning. Probably not angry, just puzzled. The Shadow Doctor seemed to be listening intently to nothing at all. *Eat your biscuit, Jack. Might as well.* He lowered his eyes, racked with embarrassment.

'Actually . . .'

It was a different voice. A confident, cultured voice, a quietly passion-filled tone. The words were directed, not to Jack, but to Aelwen.

'Actually, I have ridden an elephant. In India. I was just a little girl.'

Aelwen didn't miss a beat.

'What do you remember, Elsie?'

Elsie's eyes were wide, alight, focused, her voice quite confident and engaged.

'They put straps on me – across my knees, to make sure I didn't fall off. And I was told to hold tight to a coiled leather thing that was attached to some kind of headdress worn by the animal. A man led the elephant along with me sitting up on its back. I was a little bit frightened at first, but after a while I rather enjoyed it and I was quite sorry when it stopped and they told me it was time to get off. I had thought I might see a tiger if I was lucky. There were tigers sometimes, I believe.'

Aelwen nodded.

'How old were you when you took your elephant ride, Elsie?'

The elderly lady leaned confidently forward to answer the question.

'I know exactly how old I was. I was eight. And I remember it especially well because my dear mother died soon after we came back from India in that same year. And I remember this. One evening I was hiding on the landing of our big house back in England while my father and two uncles and an aunt and two other people I didn't know sat together in our sitting-room, talking about mother not being alive any more. I expect they thought I was asleep in bed, but I wasn't. I was not! I heard everything.'

Elsie's eyes filled. Removing her hand from Aelwen's, she extracted a delicate-looking handkerchief from her sleeve and dabbed at the tears for a moment before continuing.

'Aelwen, I heard what father said. I heard him. He asked all those people how we were going to survive without mother. We! We! I was on the landing. I had been sent to bed. I should have been there in that room being part of "we".' Her voice broke into a sob. 'But what was to become of me? How would I manage to survive? Who would look after me?'

Aelwen turned so that she was directly facing the tearful elderly resident.

'Elsie, I think Jack and Doc probably have to go now, but we'll see them again soon. And it's a good thing really, because you and I need to sit here and have a really good chat, don't we?'

The cue could not have been delivered with more clarity. Within less than a minute, the two men had left the room. They could hear Elsie's fluting voice as they closed the heavy door behind them. She was still talking.

Almost nothing was said during the journey home. Jack's mind was absorbed with just two thoughts. Doc seemed to have fallen asleep.

Having parked the X-Trail outside the cottage, Jack got out and stood with one hand clutching the top of the open car door. He was stirred in his heart, but the strands of that stirring were intertwined and difficult to separate.

Something needed to be untangled, and there was no one else available. He spoke to Doc across the top of the car.

'Doc, that question about the elephant. She had ridden an elephant.'

'That's right. Got her talking. That's good, isn't it? You asked the question and it worked.'

'Yes, but . . .'

'Go on.'

'I'm really glad it helped, but it felt a bit like a conjuring trick, with me as the not-very-involved assistant.'

Doc nodded and smiled.

'Welcome to my world, Jack. Just be glad it was useful.'

Jack still didn't move.

'Something else?'

'The girl who was there today, the one we met when we got to Green Pastures. The one who brought Elsie in and – you know – looked after her.'

Doc closed his door and crossed his arms on top of the car to reply.

'Aelwen, you mean?'

'Yes, Aelwen. I was just wondering – is that a Welsh name?'

He considered. 'I would have thought so. Martha said she was Welsh. She certainly sounds Welsh.'

'Do you think that name actually means something? It probably does, doesn't it? I don't suppose you know what it means, do you?'

He shook his head. 'No, I've no idea. It would be interesting to find out. Why don't you ask her?'

Jack squeezed his bottom lip between finger and thumb and made a grunting noise.

'I can't just ring her up or go and see her and ask her what her name means, can I? She'd think I was stupid.'

'I don't know. I'm sure she'd think exactly the right thing. Anyway, why don't you look it up if you're that curious?'

'Look what up?'

'The name, Jack. Aelwen. Google it.'

'Oh! Yes, of course. Isn't it funny? Every now and then I completely forget that I've got an encyclopaedia in my pocket.'

'You haven't.' Doc pointed downward with his finger through the roof. 'It's in the car, Jack. You've left it next to the seat.'

Jack dived back into the front of the X-Trail, emerging two seconds later with his phone.

'Right, let's have a look. How do you think she spells it?'

'Let me see. It's a guess, but I imagine it's likely to be A-e-l-w-e-n. Something like that.'

'I'll try that. Hold on. Yes, here we are. You were right. Aelwen is a Welsh name, and it means "fair-browed one". That's interesting. I remember thinking when we met her that her hair was unusual. It's coloured like the inside of a shell.'

Doc nodded seriously.

'Interesting way of putting it. But you're right. Lovely hair. Lovely name. Lovely girl. Maybe you should give her a ring.'

A flush of idiocy attacked Jack's peace. Why had he said that about her hair? What in the blue blazes was he babbling on about? Why was he talking about the girl at all? Assailed by a sudden breeze that had arisen from the direction of the lane and the open countryside, he pushed his hair back with one hand and looked directly across the top of the car into the Shadow Doctor's face. If there had been the slightest hint of the wrong sort of smile in those all-seeing eyes he would have been forced to run away into the forest and burrow under some leaves in the warm darkness so that he could hide there for ever and ever.

'Shall we go in, Jack? I feel like doing nothing at all for half an hour. Oh, by the way, did you solve that crossword clue?'

'Oh. No, not yet.'

'Never mind, Keep at it. Right, cup of tea and a Danish would just about hit the spot. What do you reckon?'

Thank you.

'Suits me. Last one in makes the tea. That'll be you, because you're a lot older and slower.'

He pushed his door shut and headed for the cottage.

Only when Jack had reached the front door and was absorbed in hunting through his pockets for the bunch of keys that he had left on the roof of the X-Trail did the Shadow Doctor allow himself the faintest of smiles.

'That took you a while. How did you get on?'

After tea, Jack had decided to take Doc's advice. The number of Green Pastures was easy to find. When he rang, it turned out that Aelwen had finished her shift and gone home. Nevertheless, the call had left Jack rather dazed. He stared into the distance, flipping his phone up and down in one hand. It took him a moment or two to register Doc's question.

'Sorry – it was a bit odd, actually.'

Doc put a marker in his book and laid it down.

'Good odd? Bad odd?'

'I'm not sure. Felicity answered the phone – you know, the manager.'

'OK. And?'

'I said who I was, and she said she remembered me coming with you, and she said lots of people were talking about how good the visit had been for Elsie, and I said that was good and we said one or two more things. But then I realised she probably thought I'd just rung to see how Elsie was. So, then I – well, I think I got a bit nervous and probably wasn't very clear about why I was actually ringing. In the end, though, I did manage to blurt out that I was also trying to get in touch with Aelwen. But then I started saying that it didn't really matter, and not to bother if it was a problem and all that sort of stuff. I could hear my own voice going on and on and on, but I didn't seem able to stop it. So embarrassing.'

'Was that it?'

'No, no, this was the odd thing. She suddenly interrupted me and said, "Hold on a moment, Jack, Aelwen's off shift now. I'll get her mobile number for you." Then she came back with the number and I suddenly realised I hadn't got a pen or paper, and completely forgot I could ask her to text it, so I was going to pretend I'd written it down when I hadn't, but I told myself, this is getting stupid, so I lied and said my pen had run out and asked her to hang on, and she said that was fine, so I went and rushed round the kitchen like an idiot until I found something to write with, and I put the number down. It's in my contacts now.'

'Is that it?'

'Yes, that was it.'

'So, what was so odd?'

'Well, there's so much stuff about – you know – protection of personal information and individual rights and all that nowadays, isn't there? It seems quite odd to me that someone as efficient and organised as Felicity seems to be would just give out a private telephone number to someone like me, who she hardly knows, without having to go off and get the permission of the person whose details she's sharing. Doesn't that strike you as odd?'

The Shadow Doctor frowned as he studied Jack's face. Unusually, he seemed to be having trouble putting his thoughts into words. He did manage it at last.

'Jack, I have to say that none of it strikes me as odd in the slightest. It's you who strikes me as odd.'

'Me?'

'Can you really not conceive of any other reason why Felicity might readily pass on Aelwen's number to you – I mean, you in particular?'

'You mean – what do you mean?'

With a slightly impatient shake of the head, Doc turned back to his book.

'Give her a call. See what happens.'

18

Aelwen

Later that evening Jack decided to take Doc's advice. Fifty metres along the soft forest path, safely distanced from the world in general and the Shadow Doctor in particular, he turned aside onto a narrower path, finding himself eventually in a secluded space occupied by what he now knew to be hornbeam and silver birch under a canopy of oak. A friendly place in which to be terrified.

The double ring sounded seven times in Jack's ear before the connection was made, each one battling against the pounding of his nervous heart. Aelwen's voice, when she replied, was slightly out of breath but vividly normal and bright.

'Hello. Aelwen Moss here. Who am I speaking to?'

'Oh, yes – it's Jack here. Jack Merton. Felicity – Felicity Carlton – gave me your number. I hope that was OK. You and I met at the place where you work – where we were with Elsie and Doc and—'

'Jack! Jack Merton. I was hoping you might ring me.'

'Why?'

The note of bewilderment in Jack's response was entirely sincere.

'Oh, one or two reasons. I wanted to have a chance to talk properly with you after all the amazing stuff that happened with Elsie. I can't tell you how much good that did her. I mean, what on earth made you ask that weird question? So, that was one thing. To talk about that. The other thing was – I wondered, that's to say, I found myself wondering if you and me might make friends. I'm sounding silly. I mean, it's all right if you don't want to, but I just thought – I don't really know what I thought. What do you think? Why did you ring me?'

Doc had propounded the truth and freedom equation to Jack quite often as a means of tackling tricky decision-making. The problem was that it could rarely be done tentatively. You had to take a firm step and then see where you ended up. Oh well, go for it. Be brave.

'About the same as you. I liked how gentle and kind you were with Elsie. But it began before that. I really liked your face.' *Aaaah!* 'I liked – you. I liked you very much.' Pause. 'I'm the one who feels silly now. I'm going red. I don't think I've ever made this sort of call before.'

'Are you doing anything the middle of the week after next, Jack? Thursday's my day off, but I get my two days in a row next week, and I always go over to see Mum then. You could come up the following Thursday if you wanted. That would be nice.'

'Thursday. Thursday week. Should be fine. I'd have to check, but – no, I think it'll be fine. Should be – fine. Where shall I come?'

'My little maisonette thing's three and a bit miles from Green Pastures, up in Northolt. That's just before you get to—'

'I know Northolt. I work – used to work – not all that far from there.'

'Oh. OK. That's good. Well, I'll be there all day. How about coming up about ten o'clock and we'll have coffee and cake. What do you say? I've got a plan about the coffee. I'm sure you'll like it. I won't tell you why, but I promise you will. Number 16B on the corner of Manor Crescent. Blue front door. Opposite a corner shop.'

'Ten o'clock. Manor Crescent.'

'16B.'

'16B. Got it. I'll see you then – there.'

Aelwen giggled.

'Then and there I hope. Thanks for calling, Jack. Byee!'

The singing notes of Aelwen's farewell rang in Jack's head all the way back to the cottage, where Doc received news of the forthcoming appointment with a nod and a smile.

'Just as well it's not next week, Jack. I've just had an email. You and I are off to Alnwick with Martha for jollies with Derek next Wednesday. We'll be away for a couple of nights.'

Two weeks later, on the Wednesday evening before his visit to Aelwen, Reed Enterprises' newest employee retired early. Jack's brain was alight with a more pungent cocktail of fear and excitement than he had known for years. Aelwen, the fair-browed one, would be waiting for him in Northolt at ten o'clock tomorrow morning. Three times he dreamt that she turned a questioning face to look into his eyes. Each time she was smiling.

The following day, after an hour's drive through a crisp and sunny morning, Jack, suitably smart and deodorised, found himself a mile from his destination with ten minutes to spare.

'Wispy white and burnished blue,' he murmured to himself, as he approached the highest point of a steep hill and for a fleeting moment appeared to be driving directly into the sky itself. As he breasted the slope and began his descent towards the flatter area around the village of Northolt, he wished he could do exactly that. For the hundredth time in two weeks he asked himself why he had volunteered for this chance to make a complete idiot of himself.

The village was not very large. Jack found Manor Crescent curving away from the south end of the High Street, and Aelwen's corner shop at the junction where the road to Pembury offered access to green, level countryside beyond the village. Number 16B was clearly marked on his left. He was still a few minutes early. Turning right, he parked in a spot where he judged he could not be seen from Aelwen's flat and took some deep breaths. Most of the excitement had drained to his boots. Fear was in charge now. Tapping the steering wheel fiercely with one finger, he toyed with the idea of ringing her from the car to say that he wasn't able to make it after all. Just dump the problem. Make it go away. But he didn't really want to do that. He didn't want it to go away. He didn't want the secret possibility to turn into a problem. Two huge questions. When he was with Aelwen, what was the best thing to do? What exactly should he say?

Panicked, he flipped his phone open and scrolled down to Doc's number. The text he sent was short, vulnerable and directly to the point.

'Sitting outside her flat. Terrified. What shall I do? What shall I say? Any ideas?'

It was two or three minutes before the familiar little notification beep announced a reply. He gazed intently at the words on the screen with a keen hope that quickly morphed to disappointment and despair. He read the words again. The Shadow Doctor was certainly offering very specific ideas, but Jack was quite certain he had neither the courage nor the capacity to accept and follow advice that, on the face of it, seemed senseless and just plain wrong.

OK, never mind that. He was on his own. Now or never. Snapping his phone shut and slipping it into his pocket, he climbed out of the car, locked it behind him and made his way, head down, towards 16B. Twitching and tugging at his shirt collar, he crossed the road, only to discover that the blue front door was ajar. He hesitated. A nervous knock brought no response. Better call out.

'Hello! Aelwen, it's Jack. I've just—'

'Come on up, Jack. Up the stairs. My flat's the top bit. I'm in the kitchen on the left.'

There was a tone of weary defeat in the distant voice. Jack cheered up a little. Maybe something had gone wrong. Something he could help with? He found Aelwen sitting at a square pine table facing the kitchen door. The room was tidy, but he couldn't help noticing small brown pellets distributed around the floor and on the working surfaces. The colour and shape seemed familiar. He hovered in the doorway.

'Hello, Aelwen.'

'Hello Jack. Thank you for coming. Sorry about this. I'm afraid I've had a bit of a disaster.'

'Oh. What happened?'

She slapped one hand on the table. Words poured out in a passionate stream.

'I'll tell you the truth. I'm not absolutely sure why, but you coming here today was a sort of special thing for me, so I wanted to do something you'd like. And when you were at Green Pastures you talked about you and your friend liking really good coffee, so this morning I bought a cheap coffee grinder from the market, and then I got some coffee beans and a lemon-drizzle cake. I thought I'd grind the coffee beans ready to put in the cafetière for when you got here, but I didn't realise you had to hold the plastic lid down on my cheapo coffee grinder while it was on, so I didn't, and – Jack, it exploded coffee beans all over the kitchen and quite a lot over me. And then – I don't want to tell you this – I decided to do it again but this time I'd make sure the plug wasn't even in the socket until I was ready with the lid on, and it would have worked fine except that I pulled the wrong plug out and left the coffee grinder one in – and on – and it happened all over again. It happened again, Jack! Two times!' She held her hands out in a despairing gesture and managed a wan smile. 'Beans all over my world! Not very impressive, is it?'

'Shall I sit down?'

She lifted an arm limply to indicate the kitchen chair opposite her.

'Of course. Just brush the—'

'Yes, I know.'

He looked at her. Perhaps the truth was a good place to start.

'I didn't do very well either, Aelwen. I wanted to come more than anything, but I nearly bottled out. I sat in the car for a while just around the corner.'

'Just round from the corner shop?'

'Yes, I think so. I was wondering if I should ring you and say I couldn't make it after all. I was really nervous. Frightened.'

She nodded. 'But you came. Why?'

Tears threatened for some obscure reason. Answering her question with a few ordinary words felt like pushing something enormous up a steep hill.

'I don't know. I want – something.' Embarrassed by his own words, Jack took refuge in an ironic laugh, and prattled on. 'You're not going to believe this, but while I was there – in the car I mean – I actually texted a friend to ask for advice.'

'About meeting me, you mean? Must have been a very good friend.'

'Oh, it was Doc. Martha's friend who was with us when we saw Elsie. I sort of – work with him.'

'Right, seems a very impressive guy. I'm intrigued. Did he get back to you?'

'After a couple of minutes, yes. You're right, he is an impressive man, and I really do respect him, but the things in his text – they weren't very helpful. I mean, he knows about relationships and things. He was very happily married earlier in his life, but I don't think he'd quite under-stand – this.'

'What did he tell you to do?'

Inwardly, Jack cursed his tendency to prattle.

'Oh, he didn't exactly tell me to do anything. I don't think he ever does, not that directly. He just – what did he do? He told me what *he* might do and say if it was him here with you.'

'Good heavens!'

Silence.

'And?'

Jack hesitated, seriously alarmed by the idea of revealing the content of the Shadow Doctor's message. He raised a firm hand.

'Aelwen, I promise you I've got absolutely no intention of taking Doc's advice about what I should do. It would be – I can't think of the right word.' It flashed into his mind. 'Presumptuous. It would be presumptuous, and – and actually, almost insulting. And I really, *really* don't want you to know what he told me to say.' His attempt at a laugh quickly died a death.

She studied his face for a moment.

'Do you trust your friend, Jack?'

Good question. Very good question. Excellent question. Do you trust your friend?

Rising to his feet, Jack stepped round the table and leaned down until his face was inches from hers. She tilted her head very slightly but did not retreat an inch. Moving a little nearer, he kissed her gently on the lips. Standing up straight again, he released a deep breath and did an awkward backward shuffle before speaking. His body seemed to be shaking with apprehension.

'That's what he suggested I should do.'

'O-O-K. And what did he think you might say to me?'

He shook his head.

'No. Look, I've already said I don't want to tell you.'

'I would like to know. What did he think you should say, Jack?'

'All right. I'll tell you.'

Another deep breath. No going back after this.

'He suggested I say that's all you're going to get. And that you're lucky to get that.'

Aelwen's mouth dropped. Her eyes opened wide with surprise. She began to laugh but stopped abruptly, seeming to trip on a thought. Then she began to laugh again, but in a different way, gazing at Jack with an expression close to awe.

He watched and waited as the laughter faded into silence, his right hand straying to a pocket, checking that the car key was handy. When she spoke at last, her voice was soft with wonder.

'Well, your friend is amazing. It's – it is amazing. How on earth could he be so – so right?' The lovely eyes suddenly filled with tears. 'A little kiss is about all I want at the moment. And I know it's going to sound strange, but I'm so very glad if it's all I'm going to get. You see, right now, I couldn't handle any more than that. And, Jack, the way I've been feeling about myself lately – you're right. I mean – he's right again. What you said – what he said: it's like me speaking to myself. I really do think I'm lucky to be given a little kiss by you. And I do feel as if I don't deserve to get even that.' She dropped her gaze. 'I'm afraid I've made one or two very, very silly mistakes in the – you know – in the past.'

Jack could feel his mouth trembling and turning down at the sides. The child in him had not wept for a long time.

'Aelwen, I'm so very sorry. That was horrible. I was only—'

'Oh no, please don't be sorry, Jack. The last thing I want is for you to feel sorry. This is so strange.' She collected herself and pointed across the little kitchen. 'Right!' She took in and released a breath loudly. 'Look – see that giant kitchen-roll? Yes? Good. Take some yourself and give the rest to me. Thank you. We'll dry our eyes first. That's it. Well done. Just drop it in the bin. Just by your left foot. I like to keep the place tidy, as you can see. Tell you what, I'll keep the roll here on the table in case we need it later. OK, now – you need to sit down and put your hands in mine.'

Jack lowered himself slowly onto the chair opposite as she had asked, but the fear of being further unlocked was so strong in him that he was incapable of raising his hands to the table, or his eyes to look into hers.

The way Aelwen spoke reminded Jack of Martha's stern words to the Shadow Doctor as she admonished him for being less than open with his new colleague.

'Come on. Come on, Jack. Hands on the table. Right. That's good – well, it's not good, but it's not bad.' She angled her hands up from the wrists, palms facing him. 'Now, you see these hands here? These are mine.' She reached across and tapped the back of each of his hands very gently with one forefinger. 'These, over on your side, are not mine. They're yours. Do you want to hear my plan? This is it. You put your hands into my hands, and I reckon there could be just the tiniest of outside chances that things will feel a bit more comfortable for both of us.'

Jack lifted his head, gave Aelwen a watery smile, and extended his hands to meet hers. Words crowded to be said. He was not looking forward to hearing any of them emerge from his mouth.

'Aelwen, I need to tell you two – no, three more things. First of all, when I got here and saw coffee beans every-where, and you looking so very forlorn, I was quite pleased. Like I said, I'd been so nervous about meeting you and not knowing what to say and – and all that. It was such a relief to find you'd had a disaster and I might be able to give you a hand clearing it up.'

She replied earnestly. 'I did it on purpose, Jack.'

'No, you didn't. Did you? No, I didn't think you did. OK, the second thing is that quite a lot of me was hoping it would all go wrong anyway. Us, I mean – not that there is an us,' he added hastily. 'That's ridiculous. The thing is, I haven't had much practice – hardly any practice – at being with someone else. I mean, we've hardly met, and you probably won't want to know me after this anyway. But I was frightened that even if we did – you know – go out together or something and we started by getting on well, I'd be sure to mess it up before long. I still think that. The thing is, I'm not sure how to feel things – no, that's not it. I don't really mean that. I do feel things, but I don't know how to talk about – feelings.' He concluded wretchedly. 'I mean – how do you do that?'

Aelwen nodded.

'And number three?'

Panic.

'Sorry, I was wrong. It was actually only two things.'

'What was the third thing? You don't get your hands back until you've said it.'

Jack's voice broke slightly.

'I don't want my hands back. All right. The third thing. And I will say it because I've got to, but it's going to sound so crude and stupid and premature when we've only just met and hardly know each other, and you might have already had enough of me as it is . . .'

'Say it, Jack.'

'Aelwen, I've never really had a girlfriend, not a real one. Kissing you like that just now, that little kiss, that was a big thing for me. I've never – you know – been with a woman in a physical relationship. In fact, the very thought of it makes me go all hot and cold. It frightens me. I can't even begin to imagine giving myself away like that. I really, really like you. I like the way you look. I love the way you were with Elsie. Even after such a little while I – well, I just love the way you are. But,' he concluded miserably, 'I think if we did . . . get on well, I'd need to take my time. If you know what I mean.'

A little smile played around Aelwen's lips.

'You know, Jack, for someone who can't talk about feelings, you're doing OK.'

She paused, stared down at the table for a few moments, then lifted her head and fixed her eyes on him once more.

'All right. Now, you listen to me, Jack Merton. You've told me exactly how you feel and what you need. It must be my turn. If it's all the same to you, I'm going to tell you exactly what I need. I'd better just check. Is it all the same to you? Let me look.' She leaned forward. Your head seems to be moving up and down. Good. That means it must be. Excellent.

'OK. What I need more than anything in the world just now is a real friend. And – I'm sorry if I'm wrong, and I have been disastrously wrong in the past, but I've got this sort of idea in my head that you might be making your journey in a small, leaky boat – not exactly the same as mine, but just as leaky. I wondered if it might be nice to have a go at travelling together in the same boat. Worth a try, do you think? Look after each other along the way. And I hope you agree with me that one of those little kisses every now and then wouldn't do either of us any harm as we go. And heh, who knows where we'll find ourselves as time goes by. You and me – we could end up having some fun, couldn't we? You never know, Jack, we might even do something useful. I do like being useful.' She dabbed a fresh trickle of tears from the corners of her eyes with another sheet of kitchen-roll and smiled hopefully. 'If you want to, that is.'

The eyes. The hands. The voice. Needing and being needed. A gentle walk instead of a panic-stricken sprint into the tantalising, terrifying unknown. At this precise moment what else in the whole wide world could he have wished for?

'If you're not quite sure, Jack, it's worth bearing in mind that we all need time. For instance, I'm confident I will work out how to master the coffee grinder before too long. These important things do take a while, you know. In fact, you could help me to get started now.'

Filled with a flood of unprecedented joy, Jack glanced around the kitchen floor.

'I suppose we could clear the coffee beans up to start with. They're not too ...' A more searching glance. 'Actually, they're everywhere really.' They both burst into laughter, then sat and simply looked at each other for a few moments. 'How about if we did that, Aelwen? I could show you how to grind some more beans if there's enough left for a cafetière, and then we could have the coffee we were going to have when I first came. What do you think? I'll go and find a brush – if you give me my hands back.'

'OK, Jack. But you've got to promise that when we're having our coffee you'll tell me all about you, and your amazing friend, and what the two of you do with your time, and especially what made you ask Elsie about that elephant. Deal?'

Jack retrieved a hand in order to rub the back of his head. 'I don't think you know what you're asking, Aelwen. Come to think of it, I'm pretty sure I don't either. You might end up thinking I'm mad, but I will have a go. It's a deal.'

'Right!' She pointed. 'Brush and dustpan are in that thin tall cupboard in the corner. Brush on a hook, dustpan on the floor. I'll rescue the beans that managed to land up on the sides and add them to what's left in the packet. Should be enough. Then I'll be ready for my first tutorial.' She squeezed his hands gently before releasing them. 'What a team, eh! Oh, don't forget, there's lemon-drizzle cake as well?'

'Perfect,' said Jack, rising to his feet, 'absolutely perfect.'

19

Two questions

'Sounds as if it went really well.'

Jack watched as Doc fastidiously trickled exactly the right amount of milk into each of the blue china cups before hefting the heavy matching teapot and pouring exactly enough tea to achieve the magical orange-brown colour that characterised perfection in the eyes and tastes of both men. He recalled how, in an early encounter, the Shadow Doctor had alarmingly named compatibility in the context of tea as a possible deal-breaking factor in any future relationship. His tone had been so serious and his face so expressionless that Jack had found himself worriedly reviewing his entire tea-drinking philosophy. He smiled to himself. He was beginning to understand nowadays. For Doc there was a genuine truth to be found and preserved through excess and exaggeration, especially when it came to something as constant and dependable as tea. How had Miriam coped with all the amiably serious madness?

'Yes, thank you, it went amazingly well – in the end.' *Stay casual*. 'We're planning to get a picnic together next Thursday. Aelwen's day off. A place called Shadwell Woods, a few miles from Tunbridge Wells. That's if you and I are not busy with anything, of course. Well, actually, she was hoping you might come as well.'

'Me?'

'Yes. Like I said, she wanted to know all about what we do, and she's very interested in you. She said you were a very impressive guy – and that was just based on meeting you at the nursing home, before all the weird stuff that happened a couple of weeks ago. She really wants you to come. Will you?'

'Do you want me to come, Jack?'

'Yes, I do, for a very important reason that I'll tell you in a minute.'

The Shadow Doctor gazed across the top of his upraised cup for a moment.

'OK. I'll come. That's over on the other side of Rusthall, isn't it?'

'What is?'

'Shadwell Woods. Down Nellington Lane from Rusthall. West of Tunbridge Wells. Used to be a lovely spot. A magical stream twisting through the bottom of the valley. Haven't been there for years. Should be enjoyable. Not sure I can guarantee to be impressive, though. Are you going to tell me this reason you have for wanting me to come? By the way, I think I'm going to have to start charging you for these question-and-answer sessions, Jack.'

'Well, not for this one. This is me, answering your question about what my reason is. So you owe me.'

He paused to take a sip of tea. *Stop talking nonsense. Find the right words and have a really good go at saying exactly what you mean.*

'It's about Aelwen. I know it's ridiculously early days and it might not come to anything, but this – what's happened so far – it's completely new to me. It's taken me by surprise. My question is, if it did go on being or becoming something special, would it get in the way?'

Doc raised an enquiring eyebrow.

'Of what?'

Jack stared helplessly into his cup, hunting for a form of words that would mean something to both of them.

'You and me. The work we've been doing. The future. Help me, Doc. Is it – could it be all right? Do you think there's some way it could fit into the plan, into the—'

'The flow?'

'Yes, all right, the flow. The eternal, blasted flow. Seriously, I need to know what you think. I really, really do. I couldn't bear to lose anything good that might happen because of a – a distraction.'

Doc slid his cup and saucer to one side of the table and sat back. Leaning both elbows on the arms of his chair, he regarded Jack steadily.

'Is that what Aelwen is, do you think? A distraction?'

Jack was horrified.

'No! I don't know why I said that. She's not just a distraction. In a way that's the problem. Right now it – whatever *it* turns out to be – feels like the most important thing in the world, and I suppose I'm frightened that I've got carried away and it's all wrong. Perhaps I shouldn't feel like that. I want you to tell me what you think.'

As though he had become aware of a noise outside, the older man raised his head and turned to stare towards the window. Jack had heard nothing, but Doc seemed to be listening intently. When he turned back, there was a gentle smile on his face.

'A story, Jack. Once upon a time, just as the sun was going down, two very sad people were trudging along the road towards their home. It was a seven-mile journey straight into the sunset, a jolly long way to walk when all you feel is disappointment and a sort of dullness about tomorrow and the day after that and every other day for as far as you can see. Just a little while earlier, there'd been someone who made the hearts of these two sad travellers burn like fire with excitement and expectancy. Now, that great man was dead, and all the flames of hope and possibility had died with him.'

Doc stopped and looked across the table as though he was waiting for something to be said. Jack said it.

'A miracle happened.'

'Yes, it did. The man came back. The fire came back. They went back. It began all over again. When did you last feel fire like that inside you, Jack?'

'Never. Not like that.' He tilted his head as tears threatened. 'I've always wanted to. Always.'

'And the feelings you had about Aelwen today – were they something new?'

'I couldn't – can't believe it. I've sometimes worried that I never would be able to feel that much for another person.'

'Something like a fire inside you?'

Jack found himself unable to speak.

'You know what, Jack, I think it's probably reasonable for us to suppose that God might be almost as kind and wise as your gran was. Dare I say, possibly a little more. I don't think it's a distraction. I think it's a generous gift. Perhaps Martha laid the fire. Aelwen seems to have lit it. You're at the very beginning of knowing how it feels to have a real sense of burning in your heart. Lots to learn, but at least you know now it's possible. Hopefully, the best is yet to come. Also, the gift isn't just for you. Sounds as though it's for her as well, if it all works out. For different reasons.

Risk and responsibility. All of God's best gifts come with that warning printed on the packet. I should know.' For an instant he was somewhere else. 'So, are you going to tell me why you want me at that picnic next week?'

Jack smiled and shook his head.

'I don't need to now. I'll tell her you're coming. Doc, before I go and get some more hot water, just tell me one thing. When I texted you from outside Aelwen's place asking for advice, and you sent that message back to me about what I might do and say, where did that come from precisely? I know you don't like tying these things up with a neat bow, but if you don't mind, I'd really like to know.'

The older man frowned and tilted his head.

'It's a fair question, Jack, but there's no easy answer, I'm afraid. It's difficult sometimes to know where one thing ends and another begins. I've done an awful lot of chatting and praying and listening and watching facial expressions and body language over the years, so – well, I've probably got into the habit of almost unconsciously drawing conclusions about people when I spend time with them.'

'You mean like those annoying times when you answer the question I'm really asking even though I've said something completely different. I hate to say it, but you're usually right.'

Doc chuckled. 'Ah, well, I'm glad to hear I don't always mess up. But that's what you do have to watch. With the stuff that comes from experience there are no guarantees at all. Magic or mayhem. It's easy to get it wrong.'

'Before you go any further – and I'm not sure if I want to hear the answer to this question – what did you make of Aelwen? You've actually met her a few times, haven't you?'

'Do you or don't you want to hear what I thought?'

'How much money would you bet on me not wanting to hear?'

'I wouldn't waste my money, Jack. What did I think about Aelwen? That's what I asked myself after I got your text. I thought she was charming, of course. I thought she has great people skills that will grow and grow as the years go by. I thought I saw that she might be dealing with a deep disappointment in herself. What else? I thought she looked determined, as though she'd made some kind of important decision. That's about it, I think.'

'All that just from meeting her a couple of times.'

'Yes, but apart from the charm and the skills, I could easily have been wrong.'

'But you based the advice in the text you sent me on the things you just talked about.'

'No, I wouldn't have done that. It was the same with Victor. I knew all sorts of things about him from his letters, and from our meeting with him at last, but the bit at the end of my prayer crossed over from those highly likely possibilities into an area that needed no conjecture from me. The crossing point is a definite phenomenon, but it's not always easy to spot the line.'

Jack hung on tight to the level of understanding he had reached.

'How do you make that crossing?'

'Could we have some more hot water now?'

'No.'

'Oh, Jack, how you do stretch me. All right, I will do my best. This is the only way I have found so far to think about it. You have to dream a little. There's an interesting thing about dreams. In that quite different world, the solid old walls of reality as we know it can come tumbling down. That applies to dreams in the night, but it can also apply to daydreams. A little girl is said to be dead, but she's not. She's asleep. There's no money to pay taxes, but, like something out of an old fairy tale, a coin is discovered in the mouth of a fish. A storm is threatening to wreck a boat, but a man who is actually asleep and dreaming peacefully at the time wakes up and sees his dream come true. A young man who is about to visit a very important young lady can think of nothing to do or say when they meet. He gets it just right. They'll be meeting again next week. Precisely where the crossing was in that case I could not begin to tell you, Jack. I'm just glad I didn't screw up, to use a theological term. Can we have some more hot water now please?'

'Yes,' said Jack.

20

Conflict in the car park

The whole thing happened with such speed and momentum that, once it had begun, Jack could hardly keep up with events as they dominoed.

It started on a very ordinary morning with a very ordinary fifteen-minute run to Rye Road Tesco in Hawkhurst. After a leisurely shop followed by coffee and a sandwich in the Service Station, Doc had gone off to look for a new satnav charger, telling Jack that he would see him back at the car in a few minutes.

After an uncommonly frustrating search in entirely the wrong section of the very large car park, Jack had finally located the X-Trail behind a large white van filling a space that had been empty when they arrived. On the other side of the Shadow Doctor's car, a sleek blue model had taken the place of the red Renault that had been parked there previously.

The blue car was smaller than the Renault, but it was not parked well. As Jack unlocked his vehicle, he could see the need to take extra care as he opened the door on the driver's side. All went well until the moment when, finally installed in the driving seat, he reached out to grasp the inner handle of the door and accidentally pushed it an inch or two away from him. There was a slight knocking noise as the outer edge of his door touched the passenger door of the blue car. Rising to check immediately, he could see no damage and he had sat back down and was about to close his own door when a loud, rasping voice made him turn and look towards the back of the vehicle.

'What have you done to that car? What have you done to my son's car? That is a very valuable car, and you crashed your door open onto the passenger side. Idiot! You shouldn't be driving a car if you can't control yourself. Have you been drinking? You should be ashamed of yourself! Idiot!'

The speaker was a short, elderly man in a suit. Between prominent ears and beneath patches of silvery-grey, pan-scraper hair, he appeared to be boiling with rage. Jack had no defence against such an abrupt and overwhelming attack. Everything in the universe was his fault anyway. His inclination was to prostrate himself and confess humbly and readily to whatever crimes he had been accused of by that horrible voice. Still in shock, he was close to tears as he tried to speak.

'I'm so sorry! I really am. I didn't think—'

'What's going on, father?'

A new voice. The elderly person had been joined by a younger, taller, conservatively dressed man who bustled onto the scene with what looked like anticipation of conflict and imminent battle already burgeoning in his eyes. The elderly man fulfilled his expectation.

'This young idiot has damaged our car by slamming his door against the passenger side. He was about to get in and drive away when I caught him. He shouldn't be allowed anywhere near a car when he's been drinking. Stupid behaviour!'

The son emitted a gasp of horror. He was about to step forward, presumably to examine the damage to his door, when the Shadow Doctor's quiet but resonantly penetrating voice sounded from behind him.

'Is there a problem? Jack, come and tell me what's going on.'

Relieved beyond words, Jack exited with extreme care from the X-Trail and moved down between the cars to stand at Doc's side. He was about to speak when the father launched into another high-volume, crackling tirade.

'I shall tell you what has happened. This young idiot—'

The Shadow Doctor lifted an arresting hand.

'No, thank you. I don't want to hear from you at the moment. Jack, why are these two people so angry?'

Doc's voice was relaxed and conversational, but the father and son were clearly silenced more by utter outrage than anything else. Jack took a deep breath.

'It's true that I accidentally knocked our door very gently against theirs when I was getting in, but I did check there was no damage, and I was about to shut the door and wait for you when this . . .' – he gestured towards the older man – 'this man began to shout at me and call me names. He said that I was an idiot and that I'd probably been drinking. He said that I'd crashed our door against theirs and that I was trying to get away when he turned up. That's about it, I think.'

'OK,' said Doc lightly. 'First of all, I'll just go and check what you said about damage.'

If the first man had reached boiling point, the younger one was now on the edge of incandescence.

'I absolutely forbid you to touch my car!'

'I have no intention of touching your car,' replied Doc mildly, 'but I am just going to take a close look at it.'

Moments later he returned, smiling happily.

'As you said, Jack. Nothing at all.' He turned to the father and son. 'Obviously, if my friend had damaged your car we would have been more than happy to pay the cost of repairing it. But he didn't. That's the end of that side of things. So – why,' he asked the older man, 'were you so rude and offensive to my friend? You shouted at him – called him an idiot and suggested that he'd been drinking. He isn't, and he hasn't. Why did you find it necessary to say things like that?'

'I accused him of neither of those things!' barked the father.

'Well – you did. Why?'

If the son had previously been on the edge of incandescence, Jack could see that he was now well and truly in the white-hot centre of that state. He drew himself to his full height, shaking his shoulders aggressively and thrusting his face close to Doc's.

'You're calling my father a liar! Are you saying that my father is a liar?'

The Shadow Doctor did not move a muscle in retreat. His manner when he replied could not have been more calm and reasonable.

'Your statement is correct, and the answer to your question is – yes, I am saying that your father has failed to tell the truth, because that is exactly what he's done.'

Jack touched the Shadow Doctor's arm. He was becoming seriously worried about the look in the other man's eyes. What if he really went off bang? What if both of these men launched themselves at him and Doc?

'No problem,' murmured Doc in Jack's ear. 'I'm getting a little bored. I'm going to finish this now.' He moved his face closer to the man who was confronting him, and said, in a cold, dispassionate tone that Jack prayed fervently would never be used against him, 'I've got just two more things to say to you. First of all, we happily forgive your father for distorting the truth and being so rude. Second, for all our sakes, I suggest that you simply get into your undamaged car and drive it away. Oh – there is a third thing. A serious word of advice. In future – don't be silly. Off you go.'

At that moment, to Jack's bewilderment, just as the father was opening his mouth and the son, arms pressed against his sides, seemed to be about to project himself from the ground with non-vented fury, the proceedings were interrupted by yet another voice, higher than the other two, but equally irascible.

'Don't bother with them. They're not worth it!'

A small, elderly lady with tightly permed hair and a small, pursed mouth, had appeared as if from nowhere. Presumably, thought Jack, this was the wife of the older man, and mother of the younger. She repeated her words, expelling them from her mouth as though disgusted by a discovery that they were soaked in something rancid.

'They're not worth it. Either of them. Come away!'

It struck Jack that both men appeared quite glad to be offered even this pale version of retreat with honour. They fumed, they growled, their eyes blazed, the younger one swayed on the spot as if thwarted in his projectile ambitions by discovering that his feet were nailed to the tarmac, but finally they clearly opted for some kind of collusion that Jack and Doc were indeed not worth it. They went. Within a very short time, the two elderly people and the younger man, and the poorly parked blue car had all, in their own ways, backed out and, to Jack's huge relief, were gone.

'Did that really just happen?'

A few minutes had passed. As he spoke, Jack was steering the X-Trail gently onto the B2099 and past Ticehurst Village Hall on their right. He was surprised to observe the smile that appeared on the Shadow Doctor's face in response to his question. It was a tad more serene than he might have expected.

'Yes, Jack, it really did happen.'

'We nearly got into a fight with those people.'

'Well, perhaps. But I think, in terms of aggression, theirs was not a very professional performance. A bit short on grand finale, don't you think?'

'I certainly agree that the two blokes seemed quite keen to go along with the mother in the end. But that was just about – you know, physical violence. Whatever you say, the whole thing was horrible.' Jack felt a shiver run through his body. 'Horrible!'

Doc turned his head as if to survey the passing delights of Ticehurst.

'What upset you most, Jack?'

Terrified of facing his own sense of diminishment, Jack hunted for a form of words that might offer escape. A waste of time. The man sitting in the seat beside him would know.

'It was the bit just before you turned up, Doc. When he shouted at me – the father, I mean. I turned to jelly. I was a wobbly mess inside. I can still see his face, all scrunched up full of anger and – and contempt. And his voice, hacking into me like a load of sharp . . . things.' *Might as well say it*. 'I nearly cried like a baby. And I was burbling about how sorry I was before I even knew if I'd done anything. He did it. That ghastly man. I wish I had scratched his son's stupid car. We're supposed to forgive people, aren't we? I can't. I hate him. I don't want to forgive him. He's left me feeling like a flabby, useless piece of rubbish.'

Without turning his head, the Shadow Doctor said mildly, 'Easy with the right foot, Jack. We're in no hurry to get back.' Then, after a pause. 'Thanks for saying all that. Can't have been easy. Take some time when we get home. We can have a chat later if you want.'

21

An absence of colour

Things had been quiet in Marlpit Cottage since returning from Hawkhurst. After stowing most of the shopping away in the kitchen, Jack had decided to take Doc's advice. It was just possible that an hour or two alone in his room would offer some sort of winding pathway towards peace. The trauma of that encounter with the angry little man in the car park remained in all its intensity, and he could see no simple means of regaining his equilibrium. The question rattled round his head like a lame hamster on a wheel. How could he have collapsed so totally – so pathetically – in the face of an accusation that was completely unjustified? His lack of ballast shocked him.

He lay quietly on his bed for some time, hoping that something or someone might intervene. Nothing did. Not even sleep. No surprise there. Sitting up on the edge of the bed after an hour or so, gazing out through the window into the dark wall of trees on the far side of the rough parking area, he felt nothing but dullness and disappointment. He had hoped and struggled to believe that something stronger and more resilient might have been growing inside him since his coming to live with the Shadow Doctor. Some sort of equipping, surely? Embarrassed suddenly by his awareness that he was reaching into the language of his old life in a vain search for scaffolding to prop himself up, he hissed a muted exclamation towards the ceiling.

'Shit!'

Then there was his attitude to the man who had made him feel so small and insubstantial. He had told Doc quite openly how he felt about that. He couldn't forgive his aggressor, and even if he could, it was not going to happen. As far as Jack was concerned, there was nothing in or about that shrivelled little despot that deserved to be loved or forgiven. On the contrary, he needed to be taught a lesson.

The voice of stern teaching from his early years filled the ensuing silence, condemning the thought, and then standing darkly back with folded arms to measure his residual worth. The horrible man had even robbed him of his capacity for forgiveness. If you don't forgive, you don't get forgiven. That was in the Bible.

Rising to his feet, Jack moved closer to the window and placed his hands against the cold glass. Outside, above the trees, the sky looked as if it might have given up. It had decided to have no colour at all. Something between putty and mud. Probably, thought Jack, it doesn't really want to exist any more. A deathlike pallor. That's what the absence of colour made him think of now. It was like death.

'Tea!'

The Shadow Doctor's voice calling from the foot of the stairs shone relief into the gloom like a flashlight in a power cut. Ridiculously, the prospect of tea and company allowed faint but unmistakable shades of perspective and possibility to flow into Jack's blank mood.

'Be right there!'

He stopped off at the bathroom to give his face a quick wash before heading down to the kitchen.

22

Flush it again, Sam

'How did you get on up there, by the way?'

Jack smiled ruefully. A piece of music that turned out to be Jaqueline du Pré's rendering of one of Haydn's two cello concertos, Doc's smiling presence, a pot of Yorkshire tea and two slices of chocolate almond Battenberg cake had restored just enough of his joy to suggest that life might after all be worth living.

'Rubbish, Doc. No sleep and an hour and a half of spiralling down into misery after what happened at Hawkhurst. I feel a bit better now, but I'd still like to seriously injure that little man who shouted at me. He made me feel stupid, and he made me feel less of a proper Christian than ever.'

'Because you don't want to forgive him, you mean?'

'Exactly.'

'Well, that's good to hear, Jack.'

'It is? By the way, I meant to ask you – after we left the car park, there was a real smile on your face. What was that all about?'

'Oh, it's a bit childish really. I think it was just that I spend so much of my time being a particular sort of person. Our little conflict-filled interlude – well, the truth is, I enjoyed every moment of it. Probably shouldn't have, but I did. I'm sorry it was such a horrible experience for you, though.'

After a brief pause, the Shadow Doctor cleared a space in front of him and retrieved his laptop from the edge of the table.

'What you were saying about forgiveness reminds me of something else. Can I tell you what I've been doing?'

'Yes, of course. You'll tell me anyway. Go on. What have you been doing?'

'I've been replying to an email from Sam. She sent it this morning.'

'Oh, good. Another Marsh-wiggle outing?'

Jack was very fond of Sam. She was an attractive, fascinatingly complex, middle-aged lady who had originally contacted the Shadow Doctor to ask for a meeting. This happened in a café called The Wayfarer, situated in an ancient building opposite a famous abbey, at one end of the Sussex town of Battle. During that first encounter with the two men, she had spoken of many things that were important to her, including the fact that she was one half of a same-sex couple.

Discovering that all of them, including Sam's partner Chris, were lifelong admirers of Puddleglum, the gloomy but determined Marsh-wiggle featured in C.S. Lewis's sixth Narnia book, *The Silver Chair*, Doc had suggested forming a Marsh-wiggle club. They would enjoy meeting for meals out, and wearing, or possibly not wearing, pointed Marsh-wiggle hats. The first meeting of the four members of the club, held (entirely hatless) in New Spice, an Indian restaurant in Robertsbridge, had been a huge success. Hopefully, more were to follow.

'I'm quite sure we'll get that sorted out soon, Jack, but this email was about something else. I'll give you the gist of it. Last week, when Sam and Chris were in church for their usual nine-thirty service, a friend of theirs stood up looking very stiff and nervous. It was the bit of the morning where, in their church, people are invited to come up and share thoughts and testimonies and things to pray for and that sort of thing, and this man said he had something to say. When the minister gave him the go-ahead, he made such an unexpected and aggressive attack on Sam and Chris that they were both reduced to tears. Apparently, this guy had always been their friend, someone who'd helped them through all sorts of stuff, and vice versa. It was devastating. Sam says the way he spoke sounded like a sort of angry confession. He'd been led up the garden path, he said, but now he'd come to his senses. Someone or something must have got to him, she doesn't know who or what. But the fact that a close friend would do something like that in public without any discussion or warning was just too much for them.

'So, Sam's problem is like yours. Even worse probably. You didn't even know the man in the car park. Imagine if he'd been someone you'd always thought was a real friend. What that man in their church did was deliberate. And it was public. Sam can't imagine ever being able to forgive him. And she can't bear feeling like that. She wanted to know what I thought she should do.'

'Poor Sam and Chris. I'm glad she's written to you. Tell me what you said. Read it out. She won't mind, will she?'

'Of course not.'

Doc pressed a key, scrolled down a little and began to read:

Dear Sam,

Thanks for your email. Apart from anything else, brilliantly written as usual. Here I am with time to sit down and write you a proper reply. By the way, a second meeting of the Marsh-wiggle club is seriously overdue. Talk to Chris and send me some dates. When you've done that, I'll give New Spice a ring and we'll make an evening of it – hats and all this time.

Oh, and I ought to mention that, today, we nearly got into a fight with a whole family in a supermarket car park. I'm not joking. More details when we see you.

You said some very kind things at the beginning of your message. Jack and I genuinely appreciate your encouraging words, but, speaking for myself, there are times when I become so weary of the sound of my own voice that, if I hadn't tried it before and found that it doesn't work, I might be tempted to commit some hugely offensive public sin, just so that my name could be removed from the list of those who have any chance at all of helping others. Having said all that, both of us are lucky enough to meet wonderful people like yourselves all the time, folk who have learned that the whole of the law and the commandments can be summed up in one four-letter word. You and Chris will know the word I mean. It's the one that, to Wimbledon contestants, means nothing.

Which brings me directly to the question you asked in your email. Sam, that was a very nasty experience you had to go through in the service. One thing that struck me about what happened to you was that, in almost any other context in what we might call the normal world, barely anyone would dream of doing something so cruel and thoughtless. If this man really did feel strongly that he needed to get something off his chest, he should have spoken to you, and to the minister as well, before even thinking of addressing the whole assembly. I am so very sorry you had to go through that. I know we followers of Jesus are commanded to exercise compassion and forgiveness by someone who really did know what that can cost, but there are times when I have simply had to say to God, 'Look, I'm about as far from being forgiving as it's possible to be. All I can offer is my honest inability to forgive, and my hope and belief that you will understand and forgive the me who cannot take a single extra step along the "£$%^&* road to heartfelt mercy and forgiveness without a helping hand.'

Having said all that, Sam, it gives me great pleasure to tell you that, after a great deal of medication and prayer, I know exactly how, in this case, you should respond to the man who caused you such pain. Here is the simple, three-step plan that has been revealed to me. Are you sitting comfortably? (I think I meant meditation.)

OK. First, contact two seriously substantial ladies in your church who are fit and trustworthy. Second, arrange a meeting to discuss with them exactly what needs to be done. Third, on the next occasion when you are sure that all three of you *and* the man in question will be present in your church, you and the two ladies should grab hold of the offender at a moment when the violence will be least distracting to others (you don't want to offend anyone), manhandle him to the church conveniences and duck his head three times in one of the Ladies toilets, flushing the toilet on the third occasion.

Calling out, 'Feeling any better, Naaman?' at the end of the procedure is something you are free to consider as an optional extra. I do believe in my heart, Sam, that this is the Jesus way, and I am confident that you will sense his presence as you strive to be obedient.

There's my advice. Simple and effective. The annoying thing is that, after me going to all that trouble to work out a solution for you, I'm almost certain that you're not going to take my advice. You won't go for the toilet option, will you, Sam? Of course, you won't. I know you too well. You are so annoying! So stubborn! Your problem, whether or not you mind me saying so, is that you are blessed or cursed, depending on how you look at it, by an inconvenient burden of compassion and forgiveness, as well as all those other frustratingly positive attributes that conspire to take the good fun out of good old straightforward revenge.

I remember the story you told us last time we met of how, years ago, you responded with such warmth and patience to a lifelong friend whose cruelty came close to breaking your heart. Others would probably have lashed out, or stomped off, or called for the toilet seat cover to be lifted, ready for the next headinsertion. You didn't – you won't – because mercy is built into you. What is your trouble?

Dear Sam, your trouble is that you are like me and Jack – and Jesus even more so, if it comes to that. You've been broken, and half repaired, and found yourself in dark, apparently endless tunnels. You know all too well that human beings are frail, and because of that they can be very foolish and unaware and cruel at times. Imagination is the real pleasure killer, though, isn't it? It is for me. Other than with extraordinarily annoying family members who have gone tribal in car parks (I promise I'll tell you about it when we next meet), I seem to be constitutionally almost incapable of NOT looking at the other person's point of view, damn it all!

However, those two incapacitating burdens of yours are a large part of why we are learning to love you. Can I ask you to please not change? It's never going to be easy, Sam. That's the bad news. The good news? Well, I know you will agree that the problems with finally discovering a crystal-clear answer to that question are never going to daunt us Marsh-wiggles.

Much love to you both, from both of us.

Jack smiled and gestured appreciatively.

'I'm glad you sent my love as well. Thank you. How do you think she'll feel about the things you wrote?'

Doc chuckled quietly.

'I hope they'll make her laugh. Obviously there's a nil per cent chance that Sam will take my advice about sticking that fellow's head down the church bog, but at least it might give her permission to own and look squarely at all those nasty turbulent feelings before tackling things a bit more constructively. That's what I meant earlier when I said it was good to hear you say you didn't think you could forgive the man with the big mouth and the Brillo-pad hair. Most of us need to start with the raw truth about how we're feeling before we embark on some fragrant act of mercy and understanding. There's so much nonsense talked about forgiveness, Jack. People make it sound as if it's something you can go and buy a sachet of from Boots.

'Poor Sam and Chris. My goodness, I can tell you from experience, you need to feel safe before planning to set out on one of the toughest journeys known to humanity. This promised land, this place where you'll truly be able to love your enemies, it can seem an awful long way away when you're still trudging through the desert.'

'But surely God helps with the transport sometimes, doesn't he?'

'Very kind and brave of you to adopt my metaphor, Jack. I think this particular one is about to die on its feet. But you're right. There do seem to be times when a divine chopper is despatched to the middle of the wilderness to pick up suffering souls who can't locate a Saharan branch of Boots, but it can take a lifetime.'

'Literally?'

'Now you mention it, I remember a man in a group that Miriam and I were leading who suddenly announced after a lull in conversation, 'I am a vengeful man!' We all perked up a bit on hearing that, as you can imagine. Something a bit juicy coming up, I expect we all imagined and hoped. Actually, it was really interesting.'

'What did he mean?'

'He was in his early seventies, and he'd been an Anglican all his life. After coming out with this headline of a confession, he explained what he meant. All his life he'd been a man who never forgave anyone who upset or hurt him. He always wanted to get his own back, and as often as he could manage it, that was exactly what he did.

'Then, one day, he was sitting in church on a Sunday morning and everyone, including him, of course, started to say the Lord's Prayer. By the way, Miriam and I wasted several minutes later on working out that he must have said or heard that same prayer somewhere between five and six thousand times during his life. Suddenly, on this particular morning, and for the very first time, he registered the bit about being forgiven by God in the same way that we forgive other people. It shocked him rigid, and it changed his life.'

Jack shook his head in wonder.

'What was left of it, you mean. That man was in your desert for longer than the Israelites.'

'About half as long again, yes.'

'No handy helicopters.'

'Apparently not. More like a bumpy rickshaw ride for the last hundred yards.'

'But why? Why would it take so long?'

'Ah, I've thought a lot about this, Jack. My own view is that some ambitious junior angel was put on the job. Probably told he'd be given something more interesting when he managed to corner that man into finally noticing something that had been sitting right in front of him every week of his life, twice a week or more, quite likely. He did well – the angel, I mean. Only took him six and a bit decades. Not too bad in the context of eternity, is it?'

Jack smiled at the idea.

'He must have enjoyed reporting back to God. Flushed and weary and a bit rough round the edges, but proud of his achievement. A happy little angel. I wonder what his next job would have been.'

'Hard to say. A.N. Wilson perhaps, just to keep him humble.'

'Seriously, Doc, why so long?'

The Shadow Doctor sighed and patted his knees a few times before replying.

'As you know, I never had children, Jack, but I have had chances over the years to get to know and watch other people's kids. And we – Miriam and I, that is – we did have pets.'

'A cat and a dog.'

Jack saw and interpreted the sharp glance that was directed at him.

'You told me about them – well, you mentioned how the business of feeding them every day got very boring. I think "grinding tedium" was the actual phrase you used.'

Doc raised a hand in apology.

'Sorry, Jack, really sorry about the evil eye. I've said more to you than almost anyone else. I forget. Sorry. What I was going to say was that, from what I've seen, small children and pets seem to have the same problem with grown-ups and owners as we do with God. I mean, the questions very small children ask are about as logical and reasonable as you can get. You know the sort of thing I mean.

'Why can't my birthday be today instead of next Wednesday? Why are you spending ages stuffing clothes into a round hole in a shiny white box instead of telling me a story? Why can't it be sunny and not wet when we were supposed to be going to the park? Why are you pressing that flat, oblong thing against your ear and talking to it when I'm trying to talk to you? Why won't we be able to see granny any more? What does dead mean?

'You see what I'm saying? Within the limits of their experience and understanding an enormous number of the things they see us doing must look random and meaningless. A waste of time as far as they're concerned. Animals are just the same. We loved Boisdale, our gorgeous Irish Setter, but he would trail behind us round the house or sit on the edge of the room, asking one silent, intense question. Setters would make great funeral directors. How long do I have to put all this canine effort into staring mournfully at you before you come to your senses, remember the reason for your existence, and take me for a long, glorious walk?'

'And we're like them, the kids and the pets. Is that what you mean?'

'You like me quoting from the Bible, don't you, Jack?'

Jack shrugged helplessly. 'Yes, I can't help it. It makes me feel safe.'

The Shadow Doctor frowned.

'Despite that I will tell you. You'll know these words anyway. They're always worth hearing again. "My thoughts are nothing like your thoughts, says God, and my ways are beyond anything you can imagine."

'If that is the case, it's all bound to look pretty random, isn't it, Jack? How else could it look? We know a very small percentage of a millionth of something very close to absolutely nothing. We ask the wrong questions. We're tempted to refuse answers that we don't like. Trust is a very tough call. It was for Jesus, as far as trusting people was concerned. We're told he backed off because he knew the hearts of men. It's the same for us. And the great danger is that we settle for a little kid's version of reality, and we sit in the sandpit squashing our idea of God down into a shape that jams grotesquely and uselessly into the limits of what we know and feel sure of.'

Jack thought for a moment.

'So what's the bottom line with all this stuff about forgiving and being forgiven by people or God or both?'

Doc sighed. 'I'm going to bore you now, Jack.'

'Go on then. There's always a first time.'

'It's truth again. Think the truth. Feel the truth. Own the truth. If I can forgive someone who's hurt me, I'll go and tell God about it. He'll probably be thrilled. If I can't manage that, I'll still go to God and tell him exactly how far up the rickety ladder of forgiveness I'm actually able to go, even if it's only the bottom rung. He'll be thrilled. I'll go to him, even if I can't get one foot on the ladder yet. I would go to him even if I was curled up in a corner swearing about old men in car parks. He'd be thrilled. I'd tell him the truth. Be who I am and ask for help. I'd be an honest, failing, foolish, flat-footed remnant of a Christian.'

'And he would help?'

'I think God is probably like the best of those wonderful old-fashioned bank managers. All those years ago when I went begging, he came up with a plan that worked for me.'

'An overdraft?'

'He hates to lose a customer, Jack.'

'Thanks, Doc, I'll make an appointment.'

23

What happened to Alice?

Jack had discovered that there was a very fine fish and chip shop in Wadhurst. It was called LONG TIME NO SEA. When, in the early days, he had asked Doc why an establishment famed far and wide for the freshness of its fish should so blatantly risk its good reputation, he said he had no idea, but that he loved the name and hoped that it would never change.

It was a pleasure and a relief for Jack to find that Doc shared his love of good fish and chips. Crispy batter that was not too heavy, quality fish that fell apart into chunks rather than mush, and chips that were crispy on the outside and soft on the inside, not too thin and, crucially, not too thick. LONG TIME NO SEA was obviously run by expert professionals. They seemed to get it right every time.

However, Jack soon discovered that the fetching of these delights was a hectic business. Experience had demonstrated clearly that, even unimpeded, the journey from the car park behind the fish and chip shop in Wadhurst to the parking space immediately outside Marlpit Cottage took nine and a half minutes. Disturbingly, extra traffic in the village or on Northfields Lane could extend this to as much as ten minutes, or even a little more.

Tension began and steadily increased from the moment a fish and chip collection was agreed, until the fetcher, always Jack since moving in with the Shadow Doctor, had returned successfully to the cottage. In his absence, Doc's responsibility was to warm plates, butter bread, boil water for tea, and ensure that nothing could stand in the way of the two men picking up knives and forks and beginning to eat seconds after the white wrapping paper was unrolled and the food landed in a golden heap on the plates.

Neither Doc nor Jack was interested in reheated fish and chips. Whatever came out of the paper was what they ate, and so far it had been good. On each occasion they scored the meal out of ten. Generally speaking, the hotter the food, the higher the score. There had once been a nine.

On the evening after the car park incident, Jack went for gold. It was a risky triumph. The journey from shop to cottage took just under nine minutes. The food was hot. For the first time, they gave their meal a score of ten.

The atmosphere later that evening as the two men relaxed in the sitting-room with a glass of excellent port was mellow, so mellow in fact that Jack decided an appropriate time had arrived to have another of his most pressing questions answered. He began casually.

'Do you think much about Alice, Doc?

'Your gran? Yes, in fact I was thinking about her on the way home from our epic battle in the car park. She would have loved to hear all about that – and about Aelwen. And if anyone ever made a film of your life, she could have told them exactly who to choose to play you.'

'Who?'

'She said you always reminded her of Matt Damon.'

Jack raised his eyebrows in surprise.

'Really? I should be so lucky. That reminds me – I meant to tell you – the other day that nice, smart lady in the garage said that you remind her of Paul Scofield playing Thomas More in *A Man for All Seasons*. I've seen that film. I remember thinking the same myself when I first met you.'

'Oh, well, I suppose I'm a man for three out of four seasons. Winter can be grim. Although, having said that, the bleak months have their moments as well. The January when I met your gran was not too bad at all.'

'You were staying in a place just up from the beach in Eastbourne, the Sheldon Hotel, wasn't it?'

'It was. Did you get that from Alice's last letter to you?'

'No, it's a divine revelation.'

Doc nodded sagely.

'Ah, I thought it must be one or the other.' He reflected for a moment. 'Yes, that was a very pleasant and productive January for me. The Sheldon was a warm and wonderfully enfolding sanctuary in the middle of a seaside storm. I met your gran and began one of the most stimulating and unspoiled friendships I've known, and later, because of that meeting, I got to know you. The rest, as they say, is—'

'Geography?'

'No.'

'Maths?'

'Definitely not.'

'Religious Studies?'

'Categorically not.'

'History?'

'It's looking that way, yes, although currently it does have a sort of strong flavour of 'now' about it. Later on, who knows?'

There are times, thought Jack a few moments later, when a silence can be so rich with goodness that you feel you

203

could almost raise a hand and touch it. This one lasted for some minutes.

'Doc, there was a reason I mentioned Gran just now. It's to do with one of the things on my list – you haven't forgotten about my list, have you?'

The Shadow Doctor somehow managed to orchestrate his sigh of response on two different notes.

'No, I have not. I have tried quite hard, though. Go on then.'

'On that night when we stayed up late in the kitchen, and warmed ourselves in front of the oven, and I made a decision that still frightens me when I think about it today—'

'Oh, do get to it, Jack.'

'One of the things you said was that you'd tell me what happened to Gran. She mentioned it in her letter, and she said you'd tell me all about it if we ever got to meet. So, how about telling me now?'

Doc considered for a moment or two, then nodded slowly.

'I will have a go. It's a rather disjointed story, but that's not very surprising when you think of the person Alice was. My friend and your gran. She was stubbornly straightforward and pragmatic in her attitude to ideas and experience, but there were times when . . . how can I put it?' – he sculpted shapes in the air with his hands – 'she managed to create a curve out of all those straight lines and changes of direction. I sound like one of those bright-eyed purveyors of cheap paradox, don't I? But Alice was unusual. If she discovered that something was true even though it didn't make any sense and hadn't happened to her before, she just went for it. Like finding a poem in a telephone directory.

The context didn't matter. Just as well, as you'll understand when you hear what happened to her, Jack.'

Jack squirmed tensely in his chair. Words were clamouring in his head, but he had no immediate plans to speak them aloud.

I want to hear that she became a Christian. That's what I want to hear. I want to know that she fulfilled the bog-standard criteria for getting into heaven. Doesn't have to be unusual. Doesn't have to be clever. Doesn't have to be original or interesting. I only want to know that some angel sitting at a desk just inside the gates of heaven will glance at his or her laptop screen on hearing the name Alice Merton and announce, 'Computer says yes!' I want to meet my gran in heaven.

Forget all that – ask an intelligent question.

'Did Gran ever ask you about what you believe?'

'Not at first, no. She told me about you, of course. Said how guilty she'd felt about shutting the door on talking about something that she could see was important to you. I understand why she did it, though. She loved you, the person she knew, so very much. It was almost impossible for her to find a way of engaging with a part of you that seemed to her, rightly or wrongly, to have no substance at all. Forgive me, that sounds very harsh, Jack, but it is truly how she felt. Here's a question. Did you spend much time praying that Alice would find faith of some sort?'

Oh, well. Say it anyway.

'Yes, whether or not you think it works, I did spend hours praying for her. Hours and hours. I think I was more worried about what was going to happen to gran than anything else in the world. Looking back, I probably went a little bit mad. I got into the way of offering God deals.'

'Ah, the deals.'

'Yes, the deals. In return for sorting gran out and making sure she was on the road to heaven I'd commit to getting up at five o'clock every morning for two hours of prayer and Bible study. Things like that. Or I remember promising to witness to at least one non-Christian every day. I even said once that I'd sell everything I'd got and give the money to the poor. Crackers! Then I'd realise what an idiot I was being because everyone says you can't twist God's arm, so I'd worry about offending him and then repent in case he took it out on me by refusing to let gran into heaven. And then I'd start all over again.'

'Did you ever manage to keep any of those promises of yours?'

'No. Not one. I mean – like I said, I did pray a lot for her, at five o'clock in the morning sometimes, but not because I'd got up specially. I was just lying awake worrying about it.' *Risk the tears.* 'I loved her so much, Doc. Just as well. Before that, I hadn't had a lot of practice so far in that area. Nothing – nobody like Aelwen. Dad for a short part of my life and gran until she died. That was it.'

A grievance, unexpressed and previously undefined, suddenly steadied and animated him.

'You know what really used to drive me mad, and I was hardly conscious of it at the time.' He twizzled his fingers and thumbs together in front of his face, as if he were rolling a cigarette. 'Little twiddly bits of insightful advice from well-meaning people. I suppose they were intended to nudge me into believing that a tiny change of attitude will make everything all right. You know the sort of thing I mean. "Jack, have you ever considered the fact that God is even more keen for your gran to come to faith than you are?" I fell for that sort of thing every time. Every single time! And I did it to other people. Lots of people. I can't believe it.'

'I think I do know what you're talking about, Jack.' The Shadow Doctor was smiling in agreement. 'It's like the thing we used to say about Chinese meals, isn't it? Quite satisfying, but it's not long before you need another one.'

Jack could sense Doc's awareness of the spark of hope in his eyes.

'I asked you how much you prayed for Alice because all that prayer, or to put it another way, all of that true desire for the best possible thing to happen in the life of someone you love, might have been a sort of tributary that ran into the main force and, however tangentially, increased the power of its flow.'

'I remember you describing it like that before. It all sounds so technical and environmental and a bit impersonal. And I don't understand. Why do you only say that it might have had an effect?'

The Shadow Doctor spread his hands apologetically.

'Because I don't know. And I've given up pretending that I do. I am not the one who deals with prayers. The one who actually deals with prayers does whatever he thinks is best, and he definitely doesn't c.c. me in on the ones he answers and the ones he doesn't.'

'But surely—'

'Let's be clear, Jack. There are three things I know for sure about all this. One is that you continually battered the gates of heaven like a crying child on behalf of your gran. The second is that, one stormy night in January, I met Alice

Merton in a dark beach shelter facing out towards the sea, and we became friends. The third thing I know is what happened to Alice after that: this thing that she wanted me to tell you about.'

'You know a lot more things. You saved her life. But never mind all that now. What did happen to her?'

'OK. Eventually, Alice began to ask me about what I believed, together with all sorts of other questions that you'd love to know the answers to, stuff that I have no intention of bothering you with now. I told her quite a bit about my own background. Didn't pull any punches. I was beginning to know a bit more about how your gran worked by then. Wisely or unwisely, I painted a picture of the Church as truthfully as I possibly could, and never tried to answer a question that she hadn't asked. In the end, presumably after giving it a lot of thought, she phoned me the evening before we had arranged to meet, and as far as I can recall, this is what she said.

' "Doc, when we're together tomorrow I want you to tell me in the simplest way you can what this Christian thing is about. Are you listening? I don't want to know what it isn't about. I think I've gathered as much of that as I need to know already. You're very fluent in the negatives." That made me laugh. "Now I want to know, from you, what it is about. After that we'll have kippers and brown bread and butter, a couple of those individual chocolate puddings, and a glass of Sauvignon Blanc. And then we'll have coffee and a game of Scrabble."

'My goodness, that gran of yours knew how to deal with a man. You probably haven't noticed, Jack, but I do tend to come at things from funny angles, and Alice knew that. She wanted the plain truth without any funny business. I arrived the next day, armed with something I'd found in a book by someone who's spent his life writing about what you find when you take the covers off. He'd very kindly done the work for me, thank God. Do you want to hear what I read to her?'

'Of course.'

'OK, hang on a moment. I'll get the book. It might be upstairs, but I think the last time I saw it was in the cupboard under the dresser in the kitchen. I'll go and hunt it down.'

Jack waited in the sitting-room, his imagination quietly aglow with a picture of Doc and Gran seated comfortably in the little room at the front of her flat. There would be the two armchairs, one large and one small, the gate-legged table, the 'Pals' print, and the portrait of Gran's beloved William on his own, beside a larger one of the devoted couple together. Doc's mellow voice drew him back to reality.

'Here we are, Jack. Took me a while to dig it out. It had fallen down the back. Let me just pour some more port and I'll read it to you.' He glanced up for a moment. 'I warn you, the chap who wrote this is not afraid to ask questions.'

Jack closed his eyes. It was odd to think that the very words he was about to hear might be the ones that had changed his gran's life for ever. A faint tinge of jealousy. But only faint. He kept his eyes closed.

Doc began to read.

Christians talk about being saved. What does it mean to be saved? What are we saved for? What on earth do we need to be saved from? Should this whole business of salvation have a big impact on my present as well as on my future? And speaking of the future, what can we expect from an eternity spent in heaven? How can we possibly make sense of heaven when our feet remain so solidly on earth? Where is the interface, the meeting point between the flesh and the Spirit? And when all the strange religious terms and voices and patterns and mantras and man-made conventions have faded away, what will be left?

I really am not a scholarly theologian. But I have been struggling to answer those questions for more than twenty years, to stop me from asking them, as much as anything else. If you are curious to know the history of those struggles, you could bore yourself to death by reading not just the rest of this book, but all my other books as well. They are shot through with passion and puzzlement and will probably continue to be so until the day I die. If, however, you are anxious to retain your sanity, here is the severely shortened version of what I mistily understand about the claims of Christianity and the meaning of salvation. Here we go.

There is one God. He made the world and everything that is in it, including men and women. He had a plan. His plan was for us to live in perfect harmony with him. He was looking forward to it. It was going to be a truly magnificent situation for all concerned. For a while it was. Then something went horribly, dreadfully wrong. Please don't bother asking me why an omnipotent, omniscient God should go out of his way to create beings in the full knowledge that they would turn against him. I have no idea, and nor has anybody else. Don't let those frighteningly certain people tell you otherwise. We understand very nearly nothing of the truth that lies behind life as we know it. However it happened, this major disaster some-how separated human beings from God, who, never-theless, apparently continues to love them, and loves us with a passion that is difficult, if not impossible, to comprehend.

Desperate to heal the rift because of this inexplic-able love, God came up with another plan. This time it was a rescue plan. Jesus came to the earth. He was the Son of God. He was also, in some mysterious way, God himself. He was also, in an equally mysteri-ous way, a real man, born of a woman, tempted by the same things as any other human being. A strange, intriguing concept. He resisted all temptation because he loved his father and wanted to please him. Jesus taught, preached, healed and told stories for three years, until, when he was thirty-three years old, he was executed very nastily on a wooden cross by the Romans as a conciliatory gesture to a section of the Jewish religious leaders. Three days later, he came back to life and was seen by hundreds of people before being physically lifted up from the earth and disappearing from the sight of his followers.

We are told that, because Jesus was executed on that cross and brought back to life again, it is now possible for any or all of us – through taking the undeserved kindness of God in both hands, making

some kind of public declaration of new life, and signing up to join Jesus behind the counter to help with
new customers – to kick-start that magnificent relationship with God that was destroyed in days gone by.
There are more questions than answers here as well,
but somehow the gap between us and God; the sin,
the breakdown, the catastrophic split, the ruin and
decay of all that was supposed to be; has been sorted
out.

The message is that if you and I accept the death
and new life of Jesus as a living, divine, working
mechanism in our own lives, we shall become his
daughters and sons. We will go home to God one day
and find peace. But because the world is as it is, and
because we are all different, life on earth will
continue to be hard for most of us, as it was for Jesus.
The Holy Spirit, another invisible presence of God,
sent by Jesus himself after his death, is on hand to
offer support and strength to those who ask him for
it.

Those are the magical, mystical, practical bones of
what I believe. But for me, the flesh of it and of
myself is continually problematic. I am what I am. I
feel what I feel. I hurt when I hurt. I sing when there
is a song in me. I weep when the dark flood comes.
Oddly, there is a song in me when that happens sometimes. I cannot alter the shape of who I am, other
than by being obediently co-operative with the will
of God in specific matters. Jesus seems to be at the
centre of it all, and he is the one who will save me in
the end, whatever that turns out to mean. He knows

that I am – that we are – weak but willing. He knows
that the level of our faith and loyalty and fortitude
rises and falls continually, but that is all right. He is
going to save you and me, not an edited version of us.
Love is in charge. Tell the truth but be wise. Hold
your nerve. Trust God – even if you don't. He is probably much nicer than we think.

Jack heard the book close and opened his eyes. Doc sat, one
leg crossed over the other, sipping from his glass. Seconds
passed. More seconds.

'Well? Go on. What happened then?'

'Alice put boil-in-the-bag kippers in a saucepan and I
buttered some bread. One of my talents, as you know.'

'But after that.'

'Oyster Bay Sauvignon Blanc, puddings, coffee and
Scrabble, which I won as usual.'

Jack could feel his hands curling into strangling shapes.

'After that!'

Doc shrugged.

'Nothing. I went home.'

'Doc, you know perfectly well what I'm asking: how did
she react to the thing you read? What did she say?'

'Nothing. She said nothing, Jack. She asked no questions
and she made no comment. Neither then, nor at any other
time, did your gran mention the words she heard that evening. What I can tell you is that when Alice and I parted that
evening in her little hall, she kissed me on the cheek with a
little extra tenderness and reached up to whisper two words
in my ear.'

'Which were?'

'Thank you.'

Jack put his glass down on the small table beside him. Rising from his chair, he crossed to the window, stood looking rigidly out into the darkness for a few seconds, then turned around and sank slowly onto the wide window seat. Hands flat on his knees, he stared at the floor, replaying in his mind the story that he had just heard. There was something missing. There had to be something missing. He looked up at last.

'It isn't enough, Doc. If that's all that happened it doesn't make sense.' He was almost pleading. 'Gran said in her letter that you would tell me what happened to her. It's not enough. There must be something else.'

The Shadow Doctor spoke very gently.

'You're absolutely right, Jack. There is something else. I know you want all the answers, but my problem is that Alice never told me anything about the journey she must have made between the night when I read to her from this' – he patted the book that lay beside him with one hand – 'and what happened about three weeks later. I've surmised – no, I am confident – that the journey must have begun on that particular evening, but . . . I could be wrong.'

Jack moved across to sit on the upright chair next to the fireplace. It was closer to the Shadow Doctor. He wanted to concentrate on every word.

'Tell me what happened.'

The air crackled like dry kindling on an open fire. When Doc finally spoke, it was almost in a whisper.

'She came here.'

Stunning, staggering news. No. It was all wrong. It was like Hamlet turning up in King Lear. No, worse. Like

Goldilocks turning up in *Lord of the Rings*. There was a hurting edge to that sentence of three words. He shook his head in bewilderment.

'Gran came here! Here? In this cottage?'

'Just the once. She invited herself. The phone went when I was at home one Monday afternoon not doing anything in particular. It was Alice. Could she talk to me about something that had happened to her? I thought she meant she wanted to talk on the phone. I told her I was doing nothing for the rest of the day, and she just said, "I'll be there at three o'clock," and put the phone down. I tried to ring back, but no answer. I knew she had my address, so I thought I might as well let her get on with it. She'd said it, so she'd come. I put the kettle on and got the biscuits out a few minutes before three, and she knocked at the door dead on time. Came by taxi all that way, would you believe? The cab had gone by the time I stepped outside, so the first thing I did was get the number of the firm from your stubborn grandmother and cancel the return trip. As you know, I can drive when I have to.'

Jack was still shaking his head. An odd mixture of pain and surprise almost overwhelmed him.

'Gran came here!' He jabbed his finger towards the floor. 'She was in this house. I can't believe it. Why did you never tell me?'

'I was a bit nervous. And I suppose I was saving it for the day when I got to this item on your blessed list. Anyway, here we are.' He pointed at the armchair that Jack had just vacated. 'She sat – just there. I sat here. We drank tea and ate shortbread biscuits – well, I ate biscuits. She talked. I listened.'

'What did she say?'

'What did she say? Let me get this right. OK. Here's what she told me.

'Two days before her visit to me, on the Saturday, Alice had decided she would go to church on Sunday morning. Don't ask me how that came about. She didn't say, so I don't know. Typically, she just got the Yellow Pages, looked up churches in the Eastbourne area, and more or less picked one at random. She didn't remember what it was called, but she said it had the word "Community" somewhere in the title. She rang the answer-phone number to find out times of services, checked the address and booked a taxi to get her there the next morning. A bit of an adventure by the sound of it.

'So, Sunday came. Andrew Marr was left to talk to William's portrait. She got to this church ten minutes before the service, and nearly didn't get out of the taxi. I know which church it was, by the way, and it's more of a cross between a shed and a hall than any church she would have ever had anything to do with in the past.

'There were a couple of very doubtful-looking characters hanging about outside. One of them she felt pretty sure must be a drug dealer. Lots of feral kids as well, racing around all over the place. Not promising. You know what your gran was like, though. She'd said she was going to this church on this day, and that was that. So, she went in, found a chair on the back row, and sat down waiting to see what would happen. You can just imagine Alice laughing, can't you, Jack, when she told me that a moment before the service started, it turned out that the most iffy of the two blokes outside was actually the assistant minister.'

'So, she stayed for the service?'

'She did. Stayed for the whole service, had a very quick, very bad cup of coffee at the end, then smiled prettily around at whoever was close to her at the time, and set off out to wait for her taxi home.'

'But she enjoyed the service.'

'Hated every moment of it.'

'Oh.'

'Hated what she called the cowboy songs. Really, really hated one or two choruses that sounded as if Jesus was asking her to be his girlfriend. Too much crying for no apparent reason.' He thought for a moment. 'What else? She didn't understand why the man who did the talk spoke in such a funny voice, and she felt a bit frightened of a lady with a huge amount of bright red hair who came up to the front and said that God had told her to pass on a message that he was angry with the church for worrying too much. Extremely worrying for all those present, Alice reckoned.

'She didn't like any of it, Jack, but by the time she got to this bit of the story I have to say that I was quite intrigued.'

'What do you mean? I would have been very disappointed.' A pause. 'I am very disappointed.'

'Well, I can understand that, but here's the thing. I'll tell you what I was asking myself. Had she really come all the way from Eastbourne to Wadhurst by taxi at enormous expense just to tell me that she went to a service that didn't suit her at all? If that church was the one I thought it was – and the lady with the red hair pretty much clinched it – I knew that it was actually quite an amazing place. Hard to run, very difficult to control, wears its leaders to a frazzle, not my scene at all, but it picked up – it still picks up – a lot of folk who can't find a home anywhere else. And I admire it. There are only a couple of churches I still go and speak at if they ask me. That's one of them.' He shifted uneasily before continuing. 'Jack, I also need to tell you that it's the church where you're going to hear me preach the Sunday after next – if you still want to come after hearing the rest of the story.'

Jack spoke very quietly.

'Tell me the rest of the story, Doc.'

'O.K. Well, all of Alice's reservations were exactly the same as mine and, judging on that basis alone, I would never have chosen that place to send her. But then, here's another thing, Jack. As usual, and you might as well get used to this if you're going to stick around, I wasn't allowed to do the choosing.'

Jack hardly dared to breathe.

'Something happened.'

The Shadow Doctor sighed.

'As I have said to you many times before, the becauses and the despites get a bit confused in the real worlds – this one and the other one. Alice walked out through the inner door of the church into a little porch and was about to open the outer door when she found herself unable or unwilling or something to take even one more step forward. The only way she could put it into words was that, in a peculiar sense, she was being invited to "Hold on for a moment." So she did.

'As she stood all alone in that small space, she said it was as if a stream of warm water began to pass gently from the top of her head right down through every part of her body to the soles of her feet. I asked her how it made her feel. She thought very carefully for a moment, and she said, "Doc, the closest I can get to it is this. It made me feel I was clean for the first time, and it made me feel that, against formidable odds, it was all right."

'Then she asked me if I was able to explain what it meant, and she also wanted to know if I thought she was going mad.'

'You told her. You explained that it was the baptism—'

Doc waved his hands dismissively.

'I did do a quick check in the drawer where I used to keep my labels, but I must have run out. I told her that it meant she was now clean, and that her feeling was a reliable one. It – she – was definitely all right. I added that I was sure she was not going mad because, in my view, she was already about as pleasantly crazy as she was likely to get.' He clasped his hands together against his chest and looked up at the ceiling. 'She did ask one other question. I knew she would.'

An image of the portrait on Gran's sideboard returned to Jack's mind.

'About Grandad. William.'

'Of course. Straightforward as ever. "Doc, where is William now?"'

'What did you say?'

'What do you think you would have said?'

After a sharp intake of breath, Jack shook his head hopelessly.

'Oh my goodness, I'm so very glad I wasn't the one who had to say anything about that. I'd probably have waffled endlessly about how you can never tell what's going on inside people. There'll be surprises in heaven. That sort of thing. It doesn't matter what I would have said anyway. What was your answer?'

'After giving the matter intense thought for about one and a half seconds, I said I hadn't the faintest idea.'

'Oh, my! And what did Gran say to that?'

'Not much. She got up, came over to my chair, leaned down to kiss me gently on the cheek, and said, "Thank you". Never mess with Alice Merton – that was my motto. Besides, if I was going to end up getting a kiss every time I hit her with a blunt truth – well, why spoil a good thing?'

24

A fondness for God

It was Wednesday evening. A storm was gathering outside. The sudden rattle of raindrops as a south-west wind gusted against the window reminded Jack of the very first evening he had spent in the Shadow Doctor's house. Peace, puzzlement, good whisky and the faintest whisper of freedom – those were Jack's dominant memories of that initial encounter with a man whose company and influence were changing his life. It seemed an age ago.

'Another question. I don't quite know how to ask it.'

The Shadow Doctor smiled.

'Try blurting. There's nothing like a bit of blurting to get stuff out.'

Jack stared at the bronze hare, standing up like an animated exclamation mark on its shelf at the other side of the kitchen. The animal glared back with its eternally sculpted expression of outraged derision. Jack took a deep breath.

'I'll try.' Another breath. He smacked the table lightly with one hand. 'OK. As you know, before I met you I only knew a few ways to talk about God – I mean, about how I or anyone else, for that matter, feel about God. I guess, to be fair, because I hadn't actually met him in the way that I meet human beings, I had to use words and expressions that fitted what the Bible or other people say he is. Most of the people I knew in the Church seemed to do that. God was awesome, wonderful, everlastingly loving, King of kings – you know the list.'

Doc nodded slowly and took a sip of his wine before speaking.

'And now?'

'Well, that's what I want to ask you about, really. Sorry, I don't think I'm very good at blurting. I wondered if you could tell me how you feel about God . . .' He raised a forestalling hand. 'Not how anyone else says you're supposed to feel – I know you wouldn't bother to do that anyway – but what you think about him. Deep down. In your . . .' Jack snatched at the air with alternating hands, hunting for a word. 'I don't know – in your *ventricles*.'

'In my ventricles? Good gracious!'

'Sorry, you're right to laugh. Silly thing to say. I suppose I'm asking how you feel – you know – after all those years of doing stuff with your wife, and then losing her and everything going so wrong, then coming back and finding a new way to – to operate. Probably the wrong word. All these years. All the things that have happened. The good stuff. The horrible, terrible, sad experiences. The brilliant things. The weird way you go about helping people nowadays. Sorry, when I say weird, I don't mean – well, you must admit, it is a bit weird. Anyway!' He shrugged. 'Anyway, after all that, how do you – feel about him? I just wondered . . .'

Jack's voice trailed into silence as his confidence evaporated. Staring hopelessly at the hare once more, he decided that the arrogant creature's expression smacked as much of triumph as outrage.

Doc lowered his glass to the table, held it between both hands like a crystal ball, and peered into the depths for several seconds. Jack's favourite scene from *Jurassic Park*, immediately before the Tyrannosaurus Rex roars into view, replayed itself in his imagination. The relationship between the two men had taken several positive turns since Jack's arrival, but those turns tended to lead off into unpredictable, irregular loops. Anticipating Doc's response to almost anything that he said or did was still beyond his powers. The thing Jack was beginning to cling to, though, was a growing belief that a significant aspect of his role in the Shadow Doctor's life was to prod or persuade him into enunciating some of the swirlingly obscure thoughts and feelings that lay behind his approach to what Jack would once have called 'ministry'. Frustratingly, Doc both resisted and encouraged these prods and persuasions, but Jack felt he was beginning to gain a few new skills and a little more bravery.

Perhaps he would need that bravery now. The older man had raised his head, studying his questioner with furrowed brows.

'Interesting, Jack.' He sighed. 'Not particularly comfortable. Damn you. Thank you.' He stared at the ceiling and waved a cupped hand from side to side in front of his chest for a few moments, as if running through the final steps in an internal argument. 'Look, I promise I will do my very best to answer your question very specifically in a moment, but first I want to tell you something that came into my mind as you were talking.'

Jack picked up a cheese straw and tapped it against his cheek.

'What came into your mind?'

'A memory. I remembered a friend called Sidney – the only Sidney I've ever known, as far as I can remember. Not that that's got anything to do with anything.'

'But fascinating beyond words.'

'Yes. Thank you. Sid was a Christian. I worked with him in the early days doing all sorts of something which, for want of a better word, we called outreach. I couldn't forget Sid if I tried. I was very fond of him. Tall, skinny, big eyes like a seal. Friendly, reserved sort of chap. Never quite stood up straight. I think, in an odd sort of way, he hated the idea of folk thinking he was showing off by being taller than the rest of us. He was about the same age as me, and we used to talk endlessly, especially when we travelled, swopping stories about being kids and growing up, that sort of thing.

'Poor old Sid hadn't been as lucky as me. He grew up in care, one of those big old children's homes that used to scoop up kids with nowhere else to go. He never had managed to find out much about where his mum and dad had disappeared to. And he said the place he lived in wasn't too bad. Quite big. Continual human flow in and out and round and round. Very well organised. Lots of activities. Staff friendly most of the time. He remembered the food being good. Traditional. Roast on Sunday, I expect. Can't really remember the details now. I think a slice of brightly coloured iced sponge-cake at teatime on Saturday was a star event. Nice, but strictly one slice only. Generally OK. In fact, and I think this was why I remembered him just now, it wasn't until he left the Children's Home to move into a foster family when he was about twelve that he realised he had no idea what people had meant when they talked about living in a "normal" family. And that's what we chatted about an awful lot, because that move changed his life.'

'You said he left the home. Did kids in care get a choice about that? Did he want to leave?'

'That's a very good question. It's years since we had those chats, Jack. He must have been given a choice but, to be honest, I would imagine he had no real idea what leaving would mean. I do clearly recall him telling me that, right up to the day when he moved out of the Children's Home, and for some time after that, he had no clear picture of what fostering would really mean. Of course, there'd been long chats with his social worker, and two or three visits to the home he was going to live in, but I guess it was a forest of words and faces and rooms and unfamiliar streets. I imagine it was all a bit of a blur. But you know what grown-ups are like. They kept telling little Sid how incredibly lucky he was to get a place in this particular family, because the foster parents were wonderful, and they only ever fostered one or two kids in addition to having two older ones of their own, and he'd have a bedroom to himself for the first time ever, so it would be a fantastic place to live.'

Jack waited. He was warming to little Sid and his hopes and dreams. Had the twelve-year-old boy succeeded in his big move? He feared the worst.

'So, he moved in.'

'That's right.'

Infuriatingly, Doc picked up a cheese straw, bit a large piece from the end, and began to chew solemnly, his eyes fixed on Jack's questioning expression as he ate.

'Doc, I'm going to go and scratch your bright, silvery car right along one side with a sweetcorn fork if you take one more bite of that cheese straw. I mean it. Tell me what happened to Sid when he went to be fostered.'

'With a sweetcorn fork? Have we really got forks specifically designed for—?' He raised a hand in mock surrender as Jack rose threateningly to his feet. 'All right, all right, I'll tell you.' He folded his arms, stretched his legs out and crossed his ankles. 'Sid stayed with that family for six or seven years – something like that. He ended up calling his foster parents Mum and Dad, and at the time when I knew him, he went back to their house two or three times a year to see them, and he spent every Christmas with the family.'

'So, it did work.'

'Yes, it worked. Amazingly well. You'd like to know why, wouldn't you?'

'You know I would. Let's not go through this again. You always know.'

'It worked because those foster parents must have been very special people.'

'Special? What sort of special? What did they do?'

Doc raised praying hands against his lips and closed his eyes for a moment before replying.

'Let me cogitate for a second. I want to get this right. OK. The secret seems to have been that they put all their intelligence and compassion into what must have amounted to an act of will. They resolved that they would understand. That's how Sid worked it out later, when he was a few years older. They got their heads round the fact that this little boy who was coming to live in their house knew next to nothing about what it meant to be in what others would call a real home.

For instance, they thought through the bedroom thing, asked the staff at the home some questions, and figured that when Sid first arrived, he probably wouldn't actually want to have a room all to himself. The grown-ups had gone on about how wonderful it would be, but it turned out that Sid was nervous and unsure about being on his own for the first time in his life. So, they let him share a room with one of the older boys for a while. That worked fine, and later on he was the one who asked if it would be all right to move into a single room so that he could do things on his own, and put his stuff on the walls, and make it special.

'Those two good folks must have seriously taken on board the fact that Sid had no experience at all of what it might mean to be loved specially and unconditionally by the adults who were looking after him. What was this "love" thing, anyway? That's what he must have asked himself. What shape does it come in? What noise does it make? How are you supposed to give it? How on earth do you take it from somebody else, and where do you put it when you've got it? I've known people in their eighties or nineties who are still asking the same questions. No wonder Sid was puzzled.'

Doc hit the table firmly with the edge of his right hand.

'Then there were the rules. Big question. Big, big question. What were the rules when there were a lot fewer of them than you'd had in the past, but you were still somehow expected to care about other people, and you couldn't learn the practical ways of doing it by looking at a list on a laminated sheet of paper stuck to the wall? Not easy.

'There was one other immediate question that seemed as big as an elephant to Sid, one of the African variety, I expect, and impossible to answer in the first weeks that he was there. And when you think about it, it's one that most people who've never lived in institutions would find very hard to understand. After all this time, how could you ever truly believe, deep down, that living your life with a Shift A and a Shift B had disappeared for ever? How could you be truly confident that people in charge of you, who you'd got to know and trust, wouldn't leave, and that you would never again experience the shock of being woken up in the morning by grown-ups you'd never seen before, people who landed smack in the middle of your life before you even knew their names?

'So, all in all, Sid's foster parents gave that uneasy little kid the time and the space and whatever information and advice he needed to become a genuine, comprehending member of this thing that more fortunate people so easily and casually call a family.

'Obviously, as I've already said, he didn't have a clue about how those things were working out at the time, but later, when he was one of the family, and able to be involved himself in helping one or two new foster children to find their feet, he said he was suddenly overwhelmed by the knowledge of what those two people had done for him. And – you know what, Jack – he loved them already by then, but he loved them even more when they explained how it had been at the beginning, and he realised just how much dedication and care and sheer concentration they'd put in to those early weeks and months.'

The Shadow Doctor relaxed in his chair, downed the last few drops from his glass and set it down carefully on the table beside him.

Jack leaned back, his head tilted to one side. A strong, uninvited feeling was threatening to surface from somewhere deep inside him. Questions might postpone a sudden eruption.

'What happened to Sid? Do you still hear from him?'

Doc shook his head and spoke very gently.

'No-o-o, not any more, Jack. He was – well, he was given the opportunity to make one more major transition. More mysterious and a lot more unpredictable in a way. I have to say, though, that in my not very humble opinion, this last move will have been even more successful than his first.'

To break the ringing silence, Jack rose to his feet, pushed his chair back loudly on the stone-flagged floor, and moved across the kitchen towards the sitting-room, pausing and turning his head before passing through the door.

'I rather fancy a Lagavulin, Doc. Will you join me?'

The Shadow Doctor swivelled briskly in his chair.

'What? What are you saying? Are you seriously suggesting that I should mix one of the finest Burgundies I know with one of the best single malts in the world?'

'Yes.'

Apparently experiencing a minor epiphany, the Shadow Doctor clapped and rubbed his hands close to his chest in approval.

'Brilliant idea, Jack! Bring it through. Two of our chunkiest glasses, and there's a packet of vegetable crisps in the cabinet. Bring those as well. We'll throw them all over the table. I'll get rid of the wineglasses. We wouldn't want them to get upset. Don't say I never do anything.'

Soon, the table was strewn with crisps of every size and colour. Two whisky tumblers, each charged with a half-inch of Lagavulin malt, stood waiting in front of the two men. Outside, the storm was gaining force. A sudden, much greater surge of wind whoomphed angrily against the swinging tops of towering trees outside the cottage.

'Why do we enjoy this whisky so much, Doc?'

Another memory of their first meeting had surfaced in Jack's mind. Aware that the cost of a single bottle of this particular whisky was way beyond anything he could afford, he had hardly dared touch a half-filled decanter that had been placed on a small table at his elbow. In conversation with Doc, however, he had learned that, incredibly, the two cases of the superlative Scotch had been gifted in return for an unspecified service to some important person at Lagavulin Bay. Jack had felt reassured, but he would never have dreamt that one day he might announce to the Shadow Doctor that he 'rather fancied a Lagavulin'. It was a good feeling. Better, it was a relatively uncomplicated good feeling.

Doc picked up his glass, lifted it to eye-level, and tilted it carefully from side to side, studying the contents.

'Why do we enjoy this whisky? Hmm, there's a bit of a list, isn't there? You like lists, don't you, Jack. It's rich, it's dry, you can actually taste the peat-smoke, it looks like dark liquid gold, and in a twisted sort of way, it's even kind of economical. A lot of people can't begin to understand why anyone would ever want to drink a real single malt, so we don't need to waste it on them. Savings there. All those things are on the list, but top of the list – absolute peak of the list on this unique evening, Jack, is the fact that we both think it's wonderful, and I cannot think of anything I would rather do right now than sit in this kitchen with you, my friend and colleague, and relish the first, second, third and all subsequent sips of such a magical elixir.' He offered his glass out over the centre of the table. 'Cheers!'

Heaven could wait no longer.

'Cheers, Doc.'

The Shadow Doctor flapped an encouraging hand over the table top. 'Have a crisp, Jack. Those big purple ones are beetroot.'

'Yes, I know; I don't like them. I'll have one of the yellowy-white ones. The funny-shaped parsnip ones. They're nice. Tasty.'

'OK, we won't fall out over our vegetable crisp preferences.'

Jack finished his crisp and toyed with another.

'Thank you for saying those nice things about – about being here with me.'

'Jack, don't thank me for telling the truth. I'm not interested in going back to that particular prison.' He considered for a second or two. 'Look, I know we still have a long way to go in all sorts of ways – both of us – but I reckon it's going to be all right. You and me, I mean. I'm very far from being sure what the future holds, and, thank goodness, I'm not ultimately responsible for steering the course, but we are on our way to becoming – a sort of team. Good heavens, I never thought I'd say anything as terrifying as that – and I look forward to us doing some very useful work together. I really do.'

Turning his head, Jack looked very directly at the Shadow Doctor. 'Why did you tell me that story about your friend Sid when I asked how you feel about God?'

'I thought you'd never ask. Two reasons, Jack. Do you remember me telling you about a list of tyrannies that continually screw the Church up?'

'Yes, you said there was one you and Miriam had trouble with. Success. Spiritual success, wasn't it?'

'That's right. Well, here's another one. We might call it the Tyranny of Superlatives.'

'And what does that mean?'

'It means that a lot of people who get interested in faith, or actually make a commitment, or whatever you want to call it, can suddenly find themselves having to make a great big, bewildering leap.'

'From what to what?'

'Well, it's a leap from a place where they know and understand virtually nothing about a thing described by someone as a relationship with God or Jesus, to a place where they find they're expected to use extravagant words and sing deeply emotional stuff and behave in prescribed ways that have very little to do with who they actually are, and, for the time being at least, are virtually meaningless. That was rather like Sid's problem when he first got fostered. So much of the stuff going on around him was completely new. Even if he wanted to join in, he just didn't know how. Fortunately, the people looking after him understood that there was a very important journey to be made by that little kid sitting anxiously on the edge of the sitting-room, nervously wondering what it all meant and how he was expected to be part of it. A lot of new Christians are the same. It takes time. And it has to be real.' He paused. 'So, how do you feel about God, and all that, Jack?'

Jack knew that his voice would break as he spoke.

'I think – I think I still feel like a twelve-year-old who's just moved in.'

'Twelve-year-olds aren't allowed to drink whisky, Jack. Take another sip. The other reason for telling you about dear old Sid was to help you understand my answer to the question you asked me in the first place. About me. How do I feel about God?'

The Shadow Doctor frowned. Jack sensed that some sort of inner debate was going on. Perhaps he could help.

'Why would I not understand the answer? You've only got to say the words.'

'That list you went through earlier on – the words people use to talk about God. What was it – awesome, everlastingly something or other?'

'Loving.'

'Oh, yes, that was it. Everlastingly loving. One or two others. And you said you had to use words and expressions like that because you hadn't met God in the same way that you meet people. Have I got that right?'

Anchoring a thumb under his chin and chewing the skin on his forefinger, Jack nodded warily.

'I think my concern is that – how can I put it? You may be disappointed with my answer and actually wish I would use that sort of language, whether it's accurate for me or not. After all, if God is anything, he's all those massive things, isn't he? It might be easier and more helpful for you to talk like that, than to get all tangled up in how someone like me feels. What do you think?'

Doc was right as usual. His warning had connected with a fear in Jack. He controlled himself with an effort. The last thing he wanted was to hear the older man expressing an emotionally limp view of the God who was supposedly entwined and invisibly present in all the work that they did. It seemed unlikely, but what if some more fundamental and disturbing truth about the Shadow Doctor's dysfunctional view of the creator was about to emerge. The innocent expression on Doc's face solved the problem for him. Perhaps he had placed it there on purpose for Jack to see. If so, it was probably all right anyway.

'No, thank you, just give me the truthful answer to my question.'

Both men seemed to relax.

'OK, I will. I'll tell you. Me and God, we're like two old friends who built a giant catapult on the edge of a cliff.'

Jack stared blankly.

'What? What do you mean?'

'We go back a long way. Don't snort into valuable whisky when I'm sharing deep personal truth with you, Jack. We go back a long way, but we do know when to let go – at least, I do nowadays. He's not so good at that. Over the years I've wished grumpily that he'd give up on me, and I've hoped desperately that he wouldn't. He's stubborn. So am I, but he's far worse than me. Tough as old boots when necessary. So, how do I feel about the creator of the universe?' He pondered for a moment. 'I wrote something about it a while ago. Do you want to hear the first four lines? Those are the only ones I can remember. I read them to Martha once, but no one else.'

In the slow, rich tones that Jack had heard him use to such great effect with folk who were feeling hurt or bewildered or lost, Doc began to recite:

I have a fondness for God, it comes from all the years,
The romance of relationship, the laughter and the
    tears,
The madness and the mercy, disappointment and
    delight,
Such hope, such desolation in the darkness of the
    night.

Jack nodded slowly. 'You have a fondness for God.'

'I do. Much more than that sometimes, Jack. He rescued me. By the way, have you decided if you're coming to hear me preach on Sunday?'

'Yes, I'm definitely coming.'

'Good.'

25

Understanding blue

The New Life Community Church was bursting and buzzing when Jack and Doc arrived. Jack had spent the last few days in a state of uneasy expectation. Might he experience something significant as he passed through the little entrance porch where Gran had been ambushed by that invitation to 'Hold on for a moment'? In fact, the volume of human traffic passing both ways through the tiny space fifteen minutes before the beginning of the service made sensitive reflection totally impossible. Much of the traffic consisted of small children, pushing and pulling and shouting at the tops of their voices, almost, thought Jack, as if they were unconsciously reflecting the atmosphere of urgent excitement that seemed to be filling and overflowing from the building.

Other than a narrow and crazily uneven centre-aisle that ran from the entrance door through to the shallow raised dais at the front of the hall, the entire space inside was packed with chairs, some matching, many not. Most were already occupied by a chattering, expectant crowd. Squashed into a corner to one side of the dais, two men with guitars were flipping through sheets of paper on black music stands. As Doc and Jack made their way towards the front, one of them, a man with long black hair, a crooked stance and an attractive, pain-creased smile, waved cheerily and pointed to the front row, where RESERVED notices had been placed on two chairs at the end nearest the musicians. As they sat down, Doc leaned across to speak in Jack's ear.

'That's your gran's drug dealer. His name's Steve. Assistant Pastor. More or less runs this place. Doesn't look too villainous, does he?'

Jack smiled and turned to take a look over his shoulder.

'Do they always pack the place out like this?'

An unfamiliar voice replied.

'Only when the Shadow Doctor gets up on his hind legs for us.' The man called Steve had joined them on the seat next to Jack. 'Half of this lot are ours. The rest come from churches all over the town – all over the area in fact. I send the word out and they come. It's your mate's fault. He's not boring like me. I'm Steve.'

'Jack.'

'Good to meet you, Jack.'

'How did you get to know Doc, Steve?'

Steve glanced quickly at his watch, looked thoughtfully at Jack for a moment, then shrugged. 'I chucked my life away a few years ago. He went and dug it out of the bin. Gave it a clean and made me take it back. Interfering git.' He gave a crooked smile and extended a hand. 'I've got to get this holy show on the road. Good to meet you, Jack.'

As Steve did a brief welcome and introduction to the service, Jack became aware that the noise of children and the children themselves seemed to have disappeared as if by magic. Puzzling. Presumably, he thought, they must have been herded off into some other, adjacent building.

As the first chorus began, and most of the people in the packed assembly rose to their feet, an unexpected tension gripped his chest. All of this was close enough to church as he had known it for much of his life to bring a stew of feelings rising like indigestion into his system. Standing in this atmosphere, next to the man who was leading and accompanying him into a new and still uncertainly shaped future, it was hard to handle his inner conflict. All of that was nothing, however, in contrast with the terror that gripped his very soul when Doc leaned and spoke with carefully enunciated urgency into his left ear in the middle of the second chorus.

'Jack, I think God wants you to do the talk instead of me. Are you up for it?'

A sense of complete paralysis was relieved with dramatic and breath-releasing abruptness when the Shadow Doctor leaned across once more and said in a sibilant whisper, 'Only joking.'

Jack was still trembling slightly as the music ended and he sat down. As the rest of the congregation stayed on their feet to offer loud applause to God, he silently planned to berate Doc on the way home for so gratuitously providing an opportunity for practising forgiveness. Soon he forgot everything else. All but one of the congregation had regained their seats. The Shadow Doctor was standing by the lectern in the centre of the dais and was about to begin his talk.

'Good morning, everybody. My name is Michael, and Steve has been kind enough to ask me if I would like to speak to you all this morning. I'm very happy to do that, but I would like to ask you all to do me one small favour. Is that OK?'

Glancing round to his right, Jack was able to witness an abundance of nods and encouraging smiles. A friendly bunch. Doc continued, his tone an endearing blend of confidence and vulnerability.

'Let me explain. I've been working really hard over the last few months to achieve something I've wanted for the whole of my life. I'm talking about humility. Yes, that's right – humility. And the problem with humility, as many of you will know, is that at the very moment when you achieve your goal, it's no longer possible to relish it, for the obvious reason that complete humility removes the capacity for experiencing the pride required for enjoyment of one's achievement. For this reason I would be truly grateful if you could be kind enough to applaud my talk at the end so that I can admire my progress for a little longer before perfection sets in. Or, if you wish, you could give me a round of applause now to save time at the end.'

Tumultuous applause and laughter from the entire room. Doc smiled and lifted a hand for quiet.

'Thank you. Thank you for just – understanding. Now, I have a passage from the book of Acts to read to you. If you've brought Bibles, do follow it as I read. If you haven't, don't worry, it's not the end of the world. Not many things are. In fact, for Christians, even the end of the world is not the end of the world. Lucky, aren't we?

'So, from the ninth chapter of Acts, here's the story.

As he neared Damascus on his journey, suddenly a light from heaven flashed around him. He fell to the ground and heard a voice say to him, 'Saul, Saul, why do you persecute me?'

239

'Who are you, Lord?' Saul asked.

'I am Jesus, whom you are persecuting,' he replied. 'Now get up and go into the city, and you will be told what you must do.'

The men travelling with Saul stood there speechless; they heard the sound but did not see anyone. Saul got up from the ground, but when he opened his eyes he could see nothing. So they led him by the hand into Damascus. For three days he was blind and did not eat or drink anything.

In Damascus there was a disciple named Ananias. The Lord called to him in a vision, 'Ananias!'

'Yes, Lord,' he answered.

The Lord told him, 'Go to the house of Judas on Straight Street and ask for a man from Tarsus named Saul, for he is praying. In a vision he has seen a man named Ananias come and place his hands on him to restore his sight.'

'Lord,' Ananias answered, 'I have heard many reports about this man and all the harm he has done to your holy people in Jerusalem. And he has come here with authority from the chief priests to arrest all who call on your name.'

But the Lord said to Ananias, 'Go! This man is my chosen instrument to proclaim my name to the Gentiles and their kings and to the people of Israel. I will show him how much he must suffer for my name.'

Then Ananias went to the house and entered it. Placing his hands on Saul, he said, 'Brother Saul, the Lord – Jesus, who appeared to you on the road as you were coming here – has sent me so that you may see again and be filled with the Holy Spirit.'

Immediately, something like scales fell from Saul's eyes, and he could see again. He got up and was baptised, and after taking some food, he regained his strength. Saul spent several days with the disciples in Damascus. At once he began to preach in the synagogues that Jesus is the Son of God.

'There we are then. One of my favourite stories in the Bible. And if you want to learn a bit more about that uber-weird encounter, you can look at the twenty-sixth chapter of Acts and hear what Paul himself has to say about it. We'll come back to that story in a moment.

'Here's a question. Why did I say yes when Steve asked me to come and speak here today? It's very simple. I've got something to say. I'm grateful to God for that. It began with a trigger. Every now and then a line of poetry or a few words spoken in conversation, or a bit from the Bible, or a scrap of dialogue in a play, can cause a mini-explosion of interest and curiosity in my mind. I'm sure it happens to lots of people in a similar way. For instance, I remember reading about a man who came across three words when he was less than ten years old that profoundly changed his life as the years went by.

' "Everybody is I."

'Those were the words. As far as he could work it out, "Everybody is I" meant that every person was as important to themselves as he was to himself. What a bombshell for a kid of that age. He was just a bit-part in the lives of every single person he met, just as they were the support cast in his. And although he didn't understand it at the time, that awareness was to become a crystal-clear insight into the heart of the creator. Every single person is a star in the eyes of God. There is nobody who does not count. As that boy grew up and became a man, that realisation stayed with him as a blessing and a burden for the rest of his life. I know exactly what that means. So do many of you. I see Steve's nodding down here like a toy dog in the back of a car.

'I've experienced my own mini-explosions. A recent one was ignited by reading one line of a poem, written by an American poet called Carl Sandburg. And this was what led me to think that I might have something worth saying this morning. I'll read you the line. It's quite short.

' "Only the fire born understand blue . . ."

'I was fascinated. The unusual mixing of ideas and images produced some unusual pictures in my head, and I had a feeling that there was some kind of deep and perfectly sensible truth embedded in those six words.

'I'll tell you what I did next. I got in touch with a friend who's an engineer. I knew he'd be able to tell me something about heat – about the characteristics of heat. I gathered from what he told me that the logic of it might have something to do with the very nature of fire. I got quite excited. Do I look like someone who gets excited? I'm not very good at showing it, but I do. Excitement starts with a slow burn in me. Very fitting in this case. I don't know about you, but I'd always thought of flames as being red or yellow or gold, but apparently, and this is where the slow burn started to speed up in me, the heart of fire, the place where it burns hottest, can be blue.

'Fascinating. So I began to wonder what kind of meaning lay underneath Sandburg's six-word metaphor.

' "Only the fire born understand blue . . ."

'I said that line over and over again to myself. My little journey of questioning ended in a place where I asked myself if the poet was suggesting that only those whose lives are forged in the central blaze of pain or sorrowful regret can really and truly understand what raging sadness really means. I've no idea if that was what the writer actually wanted to convey, but a few days later I found myself reading the chapter in the book of Acts that you heard just now. Saul is confronted by Jesus himself as he travels towards Damascus, and later learns by the touch of a hand and two crucial words from Ananias that, against all the odds, he, a man who was breathing threats against followers of Jesus, has now been unconditionally adopted into the family of God.

' "Only the fire born understand blue."

'I began to believe that the central meaning of those words could feed into my understanding of Saul's traumatic encounter, and the fierce, apparently unstoppable passion with which he went on to preach a gospel that he had previously worked so hard to extinguish. I'll tell you my thoughts.

'First, concerning when Saul was flung to the ground on the road to Damascus, I think it's important to consider what Jesus did not say.

'He did not say, "Saul, I would like to point out that you are behaving in a very aggressive and punitive manner to Christians all over the place."

'He did not say, "Here is a full list of your sins in alphabetical order."

'He did not say, "Saul, your attitude leaves a great deal to be desired."'

'And we all know, because we've been hearing it all our lives, that the Bible is too often read aloud in boringly sonorous tones, so the chances are that we've missed or never even guessed at the emotion that may well have fuelled what Jesus did actually say. Perhaps it sounded more like this.'

The hairs on the back of Jack's neck stood on end as Doc injected his expansion of the words of Jesus with a wounded passion that seemed to fill the air with pain.

' "You're hurting me, Saul! Why? Tell me why you want to do that! Why are you persecuting me? Why are you battling to stop me existing? I know all about you, Saul. I was watching you when you went through the shock of seeing Stephen's face shining like the sun as he was battered and bloodied by stones. You couldn't help but hear him when he called out, 'Look! I can see the Son of Man standing at the right hand of God!' And you puzzled over him asking God to forgive the very men who were stoning him to a horrible death. You controlled your face so well as you wrapped your arms around all those cloaks, but, Saul, I saw your eyes. They were wide with shock and yearning. You *so* wanted what he had. And you found yourself asking how it could be, that after all the education and training and dedication that had made you what you were, you were simply not able to be a Stephen. But you so wanted it. You know in your heart of hearts that all you really want is me. You wanted me then. You still want me. You want to see the Son of Man just as Stephen did. Well, here I am. You are looking straight at me. So, educated man, answer my question. Why are you hurting me? Why are you persecuting me?"

'As we know, after three days of blindness, with nothing to eat or drink, the miracle happened. Hands were gently laid on him, and the voice of brave, obedient Ananias said two gentle words that invited him to become exactly what he had so passionately longed to be in his heart of hearts. Brother Saul was home. His sight returned, he was baptised into the Christian faith, spent a few days with the disciples at Damascus, and, incredibly, immediately after that, was preaching Christ in the synagogues.

'Jesus had gone out looking for him, rescued him, turned him inside out, and set him off on the road that he was to follow for the rest of his life.

' "Only the fire born understand blue."

'I asked myself, given the intense heat of that experience, what did Saul say to Jesus in response to this startling gift of life and freedom? I'm not allowed to know, but I wonder if any of you remember the last episode of that TV series called *Extras*? There was a line where the main character, who's dumped his best friend while he goes running off looking for fame and fortune, realises that he's made a terrible, terrible mistake. On live television he calls out to his sad, abandoned friend, pleading in tears to be forgiven.

'I've never forgotten his words, and the way in which he says them. Two broken hearts lined up to be mended.

' "I'm *so* sorry! I'm so *very* sorry!"

'His friend is filled with joy. Forgives him in a heartbeat.

'Saul – later Paul, of course – certainly doesn't seem to have indulged in the kind of guilt that, as we all know, can so easily morph into a flaccid self-pity that's no use to man, woman or God, but there's no doubt that his work in the future was going to be fuelled and undergirded by the constantly present knowledge that the greatest of sinners had been personally rescued by the greatest of saviours. He was born in the fire. And he really did understand blue.

'Perhaps we people who call ourselves followers of Jesus have drifted too far from the kind of heartfelt, personal encounter that, as the eternally juice-filled parable of the Prodigal Son makes clear, is at the very heart of what is called repentance. Richer blood needs to flow into the veins of our interaction with a God who can be hurt. Coming to Jesus and coming back to Jesus is not just a question of listing sins and having them ticked off in some kind of forgiveness log. It's surely about knowing that, in hurting others and ourselves, we have hurt him, and risked a relationship with him that means so much to him and to us.

'If we need to, we might decide to say, "Look, I'm so sorry – I am so very, very sorry!"

'And that'll be good, won't it? Especially if we feel his hands laid gently on us, and hear his pleased voice saying, "Brother John, Sister Louise, Brother Adrian, Sister Jenny, Brother Jack". Hearing those words can bring the huge relief of knowing that a line has been drawn, and a new beginning really is up and running.

'I've quite often heard people say that God will laugh if we tell him our plans. It's a sort of joke, I suppose. This is not a joke. If you want to make him happy, if you want to make him smile, clear the air. Make it sweet. Say sorry.

'Those who are forgiven much, love much. Those who are forgiven very much, love very much. Their love was born in a fire. They understand blue. Amen.'

* * *

In the car on the way home Jack said, 'Your sermon made me cry, Doc.'

'That bad?'

'They gave you such a genuine round of applause at the end. So many people standing up. And it was all for real. Lots of people in tears. They all wanted to talk to you afterwards. Took ages getting away, didn't it?'

'What made you cry, Jack?'

Jack took a deep breath.

'Two things. Thinking of you. After Miriam died. Lost and angry and broken in pieces. You understand blue, don't you?'

'And the other thing?'

'Me. The thing is, Doc, I'm only me. I don't know what it means to crash and come back again – soar like an eagle, or whatever it is they say you're supposed to do. We used to sing about that. In the past I just wanted to be a Christian who helps people, probably for all the wrong reasons. I tried too hard, and it dried up and turned into nothing. That's all there was. I think things are beginning to change, but what I'm trying to say is, I've never been as far down, or as high up, as you. Do you think it matters?'

'I don't want you to crash, Jack. There's no actual virtue in misery. I don't want you to go all the way down and have to come back again. Apart from anything else, I don't think Aelwen would ever forgive me if I let that happen.'

The thought intrigued Jack.

'Can you imagine Aelwen being really angry, Doc?'

He considered.

'Let's just say I'm not anxious to go out of my way to discover the answer to that question, Jack. She's gorgeous.'

'By the way, I really liked the look of Steve.'

'Good. I'm glad. I like him too.'

'He's the one Gran thought was a drug dealer, isn't he?'

'That's right.'

'He said you got his life back for him.'

'Well, I helped clear some rubbish away, I suppose.'

'What was he doing when you first knew him?'

'I don't suppose he'd mind you knowing. He was a drug dealer.'

Jack smiled as he drove.

26

Dying to live

It was early Sunday evening. Doc was seated at the garden table, busy with pen and paper, and, unusually in Jack's experience, with an open Bible at his side. Jack took the chair opposite and watched him work for a little while. Another sweetly enfolding evening.

'What are you writing about, Doc?'

'Just playing with ideas really, Jack.'

He laid down his pen.

'Here's an unusual question for you. What do you think Paul the apostle, Wile E. Coyote, Daffy Duck, and Tom from *Tom and Jerry* have in common? I mean – other than the fact that all of them except Paul are, of course, legendary cartoon characters.'

'Just remind me who it is the Coyote character chases all the time.'

'Certainly. He spends his entire life trying to catch and eat a skinny flightless bird called the Road Runner.'

'I remember. He's the one who sprints up and down desert roads at a million miles an hour.'

'That's the fellow. Wile E. Coyote spends a fortune on defective Acme products that are supposed to catch or kill the bird, but even though all his efforts end in failure and physical catastrophe, it never seems to occur to him to give up. You know the others. Daffy Duck – well, he is to Bugs

Bunny what Wile E. Coyote is to the Road Runner. Perpetual failure. Inexplicable optimism. Tom and Jerry—'

'Large cat, small mouse.'

'Correct. Famous for its almost ridiculously precise musical accompaniment. Tom never wins. Nor does he ever have the sense to give up.'

'I can't quite see where Paul fits in with all this.'

'Patience. We'll come back to Paul in a moment.'

'I'm sure the great evangelist to the Gentiles would be deeply flattered to find himself included anywhere on that list.'

This seemed to give the Shadow Doctor a brief, wide-eyed pause for thought.

'He would undoubtedly have a view. Anyway, apart from failure and lunatic persistence, the three aggressors in this line-up have one other thing in common. It's a feature shared by hundreds of other cartoon characters over the years. It's very simple. They never die. They just – never die. It's like something out of a Beckett play. The same every time. Poor old Wile E. Coyote stares bleakly upwards, aware with dismal certainty that a massive boulder, carefully balanced by himself with the ultimate, crazily optimistic intention of crushing the Road Runner, is toppling very, very slowly in the wrong direction, and will with vicious inevitability, fall directly onto his own head. It does, of course, and there's a cloud of dust as it squishes him into what should be extinction. But he doesn't die. No matter how crushed or smashed, his body instantly pops back into shape. He never dies. Nor does Daffy Duck, nor Tom, nor the vast majority of all the other cartoon characters that you or I have ever seen.'

'What about Paul?'

Doc raised a tutoring finger.

'Bear with me. As you know, in his passionate determination to persuade the Corinthian church not to be taken in by false apostles, Paul uses some heavy satire to boast about his qualification as a genuine apostle through a passage that reads like a sort of curriculum vitae of pain and suffering. A list of all the dreadful things that have happened to him.'

Doc picked up his pen and paused for a moment, apparently unsure of how to continue.

'Jack, do you feel like doing something silly?'

Jack considered, then shrugged.

'To be honest, there can't be anything much sillier than answering yes or no to that question. Oh, go on then. Yes, I do want to do something silly.'

Doc tapped one of the sheets of paper on the table in front of him.

'The thing is – I couldn't help wondering – was Paul sitting opposite Luke the physician when he put the list together. If he was, it's just possible the conversation might have gone something like this. It's a little dialogue. I used to write them. Still do sometimes. Fancy reading it with me? Probably no one else ever will.'

A thick spider's web of fear formed like magic mist over Jack's confidence.

'You and me, you mean?'

'Yes, you and me. No one else from this vast crowd of people standing around is as qualified as you.'

'Now?'

'Yes, now. Come round this side of the table. I'll be Paul,

seeing as I'm a little weary of being called a doctor. You be Luke.'

'What about the cartoon thing?'

'We'll come back to that.'

Jack sighed. 'We spend our lives coming back to things.'

'Yes, consistent, aren't we? Come on, let's give it a go.'

Releasing tension with a deep breath in through his nose and out through his mouth, Jack joined the Shadow Doctor at the other side of the table, dragging a chair round to sit beside him. Doc slid the sheet of paper into a position where they could both see.

'It's quite short. Have a quick read-through.'

At least reading it has made me smile, thought Jack a minute later. He nodded.

'Ah well, in for a denarius . . .'

'OK, here we go.'

PAUL: I thought this seemed such a good idea when I thought of it. Just – make a list. Simple. Still, I think it'll be worth it, don't you, Luke? What's your – (*playfully*) diagnosis?

LUKE: (*a little glumly*) I hope it's worth it. It's taken quite a long time already. Where have you got to?

PAUL: The shipwrecks. (*chews the end of his quill and stares at the ceiling, then starts to count on his fingers*) One, two, three – four times I was ship-wrecked, wasn't I? Or was it five?

LUKE: (*slightly wearily – they really have been working on this for some time*) Er – three. Three shipwrecks.

PAUL: Oh! Three. Now you do surprise me. Do you know, I could have sworn it was four – or five. Surely.

LUKE: No. No, we've been through this already. That was the forty lashes minus one. Five of them.

PAUL: You said that was six.

LUKE: I did not. I said it was five, because that's what it was. (*pause*) Don't look at me like that. It was five. Look, for now, never mind the forty lashes minus one. Do the shipwrecks. Get them done.

PAUL: Right. OK. Four, did you say?

LUKE: (*restlessly*) It was three. Three shipwrecks. (*he holds up three fingers*) Three. You were shipwrecked three times. (*to himself*) As was I, in case anyone is ever remotely interested.

PAUL: OK. Got it. (*leans forward and writes busily for a few moments with his tongue sticking out of the side of his mouth, then looks up and taps his quill against the side of his head*) Right. It's going quite well now. Next question. Have I ever been in danger from my own countrymen?

LUKE: (*breathing in and out through his nose and muttering under his breath*) Yes. For sure. This very moment for example.

PAUL: Speak up, Luke, can't hear what you're saying.

LUKE: Erm – I said your wife, Thorn, will be here in a moment.

PAUL: (*standing hurriedly*) Oh! Let's go and get some tentmaking done. We can finish this later . . .

'So, what do you think, Jack?'

'It's good. Very funny. I enjoyed doing it in the end.'

'Thanks for doing that. It was like old times for me.'

Jack's silent wondering was interrupted by a high-pitched cry from somewhere far away in the depths of the forest. Both men turned towards the sound. It was cut off abruptly. Doc spoke to Jack without looking him in the eye.

'Miriam and I used to do a lot of that sort of sketchy, drama stuff. We loved it.'

Jack found himself thanking God that he was at least beginning to resist the temptation to fill potential silences with rubbish.

'Do you think Paul writing that list might have happened a bit like in your sketch?'

The Shadow Doctor turned back and smiled an acknowledgement that the bridge between past and present was adequate for purpose.

'No idea, but however it actually got written, the great apostle's CV really was impressive.' He flipped his Bible to a place he'd marked. 'A most extraordinary list. And here it is, word for word, in the eleventh chapter of Paul's second letter to the Corinthians. I'll read it to you.

Are they servants of Christ? (I am out of my mind to talk like this.) I am more. I have worked much harder, been in prison more frequently, been flogged more severely, and been exposed to death again and again. Five times I received from the Jews the forty lashes minus one. Three times I was beaten with rods, once I was stoned, three times I was shipwrecked, I spent a night and a day in the open sea, I have been constantly on the move, I have been in danger from rivers, in danger from bandits, in danger from my own country-men, in danger from Gentiles; in danger in the city, in danger in the country, in danger at sea; and in danger from false brothers. I have laboured and toiled and often gone without sleep; I have known hunger and thirst and often gone without food; I have been cold and naked. *Do you want to make a commitment?*

'I added that last sentence myself, by the way.'

'Wow! You're right, it is impressive. I'd never really thought about it like that. Must have taken ages to remember it all and get the numbers right.'

'Exactly.'

'Good, so – going back to your original question – what does the Apostle Paul have in common with all those cartoon characters?'

'The answer, Jack, lies in how we deal with one final, very serious question. Why on earth was Paul willing to go on putting up with the risk involved in all those horrible, ghastly experiences of pain and discomfort and sheer ignominy? Beaten with rods three times. Five lots of thirty-nine lashes. I mean – why would you? Why would I? Why would anybody? What could possibly be overwhelmingly important enough to drive or persuade you to live that kind of hellish life? Think about it – he could have started a very nice little church and kept his yapping mouth shut when it was likely to get him into trouble. Why not do that?'

Jack shook his head helplessly.

'I don't know, Doc. There are things I might have suggested once, but even if they're true, they just seem like random collections of words now. I don't even know how to begin to think about that sort of thing. Perhaps you answered your own question this morning. Paul had closed his mind and done terrible, cruel things to the person he really wanted to follow. He was blazing with sorrow, and I suppose he wanted to use himself up through making the fire work for Jesus. Something like that perhaps. Even then, I find it almost impossible to get my head round it.'

The Shadow Doctor executed a wave of understanding through the balmy air.

'God knows, so do I, Jack. But one thing does seem clear enough. Paul appears to have been about as confident as it's possible to get about the fact that nothing – not imprisonment, not injury, not death itself – could even vaguely threaten the life with Jesus that he'd been promised he could have for ever. Just imagine being that sure and that expectant. And that was what he had in common with the cartoon characters. In terms of the only life that will ever really matter to human beings, whatever anyone said or did to him, however extreme, he could not be killed.'

'He did have a bit of a head-start on us, though, didn't he, Doc? Stephen all lit up when stones were thrown at him, Damascus Road stuff, miracles galore, specific spot-on guidance from dreams and suchlike – no wonder he was a tad surer than I am.'

Doc smiled and nodded.

'Can't argue with that, Jack, but he did make brilliant use of the confidence all those things gave him. You're right, though. Finding a way to get anywhere near Paul's perspective isn't easy – never has been, especially for people like us who live in amazingly privileged parts of the world. Having said all that, one central truth is not going to change to accommodate our lesser selves.'

'Which one would that be, then?'

He leaned back and clasped his hands together.

'How can I put it? Something like this. If we sign on as followers of Jesus, join him behind the counter, and try our very best to do what we're told, we're going to be as totally safe in heaven, and as scarily, continually at risk in this troubled world, as it's possible to be. Begs the question, doesn't it?'

'The question?'

'Do you still fancy the journey?'

Studying the Shadow Doctor's eyes in an attempt to understand the seriousness of his question, Jack was struck by an absurd notion. For a fleeting moment he seemed to see two fires burning on the flat summit of a snow-covered hill. What could that possibly mean? He covered his face with his hands as he considered Doc's question. When he finally lifted his head and spoke, he could hear his own voice sounding small and defenceless.

'I'm not sure that I fancy the journey at all. But that doesn't mean I'm not going. Doc, what's the bottom line? What's for sure?'

27

The bottom line

The Shadow Doctor thought for a moment, then, making a sudden decision, got to his feet and disappeared indoors. Two or three minutes later, he reappeared holding a slim hard-backed volume. Sitting down, he found the page he wanted and flattened the book on the table with the palm of his hand. He took a deep breath.

'You know as well as I do, Jack, that different people would give you their own wildly varying answers to the question you just asked. It's an important question. Who would be right and who would be wrong? I don't know. Who am I to say? As for me, despite and because of everything, I have a fondness for God. It might be more than a fondness. When it comes to that sort of thing I tend to be a little more shy than is good for me – and possibly for others.' He lifted the book. 'This is a collection of works by a poet called Jalaluddin Rumi. He lived in the thirteenth century. Two of his thoughts might come somewhere near to the only way I can sum things up. This is the first one:

> Out beyond ideas of wrongdoing and right doing
>   there is a field. I'll meet you there.

'I'm guessing, of course, Jack, but here's a thought. I wonder, as the cock crew and Peter shed all those tears, if a part of Jesus would have liked to call out to this failing friend of his, "Peter, out beyond ideas of betrayal and loyalty, there's a really good place for breakfast on the shore of Galilee. I'll meet you there."

'I suppose my bottom line is somewhere in the middle of all that. Something about relationship, something that's somehow surer and a lot more attractive than what some people call certainty.' He turned a few pages in the book. 'Here's the other little piece by Rumi that you might find especially interesting, Jack. There's a question at the end of it. You never know, it might be the very question that good old George asks you the next time he comes round. This is how it goes.

There is a candle in your heart, ready to be kindled.
    There is a void in your soul, ready to be filled. You
    feel it, don't you?'

The Shadow Doctor continued as if he were asking the most casual of questions.

'Do you feel it, Jack?'

After a pause for thought, Jack lowered both hands to the table in slow motion and replied as if he might be dealing with the most important issue he had ever faced.

'I do want my heart to be alight – to be burning. I'd like it to burn like a candle I once lit in – in a cathedral. My candle, burning its own flame in its own way just for me. And yes, there is still a space in me. Not quite as empty now because of you and Aelwen and Martha and the things that have happened, but I know it's still there. I would like my soul to be filled, if that's possible.' His voice broke a little. 'I think you know it's what I've always wanted.'

Doc closed his book and stood up. The two men looked at and into each other as a silent but essential extra conversation happened.

'Good! That's very good. Well, if you want my opinion, you and Aelwen and God and Martha and me will sort all that out between us. And now, assuming that we are seeking a celebration rather than a refuge – am I allowed to check that my assumption is correct?'

Jack smiled approval.

'Good. It's time to break out the Lagavulin. Anything else to say before we do?'

'Tell me who George is.'

'All right. Here's what I'll do. I'm going to give you such a broad clue that you're bound to get it.'

'Go on then.'

'George is not his real name, and he has something significantly in common with Haile Selassie. Let me know when you've got it. I'm going indoors. Coming?'

Much later that night, Doc stopped on the landing outside the door of his room as both men were about to head for bed.

'Here's a thought to take into the night with you, Jack. It's made up of a question and an answer. The final words between Miriam and I in the middle of the night before she died. I've never told anyone this. Our very last conversation. I had to lean right down next to her mouth to hear what she said.

'Michael, when dawn breaks, what happens to the pieces?'

'I don't know. You tell me.'

'They go into morning.'

'I see. How are you spelling that last word?'

'Either way. Both ways. I'm sorry, I really think I have to go to sleep now. Goodnight, my darling.'

'Goodnight, Miriam.'

Jack waited a moment before opening the door of his room.

'Goodnight, Doc. Sleep well tonight. Thanks for everything.'

'Yes. Same to you. See you in the morning, Jack. Oh, by the way, I meant to ask you – the day we went to see Elsie – did you ever work out the answer to that crossword clue?'

'Remind me?'

'The Alpen wild creature. Eight letters. And "a" was the sixth letter.'

'No, I never did. But you're going to tell me, aren't you?'

'Yes, I am. Elephant. That was the answer, Jack. Elephant. Goodnight.'

HODDER &
STOUGHTON

Hodder & Stoughton is the UK's
leading Christian publisher,
with a wide range of books from
the bestselling authors in the UK
and around the world ranging from
Christian lifestyle and theology to
apologetics, testimony and fiction.
We also publish the world's
most popular Bible translation
in modern English, the New
International Version, renowned
for its accuracy and readability.

Hodderfaith.com   Hodderbibles.co.uk
@HodderFaith   /HodderFaith